SINISTER MAGIC

DEATH BEFORE DRAGONS

— BOOK ONE —

LINDSAY BUROKER

Edited by Shelley Holloway
Cover and interior design by Gene Mollica Studio, LLC.

ISBN: 978-1-951367-03-9

SINISTER MAGIC

FOREWORD

Thank you, regular readers and new readers, for picking up this new series. As you may know, I've been writing about dragons for years, but this is my first time bringing them to Earth. Val, the heroine of this series, is *not* pleased with this development, but I hope you will be.

Before you start reading, please let me thank the people who helped me put this book together. Thank you to my editor, Shelley Holloway, and my beta readers, Sarah Engelke, Rue Silver, and Cindy Wilkinson. Also, thank you to the cover designer Gene Mollica. Lastly, thank you to my narrator, Vivienne Leheny, for bringing the audio version of *Sinister Magic* to life.

Now, please enjoy the adventure…

CHAPTER 1

As I scooted a few more inches down the cliff, I came to the end of my rope. And swore. Vehemently and virulently, as appropriate for someone hanging from damp, gritty, *vertical* rock a hundred feet above crashing ocean waves.

Then I made the mistake of looking down and swore a little more. Heights don't usually faze me. What gets me is the thought of falling from them, landing on sharp pointy rocks, being pulverized like flank steak in a meat grinder, and then being sucked out to sea, never to be seen again.

But the mouth of the cave was less than twenty feet below. I gritted my teeth in determination. I could do this.

"Besides," I muttered to the rock, "you're the idiot who chose not to drive an hour back to a town with a hardware store for more rope."

After finding a suitable handhold, I scooted lower. Climbing back up would be easier, assuming I wasn't injured then. I had to trust that my magical weapons, my magical charms, and the agility that my half-elven blood granted me would see me through this.

Halfway to the cave entrance, my phone vibrated in my pocket. I ignored it, like any sane person would, and continued carefully downward.

But then I paused. It was Friday and almost closing time for people who worked office jobs. If this was the call I was expecting and I ignored it, I'd have to wait until Monday to get the test results.

Making sure I had three points of contact, and one foot wedged so far into a crevice that falling would be impossible, I eased my phone out of my pocket. Yes, it was the doctor's office. I had one bar of reception and the roar of the surf behind me.

"This is Val," I answered, waiting to impress the receptionist with my connection.

"Hello, this is Mandy in Dr. Brightman's office. Is this... Val... mey... jar?"

"Just Val." I didn't correct the pronunciation or explain that my Norwegian mother had thought it would be fun to name me after a Valkyrie.

"We got your test results back, and ev—"

"And what?" The tightness in my chest that had grown familiar these last few months intensified, and I rolled my eyes as I envisioned having to dig into my other pocket for the inhaler Dr. Brightman had given me. What kind of monster-slaying warrior woman developed asthma? "I'm sorry, uh, Mandy. Can you repeat that?"

I glanced at the phone, worried the call had dropped.

"Valmeyjar?" Mandy asked, clearly hearing me as well as I was hearing her. "I'm sorry. I think the connection isn't very good."

A seagull squawked as it flew by, either commenting on the stupidity of my position or wondering if I had French fries in my pocket.

"I noticed. The results?"

"I said everything is normal on your bloodwork. Are you at the coast?"

"Normal?" I used my eyes to burn a laser of skepticism into the face of the phone. "What?"

"Everything is normal."

"Are you sure? I have... issues. New issues." I barely slept, I had a ridiculous urge to take siestas, and now this new betrayal from my lungs.

"Well, your inflammatory markers are a little high, but it's nothing to worry about at this point. Your hormone levels were all good, especially for a woman of your age."

My eyes bored more lasers into the phone. "*My* age? I'm barely past forty."

"Hormones can get a little persnickety in your forties." Persnickety? Who in this century said *persnickety*? "Oh, here's Dr. Brightman." Mandy sounded relieved to pass me off.

"Everything is normal, Val," he said. "It's not uncommon to develop asthma and allergies later in life."

"I am not later in life. My *mom* isn't even later in life. She's seventy-one and hikes the Pacific Crest Trail for kicks."

"If you find yourself using the rescue inhaler more than a couple of times a month, we'll want to get you on a daily corticosteroid."

"I don't take drugs."

Dr. Brightman was diplomatic enough not to point out that my new dependence on the "rescue inhaler" counted as using a drug.

"If you change your mind or have further concerns, we can schedule another appointment, but from what you've told me of your life, you might want to relax a little."

"I've told you next to nothing about my life."

"I can read between the lines. You seem driven. How's work? How's your stress load? Are you able to take time off to relax?"

"Uh." I glanced down at the cave to make sure my target hadn't sauntered out on the ledge to contemplate my potential as a meal. "When I can."

"And how are your relationships with family and friends?"

"I fail to see what that has anything to do with—"

"Do you have a good social support group?"

I thought of Colonel Willard, the military contact who gave me assignments, and Nin, the woman in Seattle who made my magical weapons. Did they count? My ex-husband and my daughter were... people I kept tabs on but never visited, too afraid my work would endanger them.

"It's fine," I said.

"Hm." Why did Brightman sound like he didn't believe me? The connection wasn't good enough to detect lies. "I've got a friend who's an excellent therapist. I can't make appointments for you, but I can make a referral. We can set everything up so you get a text and can book online. Easy peasy. I highly recommend you work on your stress levels, your relationships, and your sleep—do you sleep well?"

No, I dreamed of all the mutilated victims that my targets had killed before I'd killed them.

"That silence speaks volumes, Val. I'll get that referral in pronto. And have you tried yoga? Some relaxation and deep breathing exercises?

Meditation? Why don't you work on your lifestyle for six months, and then we'll recheck your inflammation levels."

Yoga? Meditation? *Therapy?*

"Shit." I hung up and stuffed the phone in my pocket.

I crept down the cliff and landed soundlessly on the ledge at the mouth of the cave. Crouching, I peered into a tunnel far darker than the cloudy gloom of the Oregon coast.

"*Yeshelya*," I whispered, touching one of the charms hanging from the leather thong around my neck.

My eyes tingled as magic took hold. After a few seconds, the walls of the uneven passage grew clear, as did the spot where it curved around a bend. A few fish bones scattered the rock floor, and the pungent smells of an animal's den mingled with the salty fishiness of the ocean.

Before reaching for another charm, the feline figurine at the center of my necklace that I'd risked my life to acquire, I made myself take a hit from the loathed inhaler. I didn't want a witness to this new weakness I'd developed.

"Sindari," I whispered, a name this time, not a magical word I could barely pronounce. "Time to come out and play."

Gray mist appeared at my side, and my other *social connection* formed inside of it, the great silver tiger quickly growing as solid as any Earth animal. Only the faint glow that emanated from his black-striped silver fur and the intelligence gleaming in his green eyes gave him away as magical.

It's about time, Sindari said telepathically through our mental connection. *The air stinks of wyverns.*

There's only one left. We got the other two already. Unless you can smell more? As far as I knew, I had the telepathic aptitude of a smooth, dull rock, but when I responded in my head, Sindari always heard me.

The tiger's nostrils twitched. *There is only one. This will be a disappointingly boring battle.* His head cocked slightly. *Ah, but it is a female. Good. Females are more challenging.*

Lucky us.

Yes.

Before we headed in, I took my phone out once more, this time to play the video I'd saved. Shaky footage that someone had recorded in Thousand Acres Park outside of Portland rolled for me.

Three blue wyverns, their leathery wings flapping as they came out of the trees, dove down and attacked children playing on the Sandy River beach. Some of the kids got away. Others were pulled up into the treetops where the wyverns feasted. Four children and a mother had been killed that day.

"Let's do this," I said grimly, replacing the phone and pulling Fezzik out of my thigh holster.

The compact submachine pistol had similar features to a Heckler & Koch MP7, but Nin had made it from scratch, and the elven half of my blood recognized the magic emanating from it and from the individual cartridges in the magazine. The gun was almost as powerful as Chopper, the longsword I'd won in battle long ago and that I wore sheathed on my back. If this went to hell and the wyvern got close before I could take it down, I would switch to the blade.

Sindari led the way. Normally, I wouldn't let someone else go first, but if he was grievously injured, he could instantly return to the safety of his realm to heal.

We crept down the passage, rounding bends, and the roar of the surf grew fainter, replaced by drips and trickles deeper within the cave. Soon, we were close enough to the lair that my own ability to sense magic, one of the few powers I'd inherited from the father I'd never met, let me feel the aura of the wyvern.

The tunnel widened into a chamber twenty feet high and twice that deep. We had gone back far enough that I guessed we were under the spot where I'd parked my Jeep. A hundred feet under it.

Stalactites leered down from above, and stalagmites interfered with the view ahead. I couldn't yet see our target, but I could smell her. More bones littered the floor in here. Some were deer and some were human, with blood and gristle still clinging to them.

My grip tightened on Fezzik, anger simmering as I wondered how many people this intruder in our world had killed in addition to those caught on the video.

She is resting behind those stalagmites, Sindari said. *Your mongrel aura is weak, but you should cloak yourself.*

It's subtle, not weak. Just like me.

You are as subtle as those massive steel orbs on chains that pummel the sides of your buildings.

11

Wrecking balls, yeah, yeah. I touched the powerful cloaking charm, another hard-won prize, and faded from the sight and smell of others. My aura, my signature to those who could sense magic, also disappeared.

Sufficient, Sindari said.

Knowing I would prefer to attack from a distance and the higher ground, he led me toward a natural ramp creeping up the side of the chamber to a ledge. Just as the blue scales and folded wings of the dozing wyvern came into view, Sindari halted. His tail went rigid, and he whirled back toward the entrance.

Certain he'd sensed a second wyvern, I also turned, pointing Fezzik at the tunnel. I didn't see or hear anything.

We need to get out of here. Sindari took a step but halted. *No, we can't go that way. He's coming that way.*

My ferocious battle tiger, the same tiger who'd been worried the wyvern would be too easy an opponent, looked around, nostrils flaring in fear as he sought some back exit from the cave.

I started to ask why, but then I sensed it. Something with an aura so great that even I could feel it from far away. And tell that it was getting closer.

He's coming, Sindari groaned into my mind.

What is it? I'd never sensed anything like this.

A dragon.

CHAPTER 2

A dragon?

I wanted to be skeptical and dismissive. Dragons didn't come to Earth, not anymore. A thousand years ago, they might have, but they'd left long before the elves and dwarves had disappeared.

It was hard, however, to be skeptical when I could sense the incredibly powerful aura coming closer and closer. It—he?—was in the tunnel. And shape-shifted into something small? How else could a dragon fit in here?

We must hide. There's no way out unless we run past him. Sindari backed farther up the ramp. *Which I do not advise. Your weapons will do nothing against him, and my fangs will be like toothpicks if he shifts into his natural form. Even if he is in human form, he'll be impossible to kill.*

I followed Sindari, trusting his assessment. My only experience with dragons came through stories from other magical beings who had encountered them in their native worlds.

We scooted back to the deepest corner of the ledge. Below, just visible between two stalactites, the wyvern stirred for the first time.

Her head came up, snout opening to reveal long pointed teeth dripping with poisonous saliva. Her wings spread as she rose on her two legs to sniff the air. The wyvern was a distant relative of a dragon but much smaller, much less dangerous.

She shifted to peer around a tall stalagmite. I found a spot where I could watch her and also see the tunnel. Her talons flexed nervously on the rock floor, and she glanced around the chamber. Looking for an escape?

Her yellow-eyed gaze raked over us, and I held my breath, worried my charm wouldn't be enough to keep me hidden. Sindari, his kind masters of stealth, had innate magic to camouflage himself. *He* wouldn't be the problem.

But the wyvern's gaze didn't linger. It ratcheted back on the mouth of the tunnel as a human figure in a black robe with silver trim strode into view.

He had a tall, broad build and olive skin, a tidily trimmed beard and mustache, and short, curly black hair. My senses told me he was the dragon, even if he'd shape-shifted into this form to blend in. Not that he would blend in. That robe looked like something out of a *Lord of the Rings* movie, the silver slippers like something from Oz, and the dragon-shaped gold amulet on his chest was bling that Mr. T would have loved. Lastly, the violet eyes that glowed with inner power were nothing contacts could have achieved.

That violet gaze roamed around the cavern, skimming over us, and I held my breath again. Even if my charm worked on a wyvern, a dragon might not be fooled. I'd scrounged and fought far and wide for my collection of protective magic, and most of the centuries-old trinkets hadn't come with instruction manuals.

"*Dysnax crayell, loreth.*" The dragon's deep baritone rang through the chamber with resonance that Darth Vader would have envied. "*Crayell Zavryd'nokquetal.*"

The wyvern darted fully behind her stalagmite and hid, her pointed blue tail wrapping around the base as if she feared being torn away.

I touched another charm and mouthed the command word, hoping I could activate it without actually speaking. There was no way I was going to make a noise. Dragons could probably hear pins dropping on the moon.

"...and furthermore," the dragon said, the charm translating the words in my mind, "you fled like a coward from your home realm, leaving the slain behind you to be discovered by their families."

The wyvern was a criminal on more than one world? Not surprising. I was relieved to hear the dragon hadn't come for *me*.

"You will return with me through the portal to be incarcerated until such time that you can be judged by the Dragon Justice Court. They will determine your punishment and your subsequent rehabilitation."

Wait a minute. This guy wanted to take my target through a portal to another world? For *rehabilitation*?

Oh, hell no. The wyvern was going to die for the children she'd killed and the bones of the dead littered across the floor of this very cave. I'd been hired to kill her, not watch someone else cart her away.

I shifted Fezzik and leaned to the side enough to line my sights up with the wyvern's head.

You can't shoot her in front of that dragon, Sindari warned. *Don't be fooled by his human form. He can kill you with a look.*

I know. I'm going to need your help.

"I didn't do it," the wyvern called from behind her stalagmite.

"I see the lie staining your soul. Come with me now, or I will forcibly remove you from your miserable squalid hole."

Please say the help you need isn't for me to fight and slay the dragon, because that isn't in my repertoire of abilities.

No, just lead him away. I'll finish the job and sprint out of here. Sprint was an ambitious word considering the climb back up to the top of the cliff, but I would find a way. *If he catches up with you, go back to your realm. I'll call you back to Earth later when it's safe.*

You know he can follow me home, right?

I hesitated. *Are you sure?*

Dragons can do anything. There's a reason they rule all seventeen of the Cosmic Realms.

They don't rule on Earth.

Only because they don't care about Earth. Sindari watched as the dragon strode toward the wyvern. *Correction: They haven't cared about Earth in the past. For a dragon to come here, something must have changed. Or the wyvern committed an incredibly heinous crime.*

She did. I rested a hand on Sindari's back. *Please, lead the dragon away. I'm positive he'll be too angry with me to chase you back to your realm.*

That is not reassuring. He will kill you.

Not if I get away. Lead him far and lead him fast.

I don't think you understand the power of dragons.

Then this next ten minutes should be educational. I waved him toward the tunnel entrance.

Just don't die in the ocean. I don't want my next handler to be a whale.

Blazing yellow light flared below, stealing all the shadows in the cave.

Rocks shattered as the dragon hurled a magical attack at his foe. The wave of power pulverized the stalagmite, and dozens of others in the area, as it hurled the wyvern forty feet to the back wall.

An ominous snap erupted from the ceiling of the cave. Two stalactites plunged down, leaving my hiding spot on the ledge open and vulnerable. I could get killed simply by the raw power being hurled around.

The dragon lifted a hand, and the wyvern floated into the air and toward him. The winged creature spun, trying to flap her wings, her two legs flailing in the air, her lizard-like face panicked.

Now, Sindari, I silently urged.

Sindari didn't argue with me further. He sprang from our ledge and ran toward the dragon, mouth opening as if he would take a bite.

Despite his magical stealth, the dragon sensed him coming. The wyvern thudded to the ground as he shifted his focus toward Sindari.

The great silver tiger sprang for his head. The dragon's eyebrows twitched in faint surprise, but all he did was duck. Sindari sailed over him, snapping at the dragon's ear on the way by, but I could tell it was a feint. Even so, his snout bumped against an invisible shield and glanced off.

The dragon appeared more puzzled than afraid as Sindari, a deadly creature that would make any predator on Earth quake with fear, sailed past him.

Sindari landed and raced into the tunnel. It looked like the dragon would ignore him. My stomach sank.

Then Sindari shouted telepathically, *You hatched backward from your egg, you one-winged gimp.*

The dragon's violet eyes flared with furious light, and he whirled and started to sprint after Sindari. But he paused in the mouth of the tunnel and looked back at the wyvern. His eyes flared even brighter, and yellow bands appeared around the wyvern, entrapping her and hoisting her in the air.

The dragon sprinted down the tunnel after Sindari.

Be safe, my friend, I thought, hoping I hadn't lied and doomed him to his death.

The wyvern spit and hissed, struggling against the magical bonds, but she couldn't unfurl her wings, and her talons dangled a foot off the floor. With half of the stalactites turned to rubble on the ground, I had no trouble lining up my shot.

I hesitated, wanting Sindari to get the dragon as far away as he could—

the full mile that he could be parted from his figurine—before I killed the wyvern. I had no doubt the dragon would know when his would-be captive was dead, and I needed time to escape.

The honorable part of me regretted sniping the wyvern when she was defenseless, but I'd learned long ago that facing magical creatures in fair battles got humans killed. And this wasn't an arena. This was justice, and it was my assignment. The wyvern had committed a crime, and I was the executioner.

I fired, Fezzik's boom thundering in the enclosed space. The magical bullet left a trail of blue in the dim air as it thudded into the side of the wyvern's head.

She shrieked but didn't die instantly. Startlingly, the magical bonds holding her aloft evaporated, and she dropped to her feet. Without hesitation, she whirled, unctuous gray-red blood dribbling down the side of her head, and flew up to my ledge. I shot again, but the bullet barely sank in, her feathered torso protected by some magical armor.

As the wyvern landed, she flung a psionic attack at me—at my mind. A powerful urge plunged into my thoughts, a command to drop my weapons, fall to my knees, and expose my neck for a swift kill.

Growling, I shook it off. Once, that might have worked, but since I'd started carrying Chopper, it had grown easier to combat mental attacks.

The wyvern advanced, her large sharp beak snapping. Powerful leg muscles bunched, and she sprang toward me, talons extending toward my face.

Forcing myself to remain calm, I flicked Fezzik's selector to automatic and held down the trigger. A thunderous rain of bullets slammed into her chest. Her wing flaps faltered, but momentum carried her forward, and she landed right in front of me.

Bullets riddled her chest. Crazy with fear of death—or fear of the dragon—she was somehow still alive, still attacking.

I jammed Fezzik into its holster and tore Chopper from its sheath. As the wyvern lunged, beak snapping, I stabbed at her chest like a fencer. On the narrow ledge, with the wall looming to my right, there wasn't room for sweeping blade work.

A wing swept in as she reversed her lunge and tried to deflect the blow. I was too strong—the sword cut into the blue leathery membrane and crunched into bone.

Blood spattered, and I jerked back, but not before droplets hit my hand and sleeve. Like acid, they burned through my clothing and into my skin, acrid smoke wafting up.

I snarled and lunged in again, this time feinting high for that sneering lizard face. She whipped her wing up to block, but I was already shifting my attack to one of her unprotected legs. The blade sank deep, and she shrieked.

In my mind, I saw the children she'd killed, their crumpled bodies on that blood-drenched beach. I stabbed again and again, varying the targets, and finding her heart. Finally, she fought no more.

As the wyvern tottered, on the verge of falling, I swept my blade across her neck, not caring when my elbow clunked against the stone wall. Her head flew off, thunking to the ground far below.

My blood was roaring in my ears, my heart pounding, but I didn't pause to recover. I sprang over the body as it fell to the ledge, and sprinted for the tunnel. Already, I'd taken too much time.

Through my link with Sindari, I sensed him swimming—he hadn't been able to climb the wall, so he'd leaped to the sea far below. I also sensed the dragon shifting into his natural form—four legs, black scales, great wings that blotted out the sun when he flew—and swooping down after the tiger.

I raced down the tunnel, jamming my uncleaned sword into its scabbard with a wince. There was no time to wipe it down, and I couldn't climb with it out.

Only the knowledge that I wouldn't survive the fall if I tumbled into the sea slowed me down. Carefully, I picked my way up the damp cliff, my fingers shaking.

Wind gusted, needling me through my sweat-drenched clothing and trying to tear me from the cliff. My rope jerked and twisted like a snake on a handler's tongs. It taunted me as the end flapped against the rock to the left of my reach.

Rock gave way, and my foot slipped. I caught myself, heart lurching wildly.

A roar came from the ocean—a menacing baritone sound that made my very bones quail. The dragon.

My feline figurine warmed slightly through my shirt, and I sensed Sindari disappearing from this realm. Another roar echoed over the waves.

My charm didn't translate the noise, but I knew without a doubt that the dragon realized he'd been tricked. And was on his way back.

I lunged and finally caught the end of the rope. Gasping as I banged my knee on the wall, I hauled myself up. I climbed faster than I'd ever climbed in my life, but it was too slow. I knew it was without looking back.

The roar came again. Much closer this time.

I scrambled over the ledge, long wet grass slapping at my face, and lunged to my feet. Not bothering to retrieve the rope, I sprinted for the trees beyond the grass, hoping—praying—the dragon wouldn't be able to fly through the dense evergreens.

In the distance, I could make out my black Jeep. I doubted that it would keep me safe, but if I could get back to the highway, maybe…

The roar sounded again above and behind me. I glanced back, almost tripping at the terror that filled me when I saw those violet eyes in that furious, black reptilian face. Somewhere between a wolf and a lizard, the dragon was a million times more fearsome than either. And he was *huge*. A hundred feet long? He had to be.

I sprinted into the trees, lamenting that there was no path, no road, to help me through the soggy undergrowth. The dragon pulled up, the dense trees making him pause, and he circled.

Would he fly above them until I passed into a clearing? Or change into his human form to give chase?

The blazing light of a sun filled the air behind me, and heat scorched my back. I caromed off a tree as I glanced back again. Flames roiled after me, trees cracking and catching fire, blackening in instants. Birds shrieked and fled the forest.

The flames licked at my back, but one of the small charms on my necklace grew icy cold, and I didn't feel the pain of being engulfed. The brilliant light stung my eyes, but neither my skin, clothing, nor hair caught fire. Even with the protection of the charm, the heat was intense, and it chased me all the way to my Jeep.

I sprang in, shoving my sword scabbard aside so I could sit, and thrust the key into the ignition. I jammed my foot against the pedal and spun the wheel, groaning because I'd parked in a clearing. Who could have known?

The Jeep roared toward the forest service road that had gotten me most of the way to the cliff. There was no time to buckle my seatbelt, and my head bumped the soft top with each dip and bump. When I made it to the ancient dirt road, mud spattering as my wheels hit it, things didn't improve much, but I steered down it as fast as I could.

Branches blotted out much of the sky above me, but not so much that I didn't see that big black body following me. *Easily* keeping pace.

"Idiot, idiot," I chanted to myself. Why hadn't I heeded Sindari's wisdom?

A flat straight stretch opened up, and I pressed the accelerator. How far to Highway 101? Seven miles? Eight? An eternity? Yes.

The branches overhead grew less thick, and I knew I was in trouble. I couldn't see anything in the mirrors, but he was up there.

A roar blasted the air right above me, louder than a foghorn. Talons slashed through the soft top of the Jeep, plunging in like daggers. Like *swords*.

I jerked low in the seat and hit the brakes. A thunderous ripping filled my ears. The dragon's momentum carried him past, but he took the top with him.

"Hard top," I muttered. "Should've gotten a hard top."

As he turned, maneuvering his massive body between the trees to come back for me, I hit the accelerator again. I wasn't going to make it past him. There was no way.

More agile than anything that large should have been, he rose above me and then dove, arrowing straight toward the driver's seat.

I jerked down as low as I could while still holding the wheel. The Jeep lurched off the side of the road, underbrush tearing at the fender. The dragon grabbed its frame and lifted.

When the wheels were pulled off the road, I was so startled that I couldn't do anything but react. I sprang out the open window, almost getting my scabbard caught on the frame, as the dragon lifted my Jeep higher and higher.

My shoulder hit the ground first, hard, and I rolled into the undergrowth, crashing into a tree with a blast of pain. I sprang up, yanking Chopper free.

As powerful as Fezzik's bullets were, they hadn't done as much as I expected against the wyvern. I was afraid they'd be useless against the dragon. All I could hope was that Chopper, the longsword reputedly made in another world, could cut through scale. Because there was nowhere else to run. All I could do was defend myself—or die trying.

The dragon spun and hurled the entire Jeep into a thick stand of old-growth trees. The wrenching crash that thundered through the forest was the most horrific noise I'd ever heard. I couldn't help but gape as the four-thousand-pound Jeep *stuck*. It was wedged between three great trees and twenty feet off the ground.

Branches snapped as the dragon dropped to the road not ten feet away from me. He landed on all fours, wings spread and powerful muscles rippling under his black scales. The icy violet eyes bored into my soul, and I saw my death.

I hefted my sword, determined to go down swinging, even as I backed into a copse of trees and hoped in vain that he wouldn't be able to reach me with that big body.

He shifted back into his human form, and I groaned. How had I forgotten he could do that?

As he advanced with deadly intent, I muttered, "I am so screwed."

CHAPTER 3

"Listen, dragon," I said as he strode toward me with murder in his eyes. Could he understand English? I almost laughed at the ridiculousness of my plight. "I know you wanted to take that wyvern somewhere, but she was my assignment. She killed a bunch of humans, and my people wanted her dead, not rehabilitated, whatever the hell that means."

The dragon stopped outside of my sword range, eyeing Chopper briefly—dismissively—before locking his cold gaze on me again. He didn't have any weapons, but I'd already seen him tear thousand-pound rocks apart and hurl that wyvern across the cave with his mind.

"I don't know when you got your assignment," I went on, very slightly encouraged that he'd stopped, even if it was only to glare venomous daggers at me. "But I got mine two weeks ago. She was the last of three wyverns that attacked children here in Oregon, and she was mine to take down. I…" I what? I'd run out of things to say. Did the dragon even understand? "I had dibs," I finished weakly, as if we were squabbling over a toy on a playground.

"You are a bounty hunter?" the dragon asked in his resonant voice. His resonant scornful voice.

I had a feeling he didn't often talk to the people he was about to slay.

"No. I work for the army."

"You are a *soldier*?" He looked me up and down, skepticism joining the scorn.

With my jeans and shirt half torn off, acid burns on my hand and sleeve, and half the forest tangled in my thick blonde braid, I didn't look my best. It had been more than ten years since I'd been active duty, and if I still had a uniform, I didn't know where it was, but what did some dragon know about what soldiers on Earth looked like or wore?

"Technically, I'm a government contractor for the army now, not a soldier." No need to mention that I took the occasional freelance job on the side. "I get a modest base pay and combat bonuses for completed missions. Which means I make in a year about what it would cost to buy a new Jeep." I thrust my sword toward the mangled vehicle dangling in the trees. I couldn't believe it hadn't fallen down. "And my missions are hunting down and killing magical beings that have committed heinous crimes against humanity. Like that wyvern did."

"You are female."

"So what? I'm six feet tall, can bench more than my bodyweight, and can skin the balls off a ram with my sword."

His eyes narrowed, and a part of me wanted to skin a dragon's balls and show him that I was capable.

"Females do not fight," he said. "They rule society and command *males* to fight."

It dawned on me that he hadn't been calling me weak. "Oh, so dragons are like bees?"

That violet light in his eyes flared. "Dragons are not like *insects*."

He stepped forward, and I whipped up the point of my sword. A wave of power knocked me twenty feet, the same as it had that wyvern, and only luck kept me from slamming into a tree. A bed of wet ferns broke my fall. Sort of.

Fortunately, the dragon did not rush after me. He stood between two trees, sunlight filtering through the branches and onto his short black hair and hard face, and scrutinized me. Had I confused him? I hoped so. I also hoped that he didn't eat people he found confusing.

"Listen, dragon." I pushed myself to my feet. "I—"

"Lord Zavryd'nokquetal," he corrected.

"What?"

"My name."

"Can I call you Zav?"

"No."

24

I pushed myself to my feet. "If you'd ever heard how badly I mangle *suea rong hai* when I try to order it from Nin's food truck, you wouldn't want me to attempt to say your name."

His eyes narrowed. "You may call me Lord Zavryd. You have interfered with the will of this representative of the Dragon Justice Court. You have slain a wyvern that would have been punished and rehabilitated. We do not kill dragons or dragon-kin, no matter how weak and degenerate they are."

"Sorry, but like I said, I had the assignment first. She was mine to take down, and I did." I lifted my chin. Maybe he appreciated someone looking him in the eye. And maybe someone who worked for the justice-whatever wouldn't kill me. But he'd only mentioned dragons and dragon-kin as worthy of keeping alive, not humans.

His nostrils flared, more like the dragon he'd been than the human he was now, and he looked me up and down again. Disdainfully.

"You are part human, that verminous infestation that blights this world, but…" He sniffed, nose wrinkling. "You also smell like an elf."

"And here I thought I smelled like ferns and dirt."

I'd been twenty-one and not-dying of what should have been mortal wounds after a helicopter crash before I'd believed my mother's story that I had an elf for a father. After that, I'd accepted it and learned to appreciate the handful of atypical aptitudes it gave me, such as the ability to heal quickly from wounds. Already, the acid burns in my skin had stopped hurting. That didn't mean I could survive having a dragon snap me in half like a toothpick.

"An elf would never lower herself to be an assassin for humans." He curled his lip. "Your trinkets and cat will not protect you if you irritate the Dragon Justice Court."

He turned and walked toward the road.

It took me a minute to realize that he was done insulting me and leaving. Was I actually going to survive this day?

When he reached the road, he faced me again. "If you interfere with my work again, I will eliminate you."

His eyes sent chills through me, but I made myself meet that gaze with all the confidence I could muster. "I'll keep that in mind. Any chance you're on your way back to whatever realm you came from?"

Something flashed in the dragon's eyes, some emotion that was,

for the first time, not irritation, indignation, or pomposity. Was it...
wistfulness?

"No. I have many criminals that I must remove from this benighted
prison yard of a planet. Stay out of my way, mongrel."

He—Zav, was all I would call him—shifted from human form to
dragon in a second, then sprang into the air, muscular legs propelling
him up to the treetops before he extended his wings. He flapped them
twice and soared out of view.

I lowered my sword and looked at my Jeep. How was I going to get
home?

My phone buzzed. I dug it out of my pocket.

Great news, Ms. Thorvald. It was Dr. Brightman. *My therapist acquaintance
had a cancelation on Monday and can work you in. Here's the link to book the
appointment.*

I groaned. I'd rather talk to another dragon than a therapist.

My wounds had mostly healed by Sunday afternoon when the bus
dropped me off at the Greyhound station in Seattle. The acid burns on
my hand were gone, and I trusted any bruises I'd received in my fight had
disappeared. Healing fast was the biggest perk of having elven blood,
especially in my line of work. Some people might think it a perk that I
was in my forties and didn't yet look thirty, but I wouldn't mind getting
past the stage where guys ogled my chest.

As I left the bus station, I grimaced at the idea of walking the mile
to Occidental Square where Nin's food truck was usually set up. I'd lost
track of how many miles I'd walked this weekend, first on that dirt road
and then on Highway 101, before I'd been close enough to order a car
to take me to Portland. The outrageous receipt for that trip was in my
inbox; I planned to write it off on my taxes as a work expense if Colonel
Willard wouldn't reimburse me.

If only I could be reimbursed for my Jeep. I'd spent most of Saturday
on the phone with the insurance agency, trying to convince someone
that an act of God had hurled it into those trees. My initial attempt to
be honest and blame a dragon had gotten me hung up on. The last I'd
heard, the agency was sending someone out to look at the crash site.

Nobody had openly said I'd doctored the photos I'd sent, but it had been implied.

Hopefully, Nin would have time to see me. I needed more ammo, and Fezzik's front sight had bent during my tiff with the dragon. Since I didn't know how long I would be in town, I needed to take care of that as soon as possible.

In the morning, I had a meeting with Brightman's therapist. I'd been so tempted to blow that off, but maybe she could give me a couple of useful breathing techniques that would loosen my chest when it felt tight. I hated relying on drugs. It didn't make sense to me that someone who could heal quickly would have high inflammation markers, or whatever they'd called it.

Yes, my life was stressful, but I *liked* stress. A normal job would bore me to death.

But a few minutes with the therapist wouldn't kill me, and I would have plenty of time to make my meeting with Colonel Willard, who would give me my combat bonus and let me know if she had anything else for me. I hoped not. I needed a few days off. And to figure out how to get around until I could get another rig. Transportation was no problem in the city, but my missions regularly took me to Oregon, Idaho, and British Columbia. For good or ill, I was *the* preeminent assassin of magical bad guys in the Pacific Northwest.

Even though it was Sunday, Occidental Square was packed for the lunch hour, with tourists wandering through and snapping pictures of the totem poles. I passed a teenager on a skateboard who had the aura of someone like me with part elven blood. That was rare in people under forty since it had been that long since the remaining elves and dwarves in this world had declared Earth too populated and cleared out en masse, finding new homes in other realms. This kid was probably only a quarter elven, enough to give him some extra agility at the skatepark.

The line at Nin's Thai Tiger truck was packed, as always. I thought about pushing my way around and going in the side door, but I didn't want to interrupt her day business. Since she also had magical blood, I could sense her working inside near the fryers. Her grandfather on her mother's side had been a gnome, and she'd known him long enough to learn his trade of making magical weapons.

One of Nin's assistants was at the window, handing out wrapped paper bundles of beef and rice. My stomach rumbled as the scents of grilling meat and spicy sauces teased my nose.

People chatted amiably in line, nobody glancing at the sword or gun I carried, since their magical glamours made them invisible to people without the blood to see through such things. Nobody glanced at *me* either. My height usually made me stand out, but the men and women were in groups or pairs, more interested in their private conversations than people-watching.

Strange, but in the crowded square, I felt a twinge of loneliness. Dr. Brightman's words about my dearth of social connections came back to me, but I brushed them aside with irritation. I did fulfilling work that few others could do, and I helped people. That was enough of a social reward. Enough of a *connection*.

Besides, where would I go to seek new friends? The magical community feared and hated me, because they knew what I did. Many of them believed I would go after even the innocent among them if someone paid me enough—not true. And humans…

Unfortunately, humans couldn't be relied upon to take care of themselves if they ran into the magical, and that happened frequently in my company. I'd made a lot of enemies, so blackmail, assassination attempts, and drive-by shootings were a regular part of my life. I didn't tell anyone I had a daughter or an ex-husband who lived in the suburbs north of Seattle, just as I didn't draw attention to my mother in Oregon. Forming new relationships would only get people I cared about hurt— or killed. I'd learned that painfully from past experience.

"One *suea rong hai*," the assistant said, handing out a meal wrapped in paper.

I stepped to the front of the line. "I'll take one of those and—" I raised my voice so Nin would hear it, from where she was now putting more rice in the cooker, "—I'm in need of something off the special menu."

"They only serve beef and rice here," a shaggy guy in dreads behind me said. "It's a thing."

"Thanks for the tip." I shooed him back to give me an appropriate three feet of personal space.

Nin leaned into view, waving a slender arm and smiling. Her short black hair had been bleached as long as I'd known her, and this week, it was dyed purple. "It is not the usual hours for the special menu, but for a good client, of course, come inside, please."

I left my puzzled advisor behind and waited at the side door until it opened. I stepped into a workspace that was more like a closet than a smithy, but all manner of completed rifles, pistols, and specialty pieces hung on pegboards. Boxes under the counters held stocks, barrels, and bolts, along with boxes of wildcat cartridges for the weapons. The place reverberated with magic, at least to my senses.

Nin gave her assistant a few instructions and stepped inside with me, closing the door so the people waiting for food wouldn't see this area. That made the tight space even tighter. I had to duck my head to keep from bumping it on the ceiling.

"Thanks for slipping me in, Nin." I pulled out Fezzik and showed her the bent front sight. "I probably could have used some pliers to fix it, but I didn't know if that would void the warranty."

Her brow furrowed, but only for a second before she got the joke, then laughed. Even though Nin had only been in the country for five years, she'd about mastered American sarcasm and idioms, as far as I could tell. She spoke English slowly, but her words were precise and easy to understand.

"You are funny. What did you fight?" Nin took the gun from me and pulled out her tools. "Did my baby perform well?"

"It did. I got the last of the wyverns that killed those kids outside of Portland. And then I let a dragon throw me around."

The tool kit slipped from her fingers and clattered to the floor. I managed to catch Fezzik before it suffered a similar fate.

"A dragon?" Nin gaped at me. "You are joking again?"

"Unfortunately not." I took out my phone and showed her pictures of my wrecked Jeep in the trees. It hadn't occurred to me to stop and take a picture of the dragon himself—odd, I know—but I trusted the placement of the smashed vehicle would suffice as proof for most people. Not the insurance agents, alas.

Nin stared at the phone, stared back at my face, and then at the phone again. "You cannot fight *dragons.*"

"It wasn't my intention."

"I did not think there were dragons on Earth. I did not—do you think I need to put a warning on my weapons?" Nin glanced at the pegboards.

"People will not believe they are strong enough to slay dragons, will they? They will get themselves killed. Then they will sue me. America is *very* litigious."

"I've heard that, but since the official stance from the government is that magic and magical beings don't exist, I think you'll be all right."

Nin grabbed a pad of sticky notes. "I am going to start putting a warning on all weapons I sell."

"That's a good idea, but could you fix mine first? And give me a few more boxes of your special ammo? I had to use more than expected on the wyvern."

"Yes, certainly." Nin, her tongue stuck in the corner of her mouth, proceeded to draw a stick dragon with a circle around it and a line through it before retrieving her tools and working on my gun. "Take what cartridges you need from that box, please." She pointed without looking.

"How's business?" I wondered how many clients she had who knew what she did when she wasn't mixing sauces and grilling beef—and how many were likely to go on a dragon safari with her weapons.

"Business is good. I am saving my money and thinking of opening a restaurant next year."

That wasn't the business I'd meant, but I asked, "Will it have more than one entree on the menu?"

"In my country, it is very common to perfect one dish and sell only that."

"I guess that's a no."

"I am thinking of adding a gluten-free sauce option."

The assistant opened the door far enough to hand me the food I'd ordered. I dug out ten dollars for the meal and a hundred for the repair service. Nin, I knew, wouldn't charge me for anything but the ammo, so I stuck the cash on a shelf when she wasn't paying attention.

My phone buzzed. The number wasn't familiar, but it was a local area code.

I answered, hoping the therapist was calling to cancel my appointment. "Yeah?"

"Ms. Thorvald?" a young male voice asked uncertainly.

"Good guess. Who's this?"

"Lieutenant Sudo. I'll be meeting you at the usual place tomorrow, but I need to move our appointment up an hour. I have something *important* to do in the afternoon." His voice was snotty, and I immediately disliked him—and the insinuation that I wasn't important.

But more concerning than that…

"Where's Colonel Willard?" I asked.

"She can't make it."

"She's *always* my contact."

"Not this time."

I opened my mouth to ask for more details, but he hung up.

"Why do I have a feeling this crappy week is not about to get any better?"

CHAPTER 4

As soon as I walked into the fourth-floor waiting room and saw the marble floors, the leather couches, the counter full of free snacks and drinks, and the view of Lake Union out the window, I knew I should have asked for the therapist's rates before making an appointment. As an independent contractor, I had health insurance on the minimalist side.

I rolled my eyes through filling out the new-patient paperwork, feeling antsy because my new contact had moved up our appointment, and I was already suspicious that this was going to be a waste of time.

"Are you all right, Ms. Thorvald?" The perky twenty-something receptionist looked at me with concern.

"Yeah, why?" I glanced around.

There were two other people in the waiting room, presumably to see other therapists. If this turned out to be some surprise group share-fest, I was going to bring Sindari out to eat everyone here. Or at least cow them into fleeing.

"I can hear your pen scrawling from here. You seem to be applying more pressure than necessary."

"I like to be firm." Noting the thick dark pen strokes on the paper, I forced my fingers to loosen. Would I be judged for that? Were there cameras in the waiting room, taking note of how pissed or frustrated people appeared while filling out the paperwork?

"Of course." Perky Receptionist smiled, her artistically feathered eyebrows twitching.

Even though I attempted to finish the paperwork with less firmness, it was difficult. The guy a few seats away started muttering, "Life's a long drive, but my car's in the shop. Life's a long drive, but my car's in the shop." Over and over, too loudly to ignore.

I turned in the paperwork. The other person waiting kept straightening the magazines on the coffee table over and over.

I gritted my teeth. Dr. Google assured me that normal people went to therapy—I'd checked—but they weren't represented in this waiting room.

"Mary will see you now," the receptionist said.

Mary? How… informal. Did this mean *Mary* hadn't earned a degree that came with a fancy honorific?

"Thanks," I mumbled and walked through the door she opened for me.

Mary turned out to be a graying Japanese woman with the last name Watanabe, but she only introduced herself by her first name and waved me to a chair that faced her seat and would put my back to the door. I gritted my teeth again. The odds of danger finding me here were low, but putting my back to a door went against my instincts. It wasn't as if Ms. Perky was going to beat down invaders before they could reach us.

"Aren't you supposed to have a couch?"

"Do you need a nap?"

"No, I need a seat that doesn't put my back to the door."

That was a weird thing to admit, wasn't it? Her eyebrows climbed. Yes, it was.

Growling, I adjusted the chair so that I faced the certificate proclaiming her a Licensed Professional Counselor and could see the door. I had to turn my head to look at her, but it wasn't my fault she'd so inconsiderately set up her office.

She had my paperwork on a tray beside her chair and a notepad in her lap. The sole desk in the room was pushed up against a wall and was apparently there to hold plants and stacks of folders rather than for work.

"What brings you here today?" Mary asked.

"A referral."

She raised her eyebrows encouragingly. Oh hell, was I going to have to do all the talking? Small talk isn't my thing. Nor is pouring out my soul to strangers.

"I've developed a few… health quirks, and my doctor thinks stress may be a factor. But look, I don't want to talk about my childhood or my mom or analyze ink blots or take a personality test or any of that bullshit. I just need some breathing exercises or meditation techniques or something."

It was a struggle not to lump those latter two into "any of that bullshit" too, but I was willing to admit that I did get *tense* at times. Maybe there was a method that could relax me when I was on the road. Punching the bag at the gym always helped, but beating things up wasn't always practical.

"I see. Is work on the table?" Mary didn't appear fazed by my list. "What do you do for a living?"

"Professional killer."

She dropped her pen.

"Not of *people*." I lifted my hands. "Of magical beings that come to our world and commit crimes against people. Like the wyverns in the news a couple of weeks ago." I hoped she wasn't going to be one of those nuts who denied that such creatures existed. The mainstream news didn't cover them, but there were millions of social media posts and videos online. If she thought those were all hoaxes, I might end up with a fistful of drug prescriptions and an appointment in a sanitarium. Could medical professionals without fancy higher degrees prescribe drugs?

"I see." Mary picked up the pen. "You don't count them as people? Aren't some of them intelligent with languages and cultures of their own?"

"They usually have languages, yes. We don't talk about their art preferences and religious beliefs before I shoot them."

At least she didn't deny that the magical existed. Unless she was humoring me. I squinted at her. She'd lost some of her unfazed expression and was tapping the pen on her notepad.

"Most of my contracts come from the government," I said, deciding that flippancy might get me in trouble. "And even with the ones that don't, I do my research and make sure they've committed crimes—usually, they're horrible crimes, like killing and eating people—before going after them. I don't bug anyone who's just hanging out here on Earth."

"It's my understanding that these beings are essentially illegal immigrants, here without permission and not granted rights by most of our governments."

"Yes." I was relieved she had some facts right.

"And we lack a way to deport them, so it can be difficult to deal with them."

"Yes."

"Are they granted trials or a kind of unprejudiced judgment before you're sent in to execute them?"

"Not typically." I shrugged. "It's not my job to question that."

"Hm." For the first time, she scribbled something on her notepad.

Her writing wasn't firm. Which was too bad, because I would have had to climb into her lap to read her notes.

I frowned at her, tension replacing my relief. "Are you supposed to judge me? Is this like with the pen out there?" I jerked a thumb toward the door.

She looked confused as she followed my pointing thumb, but she recovered quickly. "I apologize if you feel that I'm judging you. That's not my intent. I'm trying to understand your job so I can see how it could be a source of stress for you."

"Well, it's like this: on Friday night, while you were going home to be with your family, a dragon threw my Jeep twenty feet up in a tree. That was after I climbed down a cliff, risking falling to my death, to get in a fight with a wyvern, who could have killed me with her poisonous blood even if her beak, talons, and psionic powers hadn't been enough. Also, I don't think my insurance is going to cover the loss of my Jeep." What did it say about me that *that* bothered me more than any of the other stuff?

"Those do sound like harrowing events, and I'm sorry you had a rough few days."

The sympathy surprised me, though I supposed deflecting and defusing anger was what therapists were all about.

I settled back in the chair. "Thank you."

"Would you say that was a typical week for you?"

"The wyverns, yes. The dragon and the Jeep, not so much. The week before, assassins broke into my apartment and tried to kill me in my sleep. But I was awake, since I hardly ever sleep anymore, enjoying some hot cocoa, so I shot them before they got me. The week before that, I was up by Stevens Pass killing a sasquatch that was eating hikers."

She scribbled more notes. "Do you enjoy your work?"

"Not that many people are qualified to do it, and I'm good at it."

Her eyebrows took another climb.

"It takes someone with a recent magical ancestor to sense magic and the magical. My father was an elf. Or maybe still *is* an elf. I don't know much about him. My mom said he took off in the mass migration that left the world free of elves and dwarves."

I hadn't meant to talk about my family. I frowned, not sure whether she'd tricked me or I'd betrayed myself. When I'd been younger, I'd dreamed of my father coming to visit, of meeting him and finding out what he was like, but I'd long since gotten over that. Maybe I'd speculated a bit in my early twenties, when I'd finally come to believe he was an elf, but I didn't care anymore. He had left Earth, and I was never going to meet him, and that was just how it was.

"So you're good at your job, and that makes you feel compelled to do it."

"Yes."

"Would you do it if you were mediocre at it?"

"If I were mediocre at it, I'd be dead."

Judging by her expression, that wasn't the answer she wanted.

"I don't dislike my job. I like helping people, and I like challenges. If I didn't do this, I have no idea what else I'd even be qualified to do."

"It's never too late to retrain for another career."

"I don't want another career."

"Good to know." Mary set down her pen. "Let's assume that you don't find hunting down these magical beings, or being hunted down in turn, stressful." Her face twisted, as if she had a hard time believing that. "I find that chronic stress, which many people deal with, often stems from a clash between what we think society wants from us and what we believe *we* want. The expectations of others, whether perceived or genuine, can be a great burden."

"No kidding."

"Does it bother you that you're sent out to kill these intelligent beings when they haven't received trials or a fair hearing?"

"No."

At least it hadn't until she'd pointed this out. Wasn't she supposed to make my life easier, not more conflicted?

"They're not ambiguous cases." Usually. "And I purposely don't get to know any of them. I just show up and do the job so they can't go on hurting people."

"So you distance yourself from them."

I shrugged. "I guess."

"And how is your relationship with your family?"

"Fine," I said tersely, debating whether to warn her that she was straying close to my list.

"Are you married?"

"Divorced. A long time ago."

"Children?"

"One."

"Does she live with you?"

"Are you kidding? Didn't you hear the part about assassins coming to my apartment? It's been broken into eight times since I moved into it last year. Twice when I was there. I have four deadbolts, and I sleep with Chopper and Fezzik on the bed next to me."

"Are those… dogs?"

"No, my sword and my gun."

"Ah." She started writing notes again. "So your daughter lives with your ex-husband?"

"Yeah."

"Do you see her often?"

"No."

"So more distance."

"Yeah, yeah. Look, let me sum this up for you. My job is dangerous, it makes my life dangerous, and so I don't form relationships because anyone close to me could become a target for someone on a revenge mission. That's not hypothetical. That's *happened* to me—to a friend. Yes, it's lonely sometimes, and yes, I get that people are supposed to be social creatures, but the only way I could get out of the loop I'm in would be to quit my job and move to the other side of the world. I've tried quitting before, but as soon as someone gets killed and I see that the mundane authorities aren't able to do enough, I have to go back to it. I can't stand by and do nothing when I know I could help." I flopped back against the backrest, more frustrated than relaxed by this chat. "I don't want to talk about my job."

"What do you want to talk about?"

"Can't you give me some breathing exercises to do when I feel tense?"

"There are about twenty thousand meditation and breathing apps in the app stores," Mary said.

"That's your advice? Go download apps?"

"Actually, I don't give advice. I'm just here to listen to you and help you figure out solutions on your own."

"And that's what pays for the leather couches and marble floors?"

"Those came with the building. I just rent the office."

"Wonderful." I checked the door to make sure there weren't any threats about to barge in and closed my eyes. A headache was burgeoning.

"If you like, you can try the 4-7-8 breathing technique. Whenever you feel agitated, inhale through your nose for four seconds, hold your breath for seven seconds, then exhale slowly for eight seconds. This helps switch your body from a flight-or-fight state to a relaxed state by activating the parasympathetic nervous system."

I opened an eye. That sounded vaguely useful.

"Are there other people like you?" Mary asked. "In your, ah, industry?"

"There are some mixed-blood humans who gather intelligence in the office I work for, and some of the police have experience with the magical, but I've been the go-to assassin in the Pacific Northwest for the last ten years. There are others in other parts of the country and around the world."

"Are there conferences?"

"Oh sure, and I get the industry magazine."

"I'll take that for a no."

"Nothing for assassins specializing in the magical. I don't do hits on humans or hang out with people who do. I'm not a bad guy, damn it." Maybe it was hypocritical of me to find killing acceptable as long as I didn't prey on my own kind, but it was what it was.

"The reason I ask is because, since you don't believe normal humans can protect themselves against your enemies—"

"They can't."

"—then perhaps you could forge friendships with other mixed-blood colleagues, people who *could* take care of themselves."

I couldn't keep from making a face. "The guys I know are cocky assholes who are in it for the money."

"And the magical themselves? Those who haven't broken laws? Would they not have the power to protect themselves?"

"Some of them do. Some are here hiding on Earth because they don't have much power. But I don't talk to them unless I'm questioning someone and trying to get a lead. They're not in love with me. They have lots of unflattering nicknames for me. They always seem to know what I do."

"All of them? I ask because it doesn't sound like you're willing to give up your job, but there is tension in how it affects your life, and this need you feel to distance yourself from everyone may be affecting you on a personal level." Mary was going to write *distance* on my chart in all caps, I could tell. "You might have more luck finding a support group or a relationship, if that is something you seek, among those who you deem capable enough to deal with your shrapnel."

"I do not seek a relationship, thank you very much. I didn't come here because I need a hookup."

"That's not what I was suggesting." Her tone was dry now.

Were therapists supposed to be dry? I thought it was a requirement that they radiate love and compassion.

"Is there anything else you want to talk about?" Mary asked.

"No." I glanced at the clock. We still had more than a half hour left, but I needed to get across town, so I didn't mind quitting early. "I have stuff to do."

She hesitated, then pulled out a card. "Here's my cell phone number if you need to call or text. I don't always answer, but if you leave a message, I'll get back to you soon."

I'd gotten a breathing technique to use, so I didn't plan to come back for another appointment, much less call her at home, but I accepted the card. "Do you always give the weirdos you see this much access to you?"

"No, but you seem like someone who may need after-hours help."

What did *that* mean? That she thought I was a suicide candidate?

"I can't be more messed up than the guy chanting to himself in the waiting room."

"Those are song lyrics, I've been told. If you want to schedule another appointment, Tara can help." Mary smiled. "I hope you will."

"Because the rent is due soon? You can't possibly have found any of that productive."

"It's about what *you* find productive. But I think you should have started talking to someone the first time you lost a friend because of your work."

"The person I would have talked to was the person I lost."

CHAPTER 5

"Yes. I sent the pictures." I made a face at the phone, specifically the insurance agent *on* the phone. This was some kind of senior agent that my case had been escalated to. "You sent someone out to see the crash site, right? I'm still trying to arrange a tow."

Arranging it wasn't the problem. Paying the huge fee for a truck to drive from the nearest city out along that dirt road was another matter. If the insurance wouldn't cover it, the wreck could stay there.

A car honked, almost drowning out the reply. I was cutting across Capitol Hill on foot to make my meeting with this Lieutenant Sudo, and the freeway traffic roared nearby.

"How did it get in a tree?" the agent asked, suspicion lacing her tone.

I wished I'd opened with reporting a tornado strike. Oregon wasn't known for tornadoes, but an internet search had revealed that a couple *had* touched down there before, if decades apart. It seemed too late to change the story now, especially when I'd already tried two.

"I was off-roading and I had to swerve to avoid hitting—" a dragon, "—a bear. The Jeep flipped and rolled and bounced off a log or something—I couldn't quite see what. I was thrown out before it ended up in the trees."

"This is the fourth accident you've been in in three years."

"I know, but I'm in a dangerous line of work."

"You said you were off-roading."

"I was. It wasn't recreational."

41

"And what line of work did you say you're in?"

"I didn't. It's top secret. I'm a government contractor."

"I don't think we can cover you anymore, ma'am."

"That's fine, but you have to pay out on this claim. That's why I've been paying *you* every month." That and because the auto loan required it.

The line went dead.

I resisted the urge to whip out Chopper and take out my aggressions on a fire hydrant. Was I supposed to eat it on the Jeep? I still owed twenty grand. My combat bonuses went to paying off informants, buying ammo and gas, and replacing the gear I lost in fights, not making extra car payments.

With an angry huff, I reached the Starbucks Reserve Roastery on Pike and stalked through the big wood doors. It was packed, as usual, and I grimaced at the noise of dozens of conversations, voices raised to be heard over the grinding and transporting of beans through the elaborate equipment on display. This was Colonel Willard's favorite place, so we always met here, but I was less inclined to endure the hordes of tourists and scents of burning coffee—people who actually liked coffee called it roasting, but it smelled burnt to me—for some substandard replacement contact.

I spotted Sudo immediately. He wore a suit and tie rather than his army uniform, but the short buzz cut screamed military, and he had a familiar manila folder on the table in front of him. As I walked over, I couldn't help but grimace again. He was even younger than I'd imagined—if he'd graduated from OCS, it must have been *that* year—and kept glancing at his phone.

"Where's Colonel Willard?" I sat down facing him, glancing at his small black mug with a pattern in the frothy milk mingling with the coffee.

Annoyance flashed across his face, but he tamped it down. "In the hospital."

I forgot my own annoyance. "What hospital? What happened?"

He gave me the name of a local hospital, not the army medical center on Fort Lewis I would have expected, then grimly said, "Cancer."

"Cancer?" I struggled to imagine the forty-five-year-old, tough-as-nails colonel being susceptible to anything so mundane. She competed in triathlons when she wasn't busting people's faces in some martial art or another. Coffee was her only vice, as far as I knew, and she ate more servings of vegetables than a goat with a tapeworm.

"Yes. I have your bonus." Lieutenant Sudo pushed the envelope across to me. "And I must let you know—"

"Wait. You can't tell me Colonel Willard is in the hospital and drop it. Is she just getting treatment or what? She didn't have to leave her home, did she?" I waved vaguely toward North Seattle where a few officers who worked in the city, running intelligence and keeping an eye on the magical beings that showed up here, had apartments.

"Her condition is quite advanced. She's in the hospital for the rest of… until they're able to get it under control."

"Quite advanced? How can that be?" The now-familiar tightness returned to my chest. And my throat. I struggled to calm the emotions welling up and squeezing everything. I wasn't going to use the inhaler in front of this kid. And I *definitely* wasn't going to cry. "She has to have been getting all of the usual screenings," I said reasonably, logically. "She's not the kind of person who would put that off."

"I'm not her doctor. Listen, here's your money—bringing cash is highly unorthodox, I'll have you know—and I'm here to inform you that we won't have more work for you until I've finished my investigation."

I blinked slowly. "Investigation?"

Was this kid old enough to investigate more than his comic book collection?

A waiter came over, so Sudo didn't answer right away.

"Can I get you anything?"

Sudo shook his head and waved at his cup. As if the guy had been asking him.

I started to also shake my head but thought of the colonel. "Do you have any bottles of that cold nitro stuff?"

"Yes. Sweetened or unsweetened?"

"Definitely unsweetened." I had laid a five on the table, then wondered if that was enough for hoity-toity coffee.

The waiter went to get the order without commenting.

Once he was out of earshot, Sudo answered my question. "I'm an accountant. General Nash—Colonel Willard's boss—ordered me sent in to see if everything is legitimate and a *genuine* expense that the taxpayers need to foot." He pinched his lips together as he regarded me.

"The taxpayers that don't want to be eaten by wyverns, orcs, or trolls are probably okay with it."

He curled a lip. The gesture reminded me of the dragon—Zav. But Zav, at least in human form, was handsome enough and old enough to make it look like that aloof haughtiness was perfect for him. Sudo just looked petulant, like someone had stolen the comic books he'd been investigating.

Suddenly suspicious, I opened the envelope to see if there was actually cash in there. I never would have doubted it with Willard.

Sudo's hand lifted toward it, but he dropped it. He glanced nervously around, as if afraid someone would see us exchanging bills. I couldn't care less if an undercover police officer came over to talk to us. Sudo could impress the guy by showing him his military ID with *accountant* stamped on it.

"This is only twenty-five hundred," I said after counting it. "I usually get a five-thousand-dollar combat bonus."

"I know. It's completely unacceptable. Soldiers who go into war zones overseas don't get that much nearly as often as you're getting it."

"Soldiers who go into war zones overseas don't have to buy their own magical weapons from people who don't accept credit cards, not to mention traveling all over the Pacific Northwest and staying in hotels without TDY pay, which I don't get because my position doesn't officially exist. Willard's whole office doesn't officially exist."

"Giving you that much money is ridiculous, and it's one of the reasons I've started an investigation. Magical weapons." He scoffed.

I was suddenly certain he'd never encountered a magical being himself. Well, too bad. If he was going to work in Willard's little unit, he'd learn soon. This wasn't Fort Lewis out in the tree-filled boonies. Seattle was a port city and a hotbed of visitors of all kinds. *All* kinds.

"I'm sure you'll find that Colonel Willard keeps impeccable files." I made my tone as reasonable and logical as I could. "And I hope you'll find the contract she has for me, the one I signed that lays out exactly what bonuses and pay I get, because I need to buy a new Jeep. Unless you want to provide me with one?"

I'd intended to ask Willard if the army would lend me a vehicle until I could get the insurance claim straightened out. I doubted this kid would lend me a bicycle.

His gaze flicked toward one of the big windows overlooking the busy street. I spotted a black sedan with government plates under a tree. I was almost more shocked that he'd gotten a parking spot around here than that someone in his office had deemed him worthy of a car.

"Absolutely not," he said. "I'll be investigating the various reimbursement papers you've submitted *very* thoroughly. And I'll be investigating *you*. All the work you've done these last ten years. I find it highly suspicious that the government is paying for your services at all. You didn't even bring proof that you'd completed the assignment. I'm hesitant to turn this envelope over to you."

"Colonel Willard thought it was gauche when I brought decapitated heads of monsters in and plopped them down on the table. This is her favorite place, you know. She likes the nitro cold brew."

"I will be investigating her too," Sudo said coolly. "Do not think I will be intimidated by her rank or your reputation. If I find out that she's been colluding with you and keeping half of the money—"

I slammed my hand down on the table, startling the kid into shutting up. "Colonel Willard has been going above and beyond at her job since before you were born. Don't you slander her in front of me."

Admittedly, I hadn't known Willard for her whole career, but based on the last four years I'd worked for her, I was positive it was true. I wished I could make my eyes glow like the dragon had, and that the kid would wet himself.

"We'll see," Sudo said tightly, standing up, his keys jangling faintly with the movement.

I wanted to punch him. On an impulse—not a *wise* impulse—I stuck my hand in his pocket instead, startling him like a deer with a semi roaring down on it. I tugged his keys out before he thought to try to stop me.

"Since you've cheated me on my bonus, and my insurance agent wants to stiff me on the Jeep, you're going to lend me your car for a few days."

"I will *not*." He lunged for my arm.

I caught his wrist and applied enough pressure to make him wince. I might not be able to kick a dragon's ass, but after the creatures I had fought, someone with purely human reflexes was no problem.

"Thanks for understanding," I said politely, noticing a couple at a neighboring table looking our way. "I'll bring it back when my claim goes through and I'm able to replace my Jeep." Whenever that was.

As I turned, I almost knocked over the poor waiter. He thrust the chilled bottle of coffee at me and skittered back. I was three inches taller than he was, and even though I'd combed the ferns out of my hair, I could look intimidating when I was pissed. Which I always seemed to be lately.

I waved and thanked him politely. The lieutenant didn't try to chase me as I strode for the door. Instead, he lifted his phone to make a call. That was probably worse. What were the odds I'd make it through the day without being arrested?

I wasn't sure I cared. Right now, all I wanted was to see Colonel Willard and—I swallowed around the lump in my throat—figure out what was going on. With her—how could she be so sick out of nowhere?—and with Lieutenant Dickhead. He couldn't possibly be in charge of her office while she was out. He was too young, too raw, and too much of an asshole.

CHAPTER 6

I knocked quietly on the door to the hospital room. Rain had started outside and beaded on the window at the end of the hallway. The muffled mumble from inside might have been, "Come in," but it was hard to imagine Colonel Willard issuing anything but a firm, crisp, and audible-through-a-door command. At least she was awake and able to have visitors.

When I opened the door, Willard blinked in surprise at me. It was probably weird for her to see me anywhere but our usual meeting spot. It was definitely weird for me to see her *here* and out of uniform. She sat propped up in the bed and wore a flimsy hospital gown, green-plaid pajama bottoms, and fuzzy orange cat slippers. Was that *Garfield?*

I squinted at her, wondering if this represented secret tastes I hadn't known about… or a descent into a childlike mental state.

No, her dark eyes were coherent as they considered me. They were the only normal thing about her. With her brown skin, she couldn't exactly be labeled pale, but she didn't look like herself. Her square face was wan, and as short as her wiry black-and-gray hair was, it managed to seem unkempt.

Forcing a smile, I walked in. My step faltered as I saw flowers in vases all over the place. I should have brought flowers, or something *nice,* not a bottle of no-longer-entirely-chilled coffee that probably wasn't allowed on whatever special diet they had put her on. At the least, I should have brought a six-pack wrapped in gift paper. Did fancy coffees come in six-packs?

"Val?" Colonel Willard's southern accent gave my name a longer vowel than usual. "What are you doing here?"

"I came to find out why a snotty lieutenant met me at *your* coffee shop." I walked to the side of the bed and plunked the bottle down on a tray full of pill bottles. "And to bring you this. I figured the flowers had already been handled."

"I'll say. I do appreciate the members of my congregation thinking of me…" She waved to the Bible resting beside her on the bed. "But they could have pooled their funds and spared the lives of a few flowers."

"I'm pretty sure those are grown in greenhouses for the explicit purpose of being ruthlessly slain for sick people."

"True." Willard took the coffee bottle and wrapped both hands around it, gazing down at the label.

I wasn't sure what to make of that reaction. "I hope that's the right kind. If it costs more than five bucks, it's possible I stole it. I flustered the waiter."

"Did you show him your sword?"

"No."

"Your tiger?"

"Also no. I did almost smack him with my braid when I turned around."

"It *is* an intimidating braid." Willard opened the bottle and inhaled deeply. "Bless you, child. It has been six days since I had a decent cup of coffee."

I eyed the pill bottles. Willard had never tried to bless me before, and I wondered anew if this indicated an altered state of mind. Or, I amended as she took a long swallow, maybe she was just missing her fix.

"Don't you have a delivery app on your phone? I saw three independent coffee shops on the way in."

"I don't think you can get coffee delivered." She tilted her head. "That doesn't seem right, does it? In Seattle of all places."

"I think you just didn't try hard enough." I bit my lip and looked her up and down, groping for something to say.

I didn't intend to *inspect* her for signs of magical energy or tampering or anything out of the ordinary, but I realized as I stared toward her lower abdomen, I sensed… something. It wasn't like when I sensed that someone had elf or dwarf or a hint of some other magical being in their ancestry. This wasn't something in her blood. It seemed more like one of my charms tucked out of sight under the blanket. A small magical artifact.

"They're my niece's slippers," Willard said, mistaking my expression and the direction I was looking. "I did enjoy Garfield as a girl. The cartoons in the paper and the little books full of them I got from the library. My mother was always encouraging me to read. She said an education was the best way to get out of the poor town I grew up in. She wasn't impressed by the comics."

"I think he's still around. Garfield, that is. Uhm, are you wearing any trinkets or anything?" I tapped mine, knowing she knew about my magical charms and weapons. I couldn't imagine her wearing anything in the vicinity of her lower abdomen—a magical belly button ring?—but she could have something under the covers.

"No. I wish. Do you have anything for cancer?"

"Uh, this one protects you from fireballs and also the UV radiation of the sun. I don't suppose it's a skin cancer?"

"No. Ovarian, and it's spread quickly." A haunted look entered her dark brown eyes.

It was as unfamiliar from her as the Garfield slippers and hospital gown, and I didn't know how to respond. A hug? A pat on the shoulder? It was hard to imagine the no-nonsense colonel wanting either. The only time I could remember us doing anything like hugging had been on a judo mat, and I'd ended up thrown over her shoulder afterward.

"I've had a fever and infection they can't pin down too," Willard added, "so they haven't let me leave the hospital. It's been a lovely couple of weeks."

"Is there a plan? How, uhm?" My gaze drifted to a folder on a tray on the other side of the bed. "Do you have scans of, er, it?"

"Yes. I asked for all the information they had. Are you a practicing oncologist when you're not slaying monsters? How did the wyverns go?"

I took the second question to mean she would rather not talk about details. She must have already started treatment.

"Got the last one. I ran into a dragon though." I moved around the bed to pick up the folder.

"A *dragon?*"

"He wrecked my Jeep. And almost me with it. We were after the same wyvern, and I... tricked him and got it first."

"How did you survive?"

I would have liked to talk about how clever or skilled I'd been, but the truth was, "He let me live. And warned me never to get in the way of his work again."

"His work? I've never heard of a dragon here on Earth, not since ancient times. They used to consider this a purgatory of a sort, at least for themselves. My understanding from the data I've gathered from the various magical informants and witnesses we've worked with is that dragons are why so many of them came here to start with, to avoid the so-called justice of the Dragon Justice Court."

"Yes." I looked up from the scan—the angry blobs on it did not look good, but I couldn't sense anything magical from a picture itself. "That's exactly what he called it. He said he was a Lord Zavryd-something-unpronounceable."

"Lord? Not an arbiter?"

"I didn't catch everything he said before I got my translation charm turned on, but it sounded like he was basically a cop, there to drag criminals back for punishment and rehabilitation—that's what he called it. The wyvern was quaking in her scales."

"Whatever he is, I'm sure he's more than a beat cop. All of the dragons consider themselves a sort of nobility. Everyone is either a king or a queen or prince or princess, though females are born less frequently than the males. They're often more powerful, and they're usually the rulers—the males fight each other, often to the death, for the right to present themselves as mates to one of the females. I guess since they kill each other off, it doesn't matter that the numbers are skewed."

"We didn't get into all that." I was more concerned about whether I would run into Zav the Self-Righteous again, not if he had the grit to find a dragon mate. "I asked him if he was going back to his realm, and he said no. He had more work to do here. That's when he warned me to stay out of his way."

Willard leaned back into her pillows, looking tired, as if the speaking wore her out. Should I leave? Maybe the coffee would revive her, though she hadn't taken much more than that first long swallow.

"If for some reason the dragons have decided to police the problems they've inadvertently caused for us, then that could be a good thing, but this is, if not unprecedented, something that hasn't happened for a thousand years. Magical beings have come here, fleeing the reach of the Dragon Justice Court since humans were smacking flint together in caves to make fire." Her eyes narrowed. "We *have* been wondering why so many more magical beings have appeared in our world lately. Wyverns didn't used to swoop down and eat children in broad daylight. Or at all. We had more than twenty years after the elves and dwarves left when there weren't any sightings of the magical at all."

"Yes, my blissful childhood."

She glanced at me. "I always forget you're older than you look."

"It's the elven blood."

"Must be nice." Willard flicked a few fingers. "If you see the dragon again, you better stay out of his path. If he's dragging off the beings that have committed crimes here, then there's no point in killing them. Though from what I've heard from talking to some of the snitches, that punishment and rehabilitation is not pleasant. There's a reason they flee to Earth and the Wild Worlds to avoid it. You may have been granting mercy in killing that wyvern before the dragon took her."

After what those wyverns had done, mercy hadn't been in my mind. "Well, if the dragon is going to handle all the criminals—admittedly, it sounded like the wyvern had committed crimes in their realm, not that he was here because of the children on Earth that were killed—then I guess I can retire."

Willard snorted. "And do what?"

Good question. A few years earlier, I'd finished my bachelor's degree in aviation, mostly so I could get a raise, but it had been almost twenty years since I'd flown anything. When the army had discovered I healed quickly and had a few other preternatural abilities, they'd hustled me off into a special program to learn to be a good killer.

"I'm pretty agile. I could probably get a gig with Cirque du Soleil."

She snorted again. Which was the closest I'd ever gotten to a laugh from her.

I set down the folder since my aviation training couldn't tell me anything about the scan, other than that the blobs vaguely resembled cumulus clouds, but my gaze drifted toward her abdomen again. There was definitely something *there*. And it seemed to be in the area of the tumors. Was it possible this wasn't a natural cancer? What if it wasn't cancer at all? Could some magic mimic the disease? Or cause it to start up and develop far more rapidly than usual? And if magic *had* caused it, could magic cure it?

"You seem pensive," Willard said. "Is it because I look that bad? Or are you imagining yourself whirling through the air, thrown by hunky male circus performers?"

I debated whether or not to tell her what I sensed. I didn't want to give her false hope about a cure, especially since I didn't know any alchemists or magical healers who might be able to suss out what was wrong and come up with a way to fix her. Maybe it was foolish to even think such a thing could be possible. But she was the only one who would know if she'd rubbed someone in the magical community the wrong way or had been attacked outright.

"I've told you about my run-in with a dragon. Have *you* had any run-ins with magical beings? Especially in the weeks leading up to this… *this.*" I waved at the hospital and her in bed.

Her brows rose.

"Unless you're wearing a magical belly-button ring or lying on some charm or artifact, there's something magical about *you.*" I pointed to the spot.

Alarm flashed in her eyes. Willard pushed the blanket aside, slid out of bed, and patted the mattress through the sheets. Then she lifted up the mattress and looked under it.

"No, I—"

The door opened, and a nurse walked in with a dinner tray. Then halted and stared. Willard, not having found anything under the sheets or mattress, lowered her bed to the proper position.

"Colonel Willard, you're not performing unauthorized exercises again, are you?"

"No, ma'am."

The nurse frowned suspiciously at me. I lifted my hands in innocence, even if I *had* been responsible.

"I'll set this here. If you need to adjust your bed, please use the remote." The nurse deposited the food tray and pointed to the device cabled to the bed frame before leaving.

"I'm a troublemaker." Willard sighed and climbed back into bed.

"I knew that already. The magic moved with you. It's definitely in *there.*" I pointed toward her abdomen.

"Shit."

"Have you made any enemies lately? Accepted candy from strangers? Scratch that. Accepted a salad or grass-fed hamburger patty from a stranger?"

She gave me a flat look. "*You're* the one who makes the enemies. I just sit in my office and collate data."

"Did any magical beings visit you in that office in the last month?"

"A couple of snitches have been by—it would have been nice if someone had given me a heads-up on the dragon *before* I sent you out—but the usual guys. The fae coffee shop owner and the female orc who had cosmetic surgery and started one of those axe-throwing businesses. But they've been coming in for years. They especially like to rat out anyone who's competition, magical or otherwise."

I'd met them both and made a note to look them up. "Anyone come by your apartment?"

"My neighbor Dan came to get my cat and take care of her, but that was after all this started."

"The demon cat? Do you like Dan or hate him?" I'd met Maggie the one time I'd visited earlier that year. She'd complained a lot about my presence. Actually, it had been Sindari that she'd objected most to.

"Funny. Maggie is chatty, not demonic. And a sweetheart in bed at night. But no, nobody came by the apartment that I remember, at least not that I know of. You know I'm not there much except to sleep." Her eyes widened. "Wait, there was one day that I came home and the door wasn't locked. I always lock up, so I thought it was strange, but nothing was missing. I assumed I'd been distracted when I left that morning and had forgotten."

"How long ago was that?"

"Just a few days before I started having pain." She rested her hand on her abdomen.

"Mind if I go check it out?"

"No. Dan has a key. He can let you in."

I tapped a key-shaped charm on my necklace. "I can unlock most doors."

"Protection from UV radiation *and* lock-picking? Is there anything your necklace can't do?"

Cure cancer, magical or otherwise, I thought glumly. "I've been collecting charms for almost twenty years. Some of these have saved my life numerous times." My finger strayed to the cat figurine. Sindari had saved my life dozens of times all by himself.

Willard's nose wrinkled. "Just don't let your oversized cat out in my apartment again, please. The scent he leaves makes Maggie crazy."

"Sindari doesn't smell like a real cat. He's magical."

"He smells like something. Maggie wouldn't come out from under the bed for a week that time you stopped by to drop off evidence."

"I'll keep your request in mind." And ignore it. Since Sindari had a cat's nose, I couldn't imagine not bringing him out to help with an investigation. "You better enjoy your dinner."

"Enjoy, right."

I wasn't sure if Willard's scoff was because of the quality of the food or if she just wasn't interested in eating because of her treatments. Thinking of all the masses on that scan, I realized I might not have much time to get to the bottom of this. Even if I found out that someone magical had poisoned her or hexed her or something, would there be a cure?

The idea of losing her was bad enough, but I couldn't also help but think of Lieutenant Snotty and what my life would be like if I had to report to an accountant for missions in the future. Would there even *be* missions? It sounded like he wanted to close down the department, not oversee it. If he did, what then? The citizens of the Pacific Northwest had to hope that a snooty dragon who had called humans a verminous infestation kept the murdering magical criminals in check?

As I walked out, Willard was ignoring her food and pulling her small laptop off the side table. Judging by the determined expression on her face, she meant to do some research. I hoped she wouldn't wear herself out obsessing over what I'd told her. And I hoped I would actually be able to do something to help.

CHAPTER 7

Twilight fell, and the rain turned to a light mist that dampened my cheeks but didn't soak through my clothing as I walked several blocks from where I found parking to Willard's Roosevelt neighborhood apartment. Even though it was past rush hour, traffic was still a snarl. I watched a guy who was trying to parallel park a Hummer give up after crunching someone's bumper, then cause a spate of honking as he rushed back to leave a note on the other vehicle's windshield. Two smart cars that were only slightly larger than scooters zipped into the abandoned space.

I watched the situation longer than I usually would have because I'd had a niggling sense, since stepping out of the government car, that I was being watched. Since I wasn't a novice, I refrained from glancing over my shoulder repeatedly. I took a few steps down a quieter side street and pretended to check messages on my phone, while leaning against a brick wall and waiting to see if anyone suspicious rounded the corner.

So far, I hadn't *seen* anyone. It was just my instincts twanging my nerves. Considering how many times enemies had hunted me down in my life, those instincts were well honed.

Had Lieutenant Sudo ordered someone to stalk me and steal back the keys to his car? I'd expected it to have been towed away while I was in the hospital, or at least to find a police officer leaning against it when I came out. Maybe Sudo had been too embarrassed to admit to his superiors that he'd let me drive off with it, and was handling the situation in an unconventional way.

Later, I'd see if I could put the down payment on a new-used Jeep with the combat bonus money. The *partial* bonus money. Unfortunately, I still had a lot of payments left on the rig hanging in the branches on the Oregon coast. I had money in savings and various retirement plans, but I was always hesitant to dip into them, since I didn't know how long I'd be able to continue the work I did.

I lived as frugally as one could in a city where the average apartment rent was over two thousand dollars a month, but my work expenses added up. The year before, I'd paid nearly ten thousand dollars for the charm that had kept me from being charred into a s'more by that dragon's fire. It had been worth it.

Nobody came around the corner to look for me, so I put my phone away and continued on a less direct route toward Willard's apartment.

After another block, I paused to consider the acupuncture and massage services advertised on the window of an old house converted into a business. Out of the corner of my eye, I glimpsed someone in black pants and a black parka with the hood pulled up. When I scratched my jaw and looked that way casually but more directly, the person was gone. For a moment, I thought I sensed…

No, there was nothing.

After passing through the small parking lot behind Willard's building—where numerous signs informed me that anyone without a permit would be towed while also thanking me and wishing me a nice day—I paused at the bottom of the exterior stairs. Nobody was nearby. I touched my feline charm and whispered for Sindari to join me.

The familiar mist formed, and the tiger coalesced on the cracked pavement.

It's about time. Sindari swished his tail and looked straight at me. *I've been wondering if you survived the dragon.*

I'm sorry. I should have brought you back right away to check on you, but I figured you had been injured and needed time to heal. As I'd learned in the past, the magic that linked Sindari to the figurine could only keep him in this world for a few hours at a time, and if he was wounded, he had to stay in his own realm longer to recuperate. *Also, the hotel I stayed at in Portland didn't allow pets.*

Pets! If tigers had eyebrows, his would have shot up higher than his ears.

I'm sorry. Are you considered more of a service animal?

I am Sindari Dargoth Chaser the Third, Son of the Chieftain Raul, Feared Stalker and Hunter of the Tangled Tundra Nation on Del'noth.

So… not a service animal?

An ambassador, if anything. Pet. His blue eyes squinted at me. *I should gnaw off your foot for that.*

I thought you couldn't eat anything in this realm.

I wouldn't eat it. I'd just leave it in that ditch over there for the carrion birds.

You're in quite the mood this evening. I decided not to ask if male tigers had anything equivalent to PMS.

Because I feared you were dead. And that you died in the ocean where my figurine would never be recovered, meaning I could never travel from my native realm again.

Again, I'm sorry. Next time, I'll definitely recall you right away if you leave when I'm in danger of being mauled by a dragon.

Good. Do.

Is being the most regal son of a chieftain not as wonderful as it sounds? I asked as we headed up the stairs to the third floor. The rain was picking up, so I wanted to get under the covered walkway.

It's not horrible, but there are six older sons who can be twits. The hunting is lovely where I grew up though. Did you know there's an elf following us?

I almost tripped on someone's doormat and glanced back before I caught myself.

She's using stealth. You may not see her. Your senses aren't as sublime as mine.

I thought *someone was following me. An elf?* I made myself keep walking toward Willard's door. *Are you sure? I've never seen an elf, unless one counts the idealized painting of one my mother has over her fireplace.* The painting was supposedly my father, but since I'd never met him, I had no idea how accurate it was. My mother had been obsessed after he left and had the largest collection of books, trinkets, scrolls, and maps related to elves that existed outside of a museum. And perhaps even *inside* most museums. *They're supposed to have all left Earth more than forty years ago.*

One has returned to stalk you.

Why?

You'd have to ask her.

Will you help me capture her? If this was the same person I'd seen in the parka, she was fast and elusive.

She's already leaving. I think she knows that I can sense her. Sindari faced the rear parking lot, the alley I'd cut through to reach it, and roared. It sounded partially like a warning and partially a threat.

"Shit, what was that?" someone who'd just driven into the lot yelled, sticking his head out the window and staring up at us.

The lighting on the walkway hadn't come on yet, and twilight and the mist made it hard to see details. Hopefully, he couldn't tell Sindari wasn't a large dog. I'd wandered around in public with him before, but not without attracting a lot of notice and having to awkwardly deflect questions. Someone had accused me of illegally breeding white tigers, even though Sindari was clearly and beautifully silver.

"Just my service animal," I called down. "He's feeling frisky tonight."

Your foot is in so much danger. Sindari planted his large paw on top of it, but he did not proceed to gnaw it off.

The man swore, rolled up his window, and didn't get out of his car.

You're not here to scare people. I need you to help me find proof of magical tampering in Colonel Willard's apartment. I summed up the details for him as I held my lock-picking charm with one hand and placed the other hand against her door. Dwarven made, the charm was for removing minor enchantments and traps from magical gates, but when I'd locked myself out of my apartment once and tried it on a whim, I'd learned it could remove impediments to mundane entrances too.

Will the small feline be there?

No, the neighbor is caring for it.

Very good. Last time, it tried to pick a fight with me while hiding under the bed. The hissing and spitting and fur-raising was ridiculously melodramatic. It is not as if I would eat a fellow predator or the mushy gunk in her food dish.

I don't think Maggie liked you either. By the way, if you could refrain from leaving your scent all over the apartment, Colonel Willard would appreciate it.

I wasn't planning to lift my leg on the couch.

Willard and I both appreciate that, but I just mean, you know, if you could refrain from shedding or shaking off. Leaving skin or fur or whatever would disturb the cat. I'm not supposed to bring you inside.

Hmmph.

The door opened. I paused in the threshold, flicking on the lights and waiting to see if anything plucked at my senses. The last time I'd been here, a hint of lemon and vinegar and natural cleaning detergents had hung in the air, but according to Willard, it had been a couple of weeks since she'd been home. A thin layer of dust marked the wood surfaces, and even though everything was tidy and put away, it definitely felt like nobody had been inside for a while. I wondered if we would truly find anything.

After a single sniff, Sindari wandered in. I watched him, suspicious that he would leave some intimidating sign of his presence that would bother the house cat when she returned home, but he merely sat on the rug in the living area and looked around. The place was as I remembered. Various sports equipment hung on racks near the door, a bicycle dangled upside down from ceiling mounts in one corner, and martial-arts trophies shared space with books on a case behind the couch.

Willard's apartment wasn't any larger than mine, so it should be easy to search. I wandered into the adjacent kitchen and dining room, the faded carpet clean but old. Willard would have had a house to herself if she'd lived on base, but I couldn't blame her for not wanting to commute through Tacoma and Seattle every day going to and from Fort Lewis.

Not sure what I was looking for, I poked into drawers and peered under the table and into cabinets. I found a pair of Garfield coffee mugs next to a fancy espresso maker and suspected the slippers hadn't represented only the *niece's* tastes. There were Flintstones pint glasses in a cabinet, and I found a cat dish with Smurfs on it. It seemed my no-nonsense boss had a fondness for the cartoons of her youth. I knew she'd been a drill sergeant before switching to the officer route, and amused myself by imagining her barking at privates rappelling down the Victory Tower while sipping from a Garfield mug.

When I walked into the bedroom, I found Sindari with his tail up and his butt pressed against the comforter on the bed.

"What are you doing?"

Scratching an itch.

"Are you scent-marking that duvet?"

Absolutely not.

"I don't believe you. You're leaving your scent all over the place to terrorize that poor cat, aren't you?"

Only in this place, and not to terrorize her, certainly. Only to inform her that a superior feline was here. I am an apex predator. It would be against my instincts to mask my scent.

"I bet the dragon doesn't do this."

We didn't discuss how dragons mark their territory while he was chasing me across your ocean.

I sighed. "Did you find anything suspicious in here?"

I do not detect anything magical in here, but I have not completed my search. He lifted his nose and wandered out into the living room again.

I found a bottle of odor-eliminating spray in a cabinet in the bathroom and liberally squirted the duvet. Did other service-animal owners deal with this?

In here, Sindari called from the kitchen. *And I know what you're doing.*

Good. Keep your butt off things.

I joined him in the kitchen as he pawed open the cabinet under the sink.

Check that black cylinder attached to the sink, he told me.

"The garbage disposal?" I leaned forward and looked into the drain dubiously. "There are blades in that thing, you know."

I sense something.

"You sure it's not in the trash can?" I poked through a bin hanging inside the cabinet door, the coffee grounds inside starting to grow fuzzy mold. Colonel Willard must not have expected to be admitted to the hospital when she'd left, or I was certain she would have taken out the garbage.

It is in the cylinder.

"Of course it is." Reluctantly, I slid my hand past the plastic flaps and probed around the blades, trying not to imagine the disposal turning on of its own accord and cutting off my fingers. "What am I looking for?" There were more grimy, still-damp coffee grounds inside, and I grimaced.

Something very faint.

It must have been. I couldn't sense anything magical. But my fingers brushed something that felt like a tiny vial, and triumph rushed through my veins.

I pulled it out, brushing off coffee grounds, and started to reach for the faucet lever but paused. If something interesting had been in the container, I shouldn't wash it.

"Is this what you sense?" I grabbed a paper towel and wiped it but not vigorously.

It *was* a vial of some kind, though the stopper was missing. Transparent and only two inches tall, with a narrow neck and a bulbous bottom, it had heft that suggested glass rather than plastic.

Yes. Sindari gazed at it. *As I said, it has a very faint magical signature. Less than what even the weakest of your charms gives off.*

"Coming from the vial itself or some residue at the bottom?" I peered inside, but I couldn't see a smudge or stain to hint at what it had contained.

I can't tell.

"I wonder if Willard has any police friends that I could send this to. Maybe someone in forensics could scrape enough residue off the bottom to look at under a microscope." Though I doubted *magic* would show up in a mundane crime lab.

Besides, whoever had left the vial had probably washed it out. Otherwise, why leave a clue behind? Unless the person had been on the verge of being caught and had shoved it in the disposal, certain someone would use it and destroy the vial before ever seeing it...

You should not let it out of your sight, since that's your only clue. Do you not have police friends you could ask?

"No. I don't have many friends. I'm discussing this dearth with a therapist." Not that I intended to go back.

Perhaps it is because you mask their scents with offensive odors.

"I'm positive that isn't the reason."

Hm. We should— Sindari spun toward the door. *The elf is back.*

He sprang into the living room. *I will chase her down.*

But before he reached the door, something clattered onto the outdoor walkway.

Danger! Sindari shouted into my mind.

Before I could do more than shove the vial in a pocket, an explosion roared, white light flashing as the windows facing the walkway blew into a thousand pieces. Glass flew everywhere, all the way to the kitchen where it pelted the side of my face even as I whirled away. Cracks and snaps echoed, and the living room wall collapsed. Flames roared to life, creating an orange wall of fire along the walkway.

Instinct told me to go out the kitchen window and get far away from the building, but there might be neighbors in danger—including the man caring for Willard's cat.

Get the elf, I ordered Sindari and sprinted into the fire.

He sprang from the third-floor walkway and raced across the parking lot.

My fire charm activated automatically, protecting me from the flames, even though I felt the heat as if I'd jumped into an oven. I ran to the next apartment, shouting warnings and banging on doors. The walkway creaked and groaned ominously under my feet.

People raced out of their apartments and fled to the parking lot.

"Is Dan here?" I yelled, not certain what Willard's neighbor looked like or which door was his.

"Here," came a call from a doorway at the end of the walkway. Smoke hazed my view as flames burned the exterior of the building and leaped up to the eaves and the roof. "I'm trying to get the—"

Cat? I rushed to the door and found a chain still holding it most of the way shut.

"Are you Colonel Willard's friend?" I asked.

"Look out," he barked.

Something furry darted through the crack in the door.

The man swore. I bent, reflexes honed from battling magical threats, and plucked up the cat. She raked me with her claws, but I grimaced and held tight.

"Got her," I said.

She raked me with her claws again, drawing blood. Lots of it. I understood she was scared, but I felt less bad about Sindari rubbing his butt on the duvet now.

Dan opened the door fully, rushing out with a cat carrier. He must have been trying to capture Maggie.

"Thanks." He hefted it, the little gate open. "Put her in—shit." He stared at the flames eating their way closer and higher on the building.

Sirens wailed. Fire engines on the way, I hoped.

Getting the scared cat in the carrier was like stuffing a fat square peg into a round pinhole. A fat square peg with vicious claws. Unfortunately,

I didn't have a charm that could help with the task. Sweat gleamed on both of our faces and blood ran down our wrists by the time we got the cat inside.

"Thanks," Dan said again. "Uh, how do we…?"

He waved to the stairs. They were blocked by the flames now, bits of the roof breaking off and burning on the treads. With my fire charm, I could run down them easily, but I doubted it would protect Dan or the cat.

"Over the side." I pointed at the railing near his door. The roof above it wasn't burning yet. "I'll go first, and you can hand Maggie down to me."

I hopped over the railing and slithered down the framework, pausing on the walkway railing below so he could hand the carrier down to me. From there, I jumped to the pavement. People were gathering in the parking lot, staring up at the flames. The air stank of burning wood and tarry roofing material.

Dan almost fell on his way down, and I was glad I'd taken the cat carrier, even if Maggie was screaming so loudly that my ears were in danger of falling off.

"My place," Dan moaned, backing up and staring at the third floor. "All my stuff. I didn't even get my *laptop*."

With glasses and a lanky build, Dan looked to be barely out of school. I had a bad feeling about what the answer to my next question would be.

"Do you have anywhere to go with… a cat?" I held up the carrier. Maggie screeched.

Dan shook his head. "Only my mom's place, but she's allergic. Uhm, can you…? You're a friend, right?" He snapped his fingers. "You knew her name. You must be."

I wasn't sure from his triumphant expression if he was delighted because he'd been afraid he couldn't care for the cat now, or because the cat was so much work that he wanted an excuse to foist the duty off on someone else.

"Yes." I traveled so much that I couldn't even keep the plants in my apartment alive, but I would figure out something.

"Good, good." Dan patted me heartily on the shoulder. "Do you know how she's doing? The sergeant?"

"She's a colonel, and she's… receiving treatment."

"Oh, is she? She yells at me a lot about my posture and cleaning up my apartment. I assumed she was, like, a drill sergeant or something."

"She was once."

"I knew it."

Fire engines wheeled into the parking lot, and uniformed men leaped off, issuing orders for people to get back. Dan went one way, and I went another, Maggie complaining loudly about her night thus far.

I paused at the sidewalk to make sure I still had the vial. If I'd lost that, I would have lost my only clue.

It was still in my pocket. I held it up to the light of the fire to make sure it hadn't been cracked. And twitched in surprise. Some kind of hieroglyph or sigil glowed red on the bottom of the clear glass.

"That was *not* there before," I muttered. No way would I have missed that.

It was surprisingly intricate considering the diminutive size of the bottom of the vial. It reminded me of the books in my mother's house, books I'd flipped through as a child, books on the elven language.

As the soft drizzle fell on the vial, the sigil faded. Was it heat activated? Or *magic* activated? I had no idea if that had been a magical explosive or a mundane one.

The elf got away, Sindari admitted from wherever he was. *She opened a storm grate, jumped through, and locked it behind her with magic. She ran into a passage flowing with water, and by the time I got into it, I'd lost the scent. And picked up odious other scents. Do your people defecate under their cities?*

Sounds like a sewer passage. I thought those were all in pipes these days, but who knew where Sindari had ended up. I was too disappointed that he'd lost the elf to worry about it. It wasn't his fault, but how frustrating that the person who'd bombed us, and might have had something to do with Willard's mysterious disease, had gotten away. I would have loved to question her, ideally while wringing her neck.

It's disgusting, not a fitting place for an ambassador.

I know. I pushed my damp braid over my shoulder. *Come back, please. If the elf is gone, we'll have to search for answers the old-fashioned way.*

Where?

I thought again of my mother's books, of how much knowledge—

useless knowledge, I'd often considered it—she had on elves. We'd barely spoken in years, and she had strong opinions about my choice to stay away from my daughter, so I didn't enjoy spending time with her, but she might be able to help.

Maggie screeched again, sounding more like a Halloween banshee than a cat.

My mother also liked animals. Maybe I could foist Maggie off on her while I hunted down Willard's saboteur.

To visit my mom, I replied.

You have a mother?

Yes.

You've never spoken of her.

We don't have a lot in common.

Does she like tigers?

It hasn't come up.

Strange.

Yes.

CHAPTER 8

It was a lot sunnier and warmer on the eastern side of the Cascade Mountains. A lot browner, too, with the densely packed firs and spruce and ferns of the western side of the mountains giving way to more sparsely distributed ponderosa pines and junipers and eventually just sagebrush as I drove down Highway 26 toward Madras. When I'd packed, I'd grabbed my duster, jeans, and durable polyester tops. Maybe shorts and tanks would have been a better choice.

Bend, where my mother lived, was another hour out and six hours total from Seattle. The cat had complained the whole way.

Maggie was part Siamese, a breed, the internet informed me, known for vocalization. Even though the car was climate-controlled, and I'd stopped often to check her food and water, it was clear she did not like her road trip. Or maybe the fact that she was stuck in a cat carrier for it. But I didn't want to risk her escaping, especially not when I'd seen a coyote cross the highway earlier.

The only good thing about the trip so far was that some of Maggie's hairs were floating out and nestling themselves into the fabric of the seats. I didn't know how much longer I would have this car, but the idea of Lieutenant Sudo getting it back covered in cat hair pleased the immature part of my soul.

At a rest stop by a boat launch, I brought Sindari out for company. For the majority of the trip, I'd deliberately avoided doing so, lest his looming tiger presence scare the cat, but there was also the possibility that it would cause Maggie to fall silent. My rattled nerves were frayed after five hours of feline complaints, and an hour of quiet would be blissful.

Have you brought me into this realm to hunt vile enemies? Sindari asked when he formed between the car and a field of waist-high yellow grass with a few meandering trails through it.

No, to babysit the cat and talk to me.

Already, Maggie had fallen silent, though that might only be because I'd opened the passenger door and she could see the roadside wilds.

Babysitting is demeaning. Sindari's nose twitched. *I smell deer.*

Which you wouldn't be able to eat here.

True, but I can still chase prey.

Let's not terrorize the prey, eh? Here. You can have the whole back seat. I opened the door and patted his spot.

He eyed the back seat of the sedan. *This is very small. Your other vehicle was also too small when the roof was on it, but it was better than this.*

I know. This is temporary.

Sindari, amid grumbling noises, climbed into the back seat, knocking my sword scabbard, pack, and gun off to make room for himself.

"Get comfortable, will you?" I mumbled.

The small feline rides next to you in the front? Sindari sniffed the ventilation window in the back of the cat carrier.

Maggie hissed.

She has to. You wouldn't be able to fit up here. You barely fit back there.

This vehicle is not suitable for my large majestic form. It is... Sindari shifted so he could look out the window and toward the sky.

"What is it?" I asked warily, tired of being followed and tired of being surprised.

The sky was blue without a cloud in sight. Just that very large bird.

No, that wasn't a bird. Nor was it an airplane.

Dread took up residence in my stomach even before it—*he*—flew close enough for me to sense.

The dragon, Sindari informed me.

Is it the same one?

How many dragons were you expecting?

I wasn't expecting any, and then he showed up, flambéing a forest to try to get to me.

You did kill his wyvern.

That was my wyvern, damn it.

I stared at the sky, debating what I would do if he landed. Would he? Was he keeping tabs on me and annoyed that I'd come back to Oregon? Did he consider the whole state his territory now? We were more than a four-hour drive from where the wyvern had been, though I supposed that was a much shorter distance as the dragon flew.

Fortunately, the dragon kept flying and soon soared out of sight.

"Let's hope it's a coincidence," I muttered.

Hissing came from Maggie's carrier.

I frowned at Sindari. "Are you doing something to that cat?"

Absolutely not.

Why is she hissing?

She finds my size and magnificence intimidating, a reminder of her small and diminutive stature, which would put her at the mercy of wolves and cougars if she were in the wilds.

Or maybe she just doesn't like you.

Another hiss came from the cat carrier.

As any feline will tell you, it is more important to be respected than to be liked.

I got into the car. As I headed back to the highway, Maggie hunkered down in her carrier. She switched from hissing to glaring frostily through the grate toward Sindari.

Even though it was the silence I'd hoped for, I felt bad about cowing the cat.

"You'll like my mother's house," I told her. "It's got all kinds of bookcases to climb on, and there's a loft with tons of junk in it. She's got a golden retriever, but you should get along fine. Rocket likes everybody. Cats, rats, squirrels, people. Everybody."

Tigers?

We'll see.

As I drove the car onto the highway, I realized something with a sinking feeling. We were heading in the same direction the dragon had been flying.

My mom had lived in the same log cabin in Bend since I'd left home at eighteen and joined the army. Back then, she'd been on the outskirts of town with a pine-tree-filled acre of land along the river. Since then, town had moved out to her and far beyond, with subdivisions full of expensive houses on tiny lots sprouting up like mushrooms after a rain. Fortunately for her sanity, her street hadn't changed that much, other than that half the little homes had been replaced by boxy four-thousand-square-foot monstrosities with walls of windows.

She hadn't cleared any of the trees on her lot, and a lava-rock cliff rose up behind the cabin, so it was still relatively private and unchanged by time, or at least it had been three years earlier, the last time I had visited. Now, as I drove down her road toward the end, a tingle raised the hairs on my arms, a warning of a magical being or perhaps magical artifacts. I hoped my mom didn't have a witch or a werewolf for a neighbor.

I turned off the paved street and onto her long gravel driveway and frowned. There was a beat-up orange camper van parked in the dirt that didn't look anything like her Subaru SUV. Was it hers? I'd spent the first twelve years of my life living in a school bus that she'd converted into a house on wheels, long before the term "tiny home" had become trendy. But after settling here, she'd seemed to give up her itchy-footed ways.

Stranger than the van were the new lawn ornaments—stands of metal flowers, miniature windmills, bears holding fish like bazookas, and peacocks made out of rusty bicycle parts. They were all over the patches of grass that managed to thrive in the splotches of sun between the trees. Not only were the ornaments of dubious design, but they oozed magic, much like the charms on my necklace. They were what I'd sensed from up the street.

"Did she *move*? Without *telling* me?" I stared around.

The log cabin itself hadn't changed much, with the roof still in need of pressure-washing—though the moss growing up there would surely object to such an activity—and the greenhouse and garden beds in use. There was a blue kayak mounted on the side of the one-car log garage that *might* have been there last time, but I couldn't remember.

What makes you wonder that? Sindari had figured out how the automatic windows worked, and his big furry silver head was hanging out from the back seat. *The magic?*

The magic and the, uh, flavor of the magic. I wouldn't have been surprised if Mom was collecting elven artifacts, but it was hard to imagine an elven or even half-elven hand involved in the making of the rusty recycled art.

Can you tell what those yard ornaments do?

No. Maybe your mother acquired a mate.

That's impossible.

Is she not sexually active?

No! I mean, I don't know. She's seventy-one. I knew people of all ages enjoyed sex, but this was my mom we were talking about. She'd never dated anyone the whole time I'd lived with her. *She always said that her elf—my father—was her one true love, and that she would never fall for another.*

That sounds lonely.

Yeah, tell me about it. Not that I did any better in the romance department. I'd never even *had* a true love. My ex-husband was… a nice guy, but I'd fooled myself into believing I was passionately in love with him and wanted to settle down and lead a normal life. That delusion had worn away quickly after we'd married. But unlike another man I'd had a relationship with, *he* was still alive, so maybe it was for the best that I'd left.

My chest grew uncomfortably tight as I surveyed the changes to Mom's property. The situation, or maybe the yellow juniper pollen dusting the street behind us, had me wanting to reach for that inhaler again. I felt like a drug addict needing her daily hit.

I made myself count through some of the slow inhalations and exhalations that Mary had suggested. I couldn't tell if it helped. What if my condition got worse instead of better? What if I ended up having some massive asthma attack while I was on a mission, and I had to go to the hospital? Or I died in front of a creature I was supposed to slay?

"Stay here and watch the cat, please," I told Sindari, giving up on activating my parasympathetic whatever.

A plaintive yowl came from Maggie's carrier.

The small feline has no wish to stay with me.

"I won't be long."

Are those geese? Sindari asked as I got out and walked up to the front door.

I glanced toward the river where a group of them were hanging out on the bank. *Yes. I'm sure they don't want to meet you.*

Such an assumption to make. I am the equivalent of royalty in your world. They will be honored to make my acquaintance.

I really doubt that.

As I walked up to the front door, I wondered if Mom even knew I was in town. The night before, I'd left a message on her answering machine, a hulking box on the kitchen counter that was attached to the landline, the only form of communication with the outside world that she had. She wasn't a technophobe, and I'd seen her throw down some sophisticated Google searches at the library, but she had zero interest in having technology in her house. That had been true in the 80s when I'd been growing up, and she'd refused to have a television, and I was sure it remained true.

I knocked on the sturdy wood-plank door, eyeing another piece of art mounted on it, a bulbous bronze thing that seemed a mix between a gargoyle and a shrunken head. The magic was faint, but I guessed it was the equivalent of an alarm system or maybe a doorbell camera. When had Mom decided she needed all of this stuff?

The door opened, and the pock-faced, scarred, refrigerator of a man looming inside almost had me running back to the car for Chopper and Fezzik. He was six inches taller than my six feet, his head almost brushing the door frame, and there was no way he weighed less than two-fifty. And none of it was fat.

See? Sindari observed from the car. *She has found a mate.*

Uh, I really doubt it.

The guy couldn't be more than twenty-five.

He is young and virile. Good for her. Your mother must be a powerful and strong female to attract such a mate at her age.

"I'm Val." I decided to get to the bottom of this rather than listening to Sindari's commentary. "Is my mom here? I left a message…"

Yes, I'd successfully left that message. That had to mean this was still my mom's home. Unless she'd moved and had the number transferred…

He squinted at me. "You made the *opekun* go off."

"If that means cat detector, there's a reason."

He glanced at the door hanging. "The guardian. It detects magic."

"There's a bunch of it in the car. My mom? Did she move or what?"

He went back to squinting at me. I couldn't tell if this guy was slow or only *looked* slow. "You say you are Sigrid's daughter, but I have lived here six months, and you've never visited. She's spoken only rarely of you."

"Yeah, we're not that close." I wasn't about to explain to the

Neanderthal why I stayed away from the people I cared about.

"The *opekun* tells me not to trust you. You may be a demon in disguise."

"Does it talk to you often? I know a therapist, if you need a referral."

The uproarious squawking of geese interrupted whatever his response was going to be. I whirled in time to see my silver tiger bounding through the trees and springing for his prey.

"Sindari!" I yelled as the birds flew away en mass, feathers fluttering down in their wake.

Only when he hit the water did I realize the geese hadn't been his target. He could have caught one if he'd wished to. He landed in the river with a great splash, then proceeded to frolic like a kitten in the shallows.

"Is that a *tiger?*" my mom's nutty houseguest asked.

"Really more of a service animal. I'll be right back." I jogged toward the bank, glancing at the house visible through the trees to the right. A dog was barking through a fence at Sindari.

"What are you *doing?*" I wrapped my fingers around the cat figurine, prepared to send him back to his realm.

Cleansing my nostrils. Sindari flopped on his side below the bank, water lapping at his hips.

"What? Cats don't like water. What are you doing?"

I am a tiger, not a cat, and swimming is joyous. I have webbed paws. He stuck one into the air, demonstrating his soggy webbing. *But I had to clean myself because that dreadful pet urinated in its cage and stank up the air. And those sitting in the air. I do not believe it is pleased to have been left in a box in the car with a tiger.*

Ugh. I dropped my forehead into my palm. *When I find the crazy elf that tried to blow up Colonel Willard's building, I'm going to slice her in half with Chopper. I don't care if she's the last elf on Earth.*

Leaving Sindari to clean himself, I headed back to the front door. A squirrel chattered angrily at me from a tree branch. It was possible I shouldn't have called Sindari out for my road trip.

The houseguest was staring back and forth from me to the tiger, a smart phone raised to his ear. Who was he calling? The police? Given the dubious way I'd acquired my current vehicle, I didn't want to deal with the law.

"Could you put that down, please?" I offered my most polite smile while resisting the urge to knock the phone from his hand.

He lowered it, but I had a feeling he'd already made his call.

"Police?" I glanced toward my bathing tiger. "Or animal control?"

The squirrel cursed me in his chatty tongue. No question which he would prefer.

"Deschutes County Search and Rescue," he said.

I almost asked if my mom was missing, but then I remembered she'd been training her golden retriever for the program the last time I'd been here. And that it would be shocking if my mom of all people got lost in the woods.

"Are she and Rocket out volunteering?" I asked, hoping to prove to this guy that I wasn't some trickster trying to pass as my mother's daughter with plans to do nefarious things to the cabin. Or the yard art.

His shoulders did grow a little less hunched when I used the dog's name. "Yeah. They found the guy. Some idiot who flipped his ATV on an old logging road in the mountains."

"It wasn't found twenty feet up in the trees, was it?" I remembered the dragon flying past the rest stop.

"What? No." There was that squint again. This guy was positive I was shifty.

"Don't take this the wrong way, but who are you, and why are you hanging out in my mom's house?"

"Dimitri, and I live in the van, but she lets me come in for showers and to use the kitchen."

"Do you pay her?" I couldn't imagine my mom letting some charity case intrude on her life. She'd risk her ass in a snowstorm to rescue a drunken idiot in the mountains, but that wasn't the same as having someone in her personal space.

"Three hundred a month. It's less than an RV park, she lets me use the shop for my projects, and it's got a great view—usually not as weird of a view as now." He pointed at the river. Sindari was now sunning himself in a sunny patch of grass, hopefully one devoid of goose droppings.

I wished I could let Maggie out to explore here, but she would probably take off and get eaten by a mountain lion or a coyote.

I have excellent hearing, Sindari informed me without looking over. *I heard you call me a service animal and that man call me weird. You're both in danger of having your feet gnawed off.*

Will that be before or after you dry off while napping in the sun?

After.

"I'm saving up for my own place," the guy—Dimitri—went on, "so it's good not to spend money on an apartment. I do some work for a landscaping company and sell my art at the farmers market."

"Does my mom need the money?" I cared less about his life aspirations than the fact that my mom had felt compelled to take on a renter. "She didn't have to get rid of her apartments, did she?"

Was I a bad daughter because I hadn't been sending money home? I already knew I was a bad daughter for other reasons, but guilt tramped into my heart. I'd assumed Mom did fine with finances. She'd won a settlement back in the nineties and used the money to buy an eight-unit apartment building. The last she'd told me, the rents had gone up enough to pay off the mortgage and give her enough to live on.

"I don't know anything about apartments, but she said the property taxes have gone up a lot." Dimitri scratched his cheek with the corner of his phone. "Maybe if I take a picture of the deadly tiger on the bank and send it to the county, they'll adjust the land value down a few hundred thousand dollars."

"He's a guard tiger. He would add to the value, not detract from it."

For that astute comment, I'll spare your foot, Sindari told me.

Thank you.

"He does look really cool. Is it legal to have a tiger?"

The rumble of a vehicle turning onto the gravel driveway saved me from having to come up with an answer. Ah ha, there was Mom's old green Subaru. The cat yowled as it drove past. The car was parked in the shade, and it wasn't that hot, so I was sure Maggie wasn't in distress—especially with Sindari out of the vehicle—but I felt bad about her being cooped up. I hoped my mom would let her out in the house.

A furry dog head thrust out of the car window and barked. Sindari sat up.

You may want to head back to your realm for a while, I told him, hoping he was listening. I had no power to project my thoughts, so he had to be monitoring me through our link for him to hear me.

It is getting tediously crowded here.

I think the geese and the squirrels feel that way, yes. I touched the charm and whispered the word to dismiss him.

Mom parked, got out of the car, and let the dog out while giving me a peculiar look. Probably a what-are-you-doing-here look. If she'd been off on her volunteer mission for more than a day, she wouldn't have heard my phone message.

Rocket, a handsome golden retriever of four or five, shot into the trees to investigate the place Sindari had been lounging. I had no idea if Sindari smelled like a real tiger or not. He was warm when I petted him, and he felt real, but maybe to a creature with a better-than-human nose, he smelled like fire and brimstone. But not, thanks to his bath, like cat pee.

"Hey, Mom." I lifted a hand as she approached, a backpack slung over one shoulder.

She wore faded blue hiking pants, a camp shirt, and nothing but dirt on her feet. Tall and rangy with blonde hair gone to gray and bound back in a braid, she was how I imagined I would look in thirty years—though I had a fondness for shoes. I'd been told my eyes were a more emerald green than was typical and that my facial features were finer, but it was hard for me to see my father's influence. As I now knew, human genes were dominant, at least to mixed-species children born on Earth, and usually won out. That was good, I supposed. I'd seen the time-travel-to-historical-Earth *Star Trek* episodes where Kirk had to explain Spock's ears.

"Val." She stopped in front of me, and we stared at each other. "It's good to see you."

"You too."

This was the part when normal mothers and daughters hugged, but as Mom had told me long ago, there was no need to hug when a handshake would do. She always said Norwegians weren't touchy-feely. I'd stopped pointing out that her mother had been the *real* Norwegian and that we had both grown up in the States.

"I don't know if you've heard my message—" I pointed a thumb toward her open door, "—but I have a problem and was hoping you could help."

"You don't need money, do you?"

"No." Not unless Colonel Willard didn't make it and the snotty lieutenant talked the army into cancelling my contract... No, even if that happened, I could get work as an independent. I was sure of it. But I liked my gig with the army, and I liked working for Willard. I had to figure out how to heal her. "Just your elven expertise."

Her eyebrows arched.

Instead of saying more, I tilted my head toward Dimitri, hoping Mom would take a hint and send him off to his van or her shop. He was watching our exchange with a curious expression—or maybe a puzzled one. Maybe his mother hugged him when they saw each other, though he looked like someone who would be easy not to hug.

"Dimitri is a quarter dwarf," Mom said. "He knows about *things*." She waved a hand.

"Dwarf?" I looked him up and down. "Are you sure?"

"Grandpa was a big dwarf, I hear," Dimitri said.

"Either that or the rest of your family were giants." That put a strange image in my head, as far as how copulation would go. I pushed it aside and dug out the vial, painstakingly wrapped in papers so it wouldn't break.

"What happened to your Jeep?" Mom asked.

"A dragon."

This time, her eyebrows flew upward instead of merely arching.

I took out my phone, flipped to the pictures of the wreck, and handed it to her while I unwrapped the vial.

"A dragon did this? Is this what you're here about?"

"No. As crazy as it seems, the dragon is the least of my problems this week." I glanced upward, half-expecting to see him flying over the trees. "This vial may have held a potion that was dumped into my boss's coffee or juice or something in her house. There's a sigil on the bottom that appears when it's heated up. I think it's elven, and I'm hoping you can identify it."

She held the vial up to the sun, then shrugged off her pack, pulled out a lighter, and used the flame to heat the bottom.

"You've given up on flint and steel and embraced modern technology?" I asked.

"I still practice making fires from scratch, but this is easier if you're stuck out looking for someone. It gets dark fast in the mountains."

Loud snuffles came from Sudo's car—Rocket had followed his nose back to it and had his feet up on the rear passenger window that Sindari had opened. Maggie, no doubt alarmed by the appearance of another predator, yowled a complaint.

Mom held the vial up to the sky.

"Can you see the sigil?" I asked.

"Yes."

"Is it Elvish?"

"No."

"Are you sure?"

"Yes." She lowered the vial and handed it back to me.

I looked at Dimitri. "Do you enjoy similarly monosyllabic conversations with my mother, or am I special?"

"I just met you, but I think you might be." He glanced to where Sindari had been before he disappeared back into his realm.

"Guess the therapist was right." I stared down at the vial in disappointment.

Mom might be wrong—she wasn't a scholar of the subject, just an obsessed and abandoned lover of an elf. But either way, it looked like I'd wasted my time coming all the way down here.

"I've got some language books we can check," Mom said. "Just to be sure. But if you're trying to figure out more about that symbol, I might know someone who can help. If you don't mind a short walk in the woods."

I almost answered immediately that I didn't mind, but past experience made me give her a wary squint. "How short is short? Will we be crossing a state line on foot?" I waved at her dusty bare toes.

I hadn't forgotten the summer vacation I'd spent hiking the Pacific Crest Trail with her. A rite of passage, she'd assured me, while speaking about how her parents had taken her on days-long hikes through the mountains. I mostly remembered being bored out of my gourd and trying to hide my face behind my hair to protect against mosquitoes.

"Just a few miles," she said. "Shoes are optional."

Maggie yowled in the car, reminding me that she needed attending. Or that she didn't like the big yellow furry head sticking in the window.

"Is that a cat?" Mom asked.

"Colonel Willard has assured me she is, though it's possible she's a demon or nefarious shapeshifter in disguise. Can you watch her for a while? Willard is… in the hospital. And her apartment building burned down."

"*Burned* down?"

Rocket, having finished sniffing every part of the vehicle and ground that Sindari had touched, came over and nosed my hand in greeting before giving Dimitri a vigorous tail wag. He squatted down to pet the dog.

"I don't know that for sure," I admitted, "but the entire side of the building was heartily on fire when last I saw it. An elf threw a Molotov cocktail at it."

"An *elf*? Elves all left the world decades ago."

"And dragons left centuries ago, and yet…" I pointed to my phone full of crash photos.

"Huh. The world is getting interesting again."

Before I could debate what that meant, Mom added, "Get the cat, and let's see what we can find."

CHAPTER 9

We had to wait until morning to head off on Mom's "short walk in the woods," since, as she'd informed me, we didn't want to be caught out in the national forest after dark. New residents had moved into the area, which made nocturnal travels a bit dicey. I asked what kind of residents were allowed to move onto government land but didn't get much of an answer. By then, she'd had her head buried in her language books, flipping through old yellowed pages full of symbols. To my untrained eye, they were similar to the one on my vial, but I reluctantly admitted that none of them were identical. Also, there were two angry slashes on the top and bottom of mine that didn't look anything like the flowing symbols in the books.

Now, we were on the highway in my borrowed government car, heading south toward Paulina Lake. Dimitri had the day off and had volunteered to watch Maggie while we were gone. She'd been set free to roam the log cabin after Dimitri had returned from the pet store with a litter box, an obvious thing that I, a non-pet-owner, hadn't thought to buy. No wonder the cat had been crabby on her trip.

"There's the turn." Mom pointed.

I took a left onto Paulina Lake Road, a paved route that meandered up to an extinct volcano. Paulina Lake, along with a smaller one to the east, was in the crater. From a previous trip, I remembered a couple of old stores up there to service the campers, kayakers, and hikers but not much else. Rocket, who was riding in the back seat, thumped his tail and milled about, as if turning off the highway meant a fabulous adventure was imminent.

"Does your friend work in one of the stores?" I glanced at Mom, her bare feet up on the dash.

She *had* brought socks and hiking boots, perhaps a testament to the length of the short walk waiting for us. "No, and she's not so much a friend as an acquaintance I met while on a mission."

"An acquaintance who will want to see you or one who might shoot us on sight?"

Her eyebrows rose. "I'd ask if that's typical of your acquaintances, but you showed me your Jeep, so I'll assume so."

"The *dragon* is not an acquaintance." I glanced skyward, though I hadn't seen him again since that rest stop, and it was silly to believe he would be loitering in the area.

He had criminals to collect, or so he said, and I hadn't heard of any magical beings wreaking havoc around Bend. Of course, my number-one resource for letting me know about such things was in the hospital. That lieutenant probably wouldn't tell me if he'd successfully found his own ass in the shower.

We drove on in silence, except for the occasional thump of Rocket's tail on the seat. Lieutenant Sudo's car was getting nicely fur covered. I wondered if we would find any mud up by the lake that I could drive through to ensure the exterior needed a wash and wax when I returned it. He deserved it for doubting Willard. Doubting me was irritating, too, but it was a more understandable affront. I was used to skepticism from people who hadn't had run-ins with the magical themselves. Half the world still seemed to think they were like UFOs, something only nuts believed in. If only they knew how many magical beings camouflaged themselves to blend into our society. Ninety percent of them weren't any trouble and never came onto my radar. It was the other ten that kept me employed.

"Amber and Thad came up this past winter," Mom said as we rounded a bend, ponderosa pines stretching up to the blue sky on either side.

"Oh?" I asked neutrally. Carefully. Mom had lectured me on my relationship with my daughter before, and I couldn't imagine anything but judgment coming out. "To ski?"

"Yes. They were going to stay in some overpriced vacation rental, but

I gave them the loft and the spare bedroom."

"Who got the spare bedroom?" I'd always thought that was an ambitious label for the little office with the twin-sized Murphy bed that flopped out of the only drywalled wall in her cabin—the bathroom was on the other side, and I was convinced the builders had only made that wall flat because they hadn't been able to figure out how to install a toilet-paper holder on a log.

"Thad. Amber always claims the loft."

"Always? I didn't realize they came that often."

"Almost every winter over the school holidays." She slid me the judgy look I'd been expecting. "Don't you *talk* to them?"

"No."

I'd been at more of Amber's swim meets and softball games than anybody knew, but I watched from a distance. Like a stalker, not a mom. It bothered me, but I wasn't going to admit it. Mom wouldn't understand. Oh, she probably grasped that my job was dangerous and would put anyone close to me in danger—I was worried that even coming here had been a mistake—but she'd told me more than once to get a new job. A *normal* job.

But I was good at this job, better than anyone else around, and with my fast healing and ability to sense magic, I was the ideal person to send after the magical. Having had special training and twenty years of combat experience didn't hurt either.

Even if I did quit, as I'd done once when I married Thad, I would feel compelled to go back to the hunt every time something like those wyverns popped up. That was what had happened thirteen years ago. The regular authorities didn't have what it took to deal with the magical.

"You shouldn't have had a kid if you weren't going to have anything to do with her," Mom said.

"You know why I have to stay away from them. I've told you." I gritted my teeth and focused on the road. "The same reason I don't come here." I lowered my voice to mutter, "I shouldn't have come this time either."

"It's that bad here? Didn't you like the cookies that Dimitri made? I thought they were good."

"He made those? I assumed it was you."

What kind of six-foot-six, yard-art-crafting landscaper had pastry chef ambitions? Dimitri looked like the kind of guy you hired to bounce people out of your strip club.

"When have you known me to bake anything using sugar?"

"You use dates and honey and maple syrup. It's all sweet. I can't tell the difference."

"You've got a refined palette. Maybe you can go to culinary school when you get tired of being shot at for a living."

"Sometimes, *I* do the shooting."

"That'll come in handy if you specialize in desserts and wield a frosting gun."

"I'm sure that's very similar to Fezzik, yes."

"Fez-what?"

"Fezzik. From *The Princess Bride*. That's the name of my gun. Nin said my weapons would have more power if I named them. My sword is Chopper, from *Stand By Me*. The dog that sics balls." I reminded myself that Mom hadn't met Nin—and probably hadn't seen more than ten movies in her life. "I don't know what the sword's real name is. The zombie lord I killed to get it neglected to give me its pedigree."

Mom shook her head. "When you joined the army, I thought you were going to be a pilot. I didn't think I'd get a hitman for a daughter."

"I'm a hit*woman*, thank you."

The first of the parking lots came into view. Thank God. I'd forgotten that keeping Mom safe from my dangerous life wasn't the *only* reason I didn't visit often.

"Go ahead and park in that one."

As I turned off the road, Rocket barked, startling me.

"He wants the window rolled down," Mom informed me.

"Sindari figured out how to do that on his own." I fiddled with the controls—better to have the dog barking out the window than in my ear.

"Which of your weapons is that?" Mom eyed Chopper and Fezzik in the seat well behind me.

"I'll introduce you to him later. He's a new acquisition." And he would be offended if I called him that. "A new *ally*," I corrected.

A new friend, I added to myself, thinking of the therapist's suggestion that I should make more friends. Did magical tigers count?

We parked, and I strapped on my weapons, having an inkling that I might need them. Mom slung a pack on her shoulders and fastened a special dog one on Rocket, who sat patiently instead of tearing off after the ducks loitering near the boat launch. She pointed toward a trail that headed through some reeds and tall grasses along the lake.

"Do you have water?" She touched her backpack, which appeared to have *everything*, including emergency flares and a hatchet strapped to the outside.

I took the bottle of carbonated lemon water I'd been drinking in the car and stuffed it in my vest pocket.

"You said it was a short walk," I pointed out to her disapproving look.

"You shouldn't go into the woods without supplies."

"Can we do this without lectures, please? I'm having a rough week."

She pressed her lips together, grabbed Rocket's leash, and headed down the trail. I followed the brisk pace she set and tried not to think about how much time I might be wasting. If this acquaintance of hers couldn't shed any light on that sigil, this whole trip would have been for nothing. Already, I wished I'd hunted down a forensics person to try scraping residue out of the vial to identify. But I still had that niggling feeling that whatever had been in there wasn't listed in Wikipedia.

A familiar tingle went up my spine, a warning that someone—or something—magical was nearby. I paused to look out over the lake, its tree-filled slopes rising up on all sides. The sky was blue and clear, which made it easy to pick out the huge black dragon soaring over the ridge on the opposite side.

"Shit," I breathed, almost calling Sindari for help.

But I caught myself. Since there was a limit to how many hours he could stay in our world each day, I had to save him for when I needed him.

"Mom?" I trotted to catch up and started to point out the dragon to her, but he'd dipped behind the ridge and out of sight. "Where does this trail go?"

"Around the lake. We'll take a detour on the other side." She pointed toward the forest the dragon had been flying over.

Wonderful.

❖ ❖ ❖ ❖

We'd gone three miles and were almost halfway around the lake when Mom walked off the path to head inland. We'd passed several groups of hikers along the way, but I doubted we would see any more. There wasn't any hint of a trail now, and if anyone else had been leading, I would have asked if she knew where she was going. But Rocket bounded ahead of us, apparently knowing where we were going. And Mom had warned me we were taking a detour.

My fingers strayed to my necklace and the cat figurine again. I could still sense the dragon. Now that we'd turned, he was dead ahead of us. He seemed to be staying in one position. Maybe he'd caught a raccoon and was enjoying a nice appetizer before the main course arrived. Did dragons eat humans? Or dogs?

"You might want to have Rocket stay close," I warned. "The dragon who wrecked my Jeep is a couple of miles ahead of us."

Mom frowned over her shoulder. "What's he doing here?"

"He neglected to file his itinerary with me."

"Is he *hunting* you?"

"I hope not." I wasn't cocky enough to believe I could have bested him if he'd truly wanted to kill me. My charm might keep me safe from fire, but he had all kinds of alternative magic he could hurl my way. Not to mention those fangs and talons. "Honestly, I don't know why he would be. I'm not here to ki— deal with anyone. Just ask some questions of your mysterious acquaintance. How far away are we now?"

I tried to make that question casual and not let on that I was nervous about going deeper into the woods with the dragon out here. Not that we'd be safe if we made it back to the parking lot and the car. As I well knew.

"Not far. There's a tunnel up ahead."

"A tunnel? Like a lava tube?"

"Originally, I'm sure it was. Now it's being used as a passageway."

"By your acquaintance?"

"Among others."

Before I could comment on Mom's deliberate vagueness, Rocket zipped past us, planted his paws on a tree, and barked at a squirrel. The squirrel chittered back at him from the safety of a branch thirty feet up. Rocket waved his tail vigorously, barked again, and looked over at us.

"I think he wants you to do your part and get that squirrel for him," I said.

"Squirrels are a lot of work to skin and debone for not much meat."

"Gross. I was joking."

"You've eaten squirrel before. Remember that stew we used to have when you were a kid?"

"The one you used to make on a campfire made in a sawn-off oil drum? Yes, and now I wish I didn't."

"Those were tight times. Sometimes, squirrels and asparagus scrounged along the roadside were all we had." Mom kept talking, wandering off into some weird nostalgia territory, which had to be for her lost youth because she couldn't possibly miss being broke and living in a bus, but something twanged my senses, distracting me.

The dragon?

No, I sensed more than one magical aura this time, spread out across the woods ahead of us. None of them were as significant as the dragon's, but the number of them was disturbing. Ten? Twelve?

"Hold up, Mom." As I stopped, Rocket caught up with us.

He bounded past, but then halted, nose in the air. His hackles went up, and he ran back to Mom's side, growling at the route ahead.

And it *was* a route, I realized, noticing that we'd gone from tramping along unbroken ground to a trail again. Not one as substantial as the hiking path around the lake, but there were prints in the dusty earth, showing recent use. Some of those prints had been made by boots, but others had been made by large canines and still others by what at first I thought belonged to bears. But they were more similar to human prints, *large* human prints. Nobody on Earth had a foot that big. Were there trolls or orcs out here?

"What is it, boy?" Mom rested a hand on the dog's back.

Rocket whined and growled at the same time.

"What species is your acquaintance, Mom? And is there a whole pack of them?"

"She's a golem, and no. There *is* a village up here with a lot of the magical living together."

"Such as werewolves?" The large humanoid prints could have been made by a golem, but not the canine prints. Those were too large to belong to the coyotes that roamed these forests. Even wolves wouldn't have left prints that big. Not *normal* wolves.

"No. I've never met a werewolf."

"I think we're about to." I could feel the auras of the pack drawing closer.

The sheer number of them made me uneasy, especially with Mom and her dog here. I would have suggested running back to civilization, but we were too many miles from the parking area and campgrounds, and werewolves could move a lot more quickly than we could.

"Do you have a gun or just that axe?" I waved to the hatchet strapped to her pack, one more suitable to cutting branches than clubbing hostile magical enemies.

I already had Fezzik out and was loading a magazine of Nin's special cartridges. Even though I rarely hunted werewolves—they usually only killed livestock, and the government didn't consider that enough of a crime to send out an assassin—there was some silver twined in with the other magical stuff in the ammunition.

"I've got a Glock in case the coyotes come after Rocket," Mom said. "Up until a couple of years ago, I never saw anything weird in these hills, and coyotes and the occasional mountain lion were the only things you had to worry about. Maybe some black bears, but they're usually easy to scare away. Rocket has a big bark."

"I don't think he's going to keep werewolves away."

Nor did the dog look like he had barking in mind, not anymore. Maybe he had a sense of what was out there.

Rocket tried to jerk away from Mom, but she caught his collar.

"Get him leashed up and stay here. I'll go ahead and talk to them." I hefted Fezzik meaningfully and didn't miss the irritated look Mom gave me as I stepped past her. She wasn't used to me giving her orders, but this was my expertise, not hers.

"I'm not letting you go up there alone," she said. "Can we back down the trail? Maybe they won't follow."

I saw the first glimpse of gray fur between the trees ahead of us. My senses told me more accurately than my eyes that they were closing in on us from multiple directions.

One howled, an ear-splitting wail that wasn't at all romantic, despite what the stories liked to say. It sent a chill down my spine. It was the sound of wolves on the hunt, not a friendly greeting or a mere warning that we should get out of their territory.

"They want something," I said, sure of it. "Probably me."

"You, why?"

I'd taken out werewolves in Idaho after one had contracted rabies and killed a bunch of people on the Washington border. I wondered if this pack knew about that.

"Because of my job." I took a few more steps, hoping Mom would back away, and touched the cat figurine. "Sindari, I could use some tiger intimidation."

Mist formed at my side as the wolves drew closer, massive beasts that were over four hundred pounds, their heads level with my chest. Fortunately, Sindari was even larger, and he glowed with magical power that should give them pause. Unfortunately, there was only one of him. I could pick out twelve werewolves now.

Mom let out a startled gasp, though I didn't know if it was because of Sindari or the wolves.

One black male with yellow eyes stopped on the trail twenty feet ahead of us. He rose on two legs as he morphed into a human form, a powerful, tall, broad-shouldered, and noticeably naked human form. He had to be seven feet tall, maybe more. The alpha, I assumed, unless he'd been sent out as cannon fodder to speak with us. Maybe all the others were *nine* feet tall in human form.

Are we hunting wolves? Sindari's gaze locked on to the one on the path, as his ears twitched, following the noises of the others. His magic would doubtless tell him exactly where they were even without sound.

That wasn't the plan, but they've placed themselves in our path.

Canines are rude.

Yes.

I lifted my chin and met the werewolf's cold eyes. "Will you let us pass? We're not looking for any trouble."

"You are well-armed for one who seeks no trouble." His voice had an alien edge, the accent unplaceable, but I had no trouble understanding him. "Maybe you are here to hunt the pack, no?"

"No. Today, my weapons are for defense only."

"Humans are always so full of lies. They spill out, like owl pellets hacked up in the forest."

"I'm capable of lying without making gagging and coughing noises, actually. We're looking to talk to someone out here. Not you."

He tilted his head, glancing past me.

I hoped Mom wasn't doing anything to draw attention. I could hear Rocket whining and growling, but I didn't risk taking my eyes from the speaker. Even in human form, werewolves could move like lightning.

"We are the protectors of this forest," he said. "If you wish to *talk* to someone, you must go through us."

To either side of the trail, wolves prowled closer, all focused on us, all watching. I sensed from the leader that he wanted a fight.

I didn't want a fight, not with my mother here, and not against so many. While I didn't doubt my own abilities, I also wasn't usually dumb enough to take on a whole pack at once. I wished I hadn't been so focused on the dragon—I should have sensed these guys earlier.

"Will you let us go if we walk away?" I doubted it, but I wanted confirmation. Mom's vague resource wasn't so exciting to me that I would risk her life to get to him or her.

"The Ruin Bringer fears to fight us?" He tilted his head to the other side. "This is not what I expected from you."

"The name is Val, thanks. I only fight critters that commit crimes—or that pick fights with me."

"Critters. You diminish us and belittle us. This is unacceptable. You shall not pass. Nor shall you run away. There are many who will be pleased to learn of your death, and our pack will grow in status when we slay you."

"Or we'll slay *you*, and your pack will be plucked apart by crows and vultures. Maybe owls that will later hack you up in pellet form."

He threw his head back and laughed.

The attack came not from the front but the sides.

Be ready, Sindari warned me as four massive wolves rushed toward us.

Back to back, I replied, already firing.

The wolves zigzagged, trying to dodge my shots. They were fast, but not faster than Fezzik. All four of my first rounds thudded into the chest of one of the wolves rushing me. It yowled in pain as one of its legs gave way, and it tumbled to the side. The one beside it sprang for my throat.

I fired at its chest even as I ducked. More of Fezzik's rounds thudded into fur and flesh.

The wolf snarled instead of screaming, jaws snapping, but I squatted lower to avoid them. Its momentum took it over my head, and Sindari, even though he was fighting his own battle, facing two that had come at him from that side, found time to leap up and eviscerate the wolf as it passed over him. His great claws slashed into its belly. This time, the wolf screamed, its entrails falling out.

In my peripheral vision, I saw the rest of the pack rushing in and spotted my mom with her back against a tree. She wrestled with Rocket's leash even as she pointed her handgun at one of the wolves.

"I have to help Mom," I shouted, warning Sindari that I was leaving his back.

She fired at a wolf, the bullet taking it square between the eyes. But the magical creature shook his head as if it were armored and that barely hurt. He snarled and crouched to spring.

As I charged toward Mom, yelling to divert the pack's attention, I yanked Chopper out. I couldn't fire, not when that wolf was so close to her.

The crouching wolf saw me coming and switched his target, springing for me instead. His powerful muscles bunched and propelled him straight toward my head.

Keeping my cool, I sidestepped quickly as I swept my longsword up, the blade flaring with blue light as if Chopper anticipated battle. The wolf saw the threat and twisted in the air, snapping at my head and trying to rake me with its claws.

Even as I dodged the attack, I lunged for an unprotected flank. Chopper found his side and cut in deeply. The wolf squealed and huge back paws kicked at my face. I glided out of the way, tearing my blade free as the claws flashed past, an inch from my eyes, the smell of his earthy pads hitting my nostrils.

Mom fired her Glock, and I knew another wolf was after her.

With fear for her and fury at our enemies warring in my heart, I rapidly finished off my attacker as he hit the ground. Blood poured from his half-severed neck, but he twisted and lunged one more time, jaws snapping. Hatred roiled in his yellow eyes, as if we'd met before and he had a reason to detest me. To risk his life to kill me. Maybe he did.

I shifted my grip on the hilt as those fangs darted closer, braced myself, and drove Chopper into his mouth. He saw the blade coming but was too committed to the attack and couldn't dodge quickly enough. My blade pierced the vulnerable flesh of his throat and drove deep.

But one of his paws whipped up reflexively, or in a last effort to get me, and caught me on the side of the head. Pain erupted, and I leaped back, yanking my sword from his throat. I landed in a fighting stance, ready for another attack, but the wolf crumpled, the hatred fading from his eyes as he collapsed.

I whirled to help Mom with her fight, but Sindari sent a mental warning that made me hesitate.

The dragon is back. Right above us.

Shit.

I don't think dragons do that.

Nobody's that magical.

With another wolf harrying my mom—she still had her back to the tree, but they knew her gun couldn't hurt them—I didn't have time to say anything else. I rushed at her assailant, my bloody blade raised, my heart hammering from the exertion of the fight.

I sensed the dragon swooping down from above, but I couldn't do anything about it. Would he join in with the werewolves to finish me off? Or maybe he would stop them from killing me so *he* could have the pleasure.

CHAPTER 10

An unnatural darkness fell over the forest, as if a solar eclipse had blotted out the noon sun. The werewolves broke off their attack, snapping jaws and snarls halting all at once.

A roar blasted through the trees, hammering my eardrums with more than noise. Some power rode on that roar, and even with Chopper's protection against mental attacks, it ached in my mind and almost dropped me to my knees.

The remaining wolves shook their heads and pawed at their sensitive ears.

I took the brief respite to look around and count our enemies. I'd killed two, and Sindari had killed three. They had been doing their best to avoid him and circle around to get at me and Mom, but he wasn't easy to avoid. The werewolf in human form remained, crouching on the trail and watching me.

Four other wolves turned to watch the trees and a jumble of boulders to one side of the path. I sensed the dragon there. He'd landed.

I backed up, finding a tree and using it for partial cover as a single figure strode into view. If he'd been a dragon when he roared, he had shifted into human form quickly. He wore that same black robe, had the same trimmed dark beard and mustache, and not a single curly black hair on his head was out of place. His violet eyes glowed, marking him as inhuman, even to someone who couldn't sense his aura. But I thought even the most mundane and non-magical human would have felt the power emanating from him, known that he was a deadly threat.

Gunshots fired, and I jumped.

"Mom, no," I barked.

But it wasn't she who'd fired. One of the werewolves had shifted into human form and gotten her gun from her. She was leaning against a tree, bleeding from her temple, with a dazed expression on her face.

The bullets never struck the shape-shifted dragon. Zav, I remembered. That was his name. They burst into flames in the air before they hit him, and tiny thimblefuls of ash fell to the ground. Only after he'd incinerated the bullets did his gaze turn to the werewolf.

Without making a gesture, he hurled a surge of raw power. It knocked the werewolf a hundred yards through the air, until he slammed into a tree and dropped to the pine-needle-strewn ground. He didn't get up.

When Mom scurried forward to grab her gun—he'd dropped it as soon as he was struck—Rocket tugged away from her. Mom swore and lunged too late. He raced back toward the lake, his leash flapping along the ground behind him. She hesitated, glancing between me and Rocket.

"Go get him," I said, wishing I could have convinced the dog to run away earlier so she would have gotten out of here before the trouble started.

She backed slowly away, and I wasn't sure if she would obey, though she had to be worried about her buddy.

Zav strode toward me and the remaining werewolves, glancing at the two I'd killed. I kept Chopper up, ready to defend myself if I had to—was he about to object to me killing them too? This time, I'd only been defending myself, but did *he* know that?

He ignored me and faced the human-formed werewolf on the trail ahead. I tapped my translation charm to life in time to hear him speak.

"You are Thymust Fast Claw," he stated to the werewolf.

"I am. What are you doing here, Dragon? This is not your world, and this forest is ours. We have claimed it."

"I am Lord Zavryd'nokquetal. I go where I wish, and I enforce the laws of the Dragon Justice Court." He lifted a hand.

The werewolf must have sensed what was coming, for he tried

to spring away. But yellow bands of power formed around him, restraining him and halting his escape. They lifted him into the air, his feet dangling a foot above the trail.

"You have violated the laws of Serinmoor by slaying the lover of the princess of Darkenthrall. For this, I will take you to the Court for punishment and rehabilitation."

The wolf-man threw back his head and howled. I couldn't tell if it was an objection or if he was already in pain, already being *rehabilitated*.

Several of the other wolves, all of them ignoring Sindari and me now, slunk forward, sniffing their leader and eyeing Zav. Two of them shape-shifted into humans, almost as large as the dangling werewolf. Zav wasn't small in his human form—he was several inches taller than me—but he wasn't as large or as brawny as they were. They puffed out their naked chests and flexed those big muscles.

"Let him go, Dragon. The laws of Serinmoor mean nothing here."

Not worried about their posturing, Zav didn't back down. "The law established by the Dragon Justice Court is applicable in *all* worlds, and it will be upheld everywhere. Leave now, or you will regret testing my mettle. And my patience. If I have to spend another moon on this benighted world, it will be a moon too many."

"Release him, Dragon. Or you'll know the ferocity of the pack—and your own mortality."

This would be an opportune moment for us to leave, Sindari noted. *To either go back for your mother and her pet or to continue on while they are distracted.*

Good point.

I backed slowly away, though I was curious if the combined ferocity of the pack could actually hurt someone who could incinerate bullets faster than they could travel from the gun to his body.

Can you lead me to my mom and Rocket? I had no trouble sensing the dragon or werewolves, but I had no extraordinary abilities to help me find normal people—or dogs.

Yes. She recaptured him. They aren't far. She's heading back to check on you.

We'd barely moved ten yards away when the werewolves sprang at Zav. Two of them burst into flames, the same as the bullets. They weren't incinerated, but the squeals of pain as they ran off, fire burning their fur, would haunt my memory for a long time.

I turned and jogged back down the path. By the time I found Mom and Rocket, the skirmish was out of sight, but more yelps of pain filtered down through the forest.

"Are you okay?" I waved at her and Rocket, whose tail was clenched between his legs.

"For now." She looked warily up the hill. "Do we try to get around them or go back?"

"I don't think the werewolves will be a problem after this."

"And the dragon?" Mom's usually stoic face was ashen.

"He captured one and said he was hauling him off for judgment." I was tempted to abandon this mission and go back, but to what? I didn't have any other leads, and who knew how much time Colonel Willard had? "Why don't you tell me how to get to the tunnel, and I'll go in without you. You could wait here or go back to the car."

"If that's the reception you get when you meet magical people, I think I should offer to go in and *you* go back." She held out her hand. "Give me that vial, and I'll go ask about it."

"They're not going to be happy with you, either, after you shot their guard dogs, if that's what the werewolves were."

"My bullets didn't do anything." She shook her head in disgust. "Do you have special ones?"

"Yes."

White light flashed up the hill. I whirled toward it, prepared for some new attack. But the dragon vanished from my awareness—from this world. The lead werewolf had too. The others were still out there, the handful that had survived, but I sensed their auras getting farther and farther away. They were running.

"This is our chance." I cleaned off Chopper and sheathed the sword, though I kept Fezzik out. When I brushed a hand through my hair and pushed my braid over my shoulder, it came away damp, and raw pain burned my scalp. Blood smeared my fingers. Well, if that was the worst I'd gotten, that was a win. But was the battle truly over? "What exactly is waiting for us in your tunnel? A village, you said. Are we likely to have to fight again?"

"I think they'll let me in—they have before. I'm not sure about you. Did that one call you *Ruin Bringer?*"

"Yeah. The magical have a lot of names for me."

"Flattering."

"Most of them aren't, no."

"Is the dragon gone?" She squinted suspiciously at the route ahead.

"He opened a portal and left—that was that light. He could come back, but hopefully, he's busy locking up his prisoner in the dragon equivalent of a jail cell in his own realm."

I'd never been through a portal, and I'd only seen them a couple of times. From what I'd heard, they were very difficult to create, and only a few magical beings had the power and knowledge to do so. Some of the other worlds had permanent ones that could be used by travelers, but Earth supposedly didn't have any. This was a one-way trip for most of the beings who came here to hide.

Mom shook her head slowly. "All the years I lived near and in the woods, and I never saw anything other than elves, and elves only when they wished it. The last few years have been..." She looked at me with a frown. "What's changed?"

I waved for us to walk while we talked, worried that our enemies would return. "I don't know what's changed for them, but the magical have been coming to Earth in droves to hide out here. Colonel Willard and her intel team have theories—overpopulation in their worlds, new and stricter governments, an oppressive tyrannical overlord making their lives hell..." I thought of Zav and had no trouble imagining him oppressing someone tyrannically. "But few of her contacts say anything concrete. They get a haunted look in their eyes and refuse to talk about it."

Do you know, Sindari?

With the battle over, the great tiger walked at my side. Rocket kept shooting him suspicious looks, and his hackles remained up. Poor dog. He should have been left home to entertain Maggie.

Do I know what's happening to cause the magical to flee other realms? No. Del'noth is not like the seventeen worlds in the Cosmic Realms. It is not a place that you can travel to. Long ago, my ancestors were fleeing hunters who felt it a great triumph to slay a magical tiger—the Zhinevarii, as we call ourselves. We did not wish to start a war, only to be left alone to hunt our prey and enjoy the company of our kind. The most powerful of my kind attempted to create their own special realm, but they lacked the magic necessary. They made a deal with a pair of dragons, who assisted them in the gargantuan task in exchange for the promise that some of our warriors would allow themselves to be magically linked to figurines and called upon to help the owners in battle when the time came.

I touched the figurine on my necklace. I'd had to kill a powerful ogre wizard to claim it, but not a dragon. Sindari had told me the ogre had stolen it, but I hadn't realized from whom—or what.

The realm they created is not like the others, Sindari added, *not a planet that orbits a sun in a star system in this galaxy. It exists in between in another plane, another dimension. It is pure magic. Only those bound by one of the magical figurines can travel between it and other worlds.*

Bound? Are you a prisoner, then? A surge of guilt filled me. When I'd gotten the figurine, I'd considered it a prize, fairly won in battle. It hadn't occurred to me to ask if Sindari was an unwilling prize. Of course, it had taken a month before he'd deigned to talk to me, so learning anything about him had been difficult. *Should I try to find a way to free you so you can go home and stay there?*

The thought stirred anxiety, as I imagined losing the first new friend I'd made in a long time. The first I'd felt safe enough befriending, since he could take care of himself.

That is not possible—and it would not be permitted. Even though you are not supposed to be my handler—nor was the thief that had me before—because of the deal my ancestors made, I must wait until we are called to serve the dragons. Then, perhaps when that battle has been fought and the deal has been satisfied, I will be released to live always among my own kind.

Would it help if I never called you away from your world? I hated the thought and wasn't sure I could give up such a powerful ally now that I'd gotten used to having him at my side in battles.

Do you not need me?

Of course I do.

Then you should call me. I would not wish you to be slain by some furry wolf pup because you lacked a proper nanny.

I smiled, wondering if that meant he'd come to care about me. What would I do if a dragon—maybe this Zav himself—showed up and tried to take the figurine from me, to use Sindari in some war that might be fought one day?

How long ago was your realm formed and that deal made?

Before your people existed.

Ah, and in all that time, the dragons hadn't yet fought their war? Maybe there was hope that nobody would come for Sindari in my lifetime then.

Rocket wanted to sniff one of the dead wolves, but Mom hurried him past the area of the fight. She still had him on his leash. She was almost jogging as she led the way up the path, a path that grew wider and more tamped down, more covered with all manner of prints.

She slowed to a halt in front of a jagged cliff formed of jumbled lava-rock boulders. They had been there a long time, and massive pines grew up from dirt-packed crevices between them, their roots dangling over the sides. The path ended right in front of a huge slab of rock.

"Has that always been there?" I pointed at it.

"No. It's usually a tunnel entrance. This looks very permanent." She looked down at the tracks for confirmation that we were in the right spot, then touched the boulder. Suspecting an illusion?

Her hand landed on solid rock. Dead end.

CHAPTER 11

I sensed a hint of magic in the rock wall we faced. *What do you think, Sindari?*

It is an enchanted doorway. The tiger sat on his haunches and watched me. *You should have brought your new dwarf friend.*

Dimitri? We just met him yesterday. I wouldn't consider him a friend yet.

He's watching the small demon feline. Is this not an act of friendship?

Good point.

"Sindari says it's an enchanted doorway," I told Mom.

She was patting all along the rock face, looking for a gap or some magical switch to throw.

"They probably sensed the werewolves—and the dragon—and locked up tight." I fingered my key-shaped charm, wondering if it would be up to the task.

"He... says?" For the first time, Mom paused and studied Sindari. "Your, uh, tiger speaks?"

Sindari lifted his head and puffed out his chest under this perusal.

"Telepathically to me, yes. I think he can only communicate with people who are capable of telepathy themselves and the person who has his charm." I touched the figurine. "You'll have to trust me that he's wise and witty."

I'm positive she can tell that from the regal way I carry myself.

You've got werewolf blood spattered on your tail.

Regally.

"Let me try, Mom." I waved her back from the rock, rested my hand on the rock face, and grasped my charm.

This one didn't have an activation word that needed to be voiced. Closing my eyes, I willed it to thwart whatever locking mechanism or enchantment lay before us.

It warmed in my grip, and the rock under my hand grew less solid. As it wavered, becoming opaque and then translucent, something came into view. A blue-green troll with spiky white hair—and a club.

It roared, staring straight at me. I jumped back, yanking out Chopper instead of my gun. Trolls were next to impossible to kill even with magical ammunition.

"Wait." Mom stepped up beside me, lifting her empty hands. "I'm friends with Greemaw. I've been here before."

Would the troll understand her? It wore a necklace of teeth, but nothing appeared magical and able to translate.

"You bring the Deathstalker here?" The troll pointed its club at me. *Her* club, I decided, noticing something akin to breasts pressed against her leather tunic. "This is not the act of a *friend*."

"I can't understand her," Mom whispered. "Can you?"

"Yes, she doesn't like me."

"I gathered that from the club."

"This is my mother." I tilted my head toward her without lowering my sword. "She said someone here—ah, Greemaw—might be able to answer a few questions. I don't want a fight, just information."

I wondered if the troll knew about the werewolves and would call me a liar, since I'd been fighting them.

She looked over our heads, an easy feat since she was almost ten feet tall, and out toward the forest. The nostrils in her wide squat nose flared. I don't know what the winds told her, but she gave me a flat, unfriendly look.

"The price of information will be high for the Deathstalker."

"If I introduce myself as Val, will that help?"

"No. Come." The troll lowered her club, turned, and strode into the tunnel.

"Are we invited in?" Mom asked.

"Something like that."

I started to go first, but she lifted a hand and caught my arm. "Rocket and I have been here before. I stumbled across this place when I was searching for a kid who'd gone missing from a campground."

"The troll didn't eat him, did she?" Reluctantly, I let her lead, but Sindari and I followed right after her. Which made Rocket nervous—he kept glancing back, not ready to accept a tiger as a hiking buddy yet.

"No. An orc who'd lost her own child found him and wanted to adopt him into the clan."

"There's a whole *clan* in here?"

The passage we'd entered looked like the other lava tube caves I'd seen in the area, wide with a high curving ceiling and veering slightly downhill. The ground was covered with flat sandy dust, packed down from the tread of countless feet.

"Among other things," Mom said.

The temperature dropped as we walked farther from the entrance. A shadow fell behind us, the solid rock reappearing and blocking out daylight. Magical torches sputtering in holders on the rock walls provided light, but the uneasy feeling of being trapped crept into me. I reminded myself that I had the key to the door.

A small, round shape on the ground against a wall came into view as the passage curved around a bend. My first thought was that it was a skull and that we would soon pass all manner of discarded bones from some predator's meal—some troll's meal—but it was a ball. Rocket trotted forward and sniffed it, but it was too large for a dog's mouth. Sindari could have picked it up in his teeth if he were so inclined, but he was probably too regal to play with a ball. Or play at all. Once, I'd shown him a video of panthers, lions, and tigers in a big-cat rescue having fun with boxes. He'd been unimpressed. Someday, I was going to find a box big enough for him and see if it tempted him.

Another bend took us past a natural pool against one wall, droplets of water dribbling down from a crack in the ceiling to fill it. On one side, a pair of swimming pool noodles bobbed, along with an inner tube that might have escaped from someone doing the river float through town.

I sheathed Chopper. Whatever this place was, I didn't think I was walking into a war zone.

What I didn't expect was for the tunnel to end and open back up into the outdoors. We walked into a valley filled with a surprising variety of wood, stone, and hide dwellings, everything from one-room huts to sprawling complexes surrounded by fences. The path turned into a road that meandered down the middle of the valley, past the residences and also a number of service tents and market stalls.

There were magical beings everywhere, the most orcs, trolls, dwarves, gnomes, kobolds, and goblins I'd seen in one place. There were a few more exotic beings as well, ones I'd heard about but never run into, such as firbolgs, a satyr, and a minotaur. Mom looked toward a handsome elf who looked like he'd walked off the set of *Lord of the Rings*. A wistful expression crossed her face.

Interesting, Sindari remarked as we followed the troll down the road, almost all of the beings turning to watch our passage. *These people represent several different worlds and wouldn't usually be found together. Historically, many of them have made war on each other.*

It's got to be a refuge of some kind. Maybe someone powerful—this Greemaw?— keeps the peace. What was more surprising to me was how this place could have avoided notice from the outside world.

Though the trees along the steep valley slopes were massive, with branches that stretched much more expansively than normal over the valley floor, sunlight filtered down through the leaves and needles. It was hard to imagine that this wouldn't be visible to the various helicopters and planes that flew around the area, taking visitors over the mountains and volcanoes. I'd seen a pamphlet for a tour that flew people around to remote locations to look for sasquatch.

But as I eyed the branches, I noticed a hint of magic about them. It was hard to pick out, since the auras of magical beings and artifacts bombarded me from all sides here, but an enchantment was definitely up there, hiding the valley from outside detection.

A few beings whispered as we passed, and with my translation charm still active, I picked out *Ruin Bringer, Slayer,* and *Deathstalker* along with other less flattering names I'd heard before. Even so, I hadn't realized I was this notorious among the magical. A few of the speakers were children, gnomes and dwarves wearing the tattered clothing of true refugees. I decided I didn't want this fame—this infamy—and wished I could let them know they had nothing to fear from me, so long as they didn't prey on humans.

One boy called out a semblance of Rocket's name, the accent putting the stresses in odd places, and threw a grubby tennis ball. The dog bounded off to get it. Mom lifted a hand, as if to call him back, but she dropped her arm and let him retrieve the ball. He brought it back to her instead of the skinny gnome kid who'd thrown it, but she passed it along to the owner. Rocket wagged his tail for the first time since we'd encountered the werewolves.

"There she is." Mom pointed to a cave set into the back of the valley and framed by a pergola made from wood and the porous lava-rock boulders.

The huge golem sat on a stone bench the size of a conference table, her dark gray skin almost matching the surrounding rock. She looked like she'd been carved from it, with waves of green hair akin to moss falling to her broad shoulders. Very old eyes like polished pieces of obsidian gazed at me as we approached.

I would not wish to fight a golem, Sindari informed me. *Their skin is as hard as the rocks of their native world.*

So I shouldn't piss her off?

I recommend against it. She is a lava golem. They are slow to anger, but when they lose their temper, it is as bad as a volcano erupting. They can melt pieces of their stone flesh and throw flaming lava balls at enemies, assuming they don't simply grab you and crush you to pieces.

Our troll guide bowed to the golem and backed away without a word, heading back to her post.

"Hello, Greemaw," my mother said. "I apologize for intruding in your world again, but my daughter has a mystery it's important for her to solve, and I thought you might be familiar with a sigil that's her only clue."

"Your daughter is the Ruin Bringer?" The golem spoke slowly and precisely, her deep rumble reminding me of a cement mixer.

"Apparently."

"She is not welcome among our kind."

"I'm not here to bother anyone," I said. "And I'll pay for the information. In money or tennis balls and pool noodles. Whatever excites people here."

The obsidian eyes regarded me without warmth. Mom frowned at me. I felt like the delinquent teenager who had been dragged home by the police.

"I thought," Mom said to Greemaw, "that since you told me before that you've been here since the last volcanic eruption, you might be familiar with all the races that have come and gone in that time period."

"Hasn't it been over a thousand years since the volcano erupted?" I waved in the direction of the lakes and Paulina Peak.

Mom nodded. "Golems are long-lived, she tells me."

"It is true," Greemaw said. "I was alone then and for many centuries afterward, except when travelers passed through. Now, the village is full of life. It is very busy to one such as myself, but I cannot turn away refugees." Her gaze fell on me again. "There are so few safe places for them in this world."

Because this isn't their world, I kept myself from saying. Instead, I pulled out the vial and warily approached the golem. Even sitting, Greemaw towered over me, with shoulders four times wider than mine. She had to weigh thousands of pounds. But she didn't make any sudden movements.

"Will you look at the sigil on the bottom of this and let me know if you recognize it?" I waved the vial. "I'll pay," I repeated, though I didn't know if money was useful to these people. It wasn't as if a golem could walk into a 7-11.

"Did you slay the werewolf protectors?" she asked. "Or did the dragon?"

Uh. They had called themselves protectors, and she called them that too. I'd hoped they hadn't been allied. If I told her the truth, she probably wouldn't help me. More than that, she might order everybody here to attack me.

The children, I noticed, had disappeared, and only adults were present now. More than fifty of them watched our exchange, some with clubs, short swords, or bows. A couple of flinty-faced dwarves had guns.

Though I was tempted to foist the deaths of the werewolves off on Zav, it was possible the golem could communicate with him and that I would be caught lying. I didn't like lying anyway. I didn't think I had been at fault when it came to the werewolves, but if I'd made a mistake, I preferred to own up to it. The only thing that made me pause was all the baleful looks—and the weapons—aimed in my direction.

"They attacked me," I said, "and I defended myself. I asked if they would let us turn back without a fight, but they said no. So, yes, I killed several of them. Five, I believe, between myself and Sindari. I'm not sure how many the dragon killed, if any. He captured one and lit a couple others on fire. They may have survived."

The golem listened to my tale, then looked to one of the side walls in her cave. It was more of an alcove, and I didn't sense or feel anything magical in the stone itself, but she spoke to the wall.

"Is that correct?"

The rock wall shimmered, and a surge of magical awareness flooded me even before Zav walked out in human form to stand next to the golem and face me. Physically, he appeared small next to Greemaw, but magically, he was like the sun compared to a distant star.

I couldn't read the haughty expression he leveled at me, but I made myself stare back at him with determination. I didn't care if he radiated the power of a supernova. This was my world, not his, and he didn't have any right to judge me or tell me what I could do here.

"It's correct," he said, still looking at me, though he replied to Greemaw. "I let the werewolves who fled live, though they *should* have been punished. They were arrogant and did not properly defer to a dragon."

"Yeah, I had the same problem with them." It probably wasn't the time for lippiness—the dark frown my mom sent me assured that—so I resolved to keep my mouth shut, unless it was about the vial.

"It is no surprise that a werewolf would not defer to a *human*." Zav's violet eyes closed to slits but remained locked on me. "Even a mongrel with the blood of an elf who lowered himself to rut with a human."

Mom turned her frown on Zav, and indignation burned in her eyes. Probably more at the insult to her former lover than for me or herself. But Rocket slunk back to hide behind a hut, and she must have remembered how dangerous this guy was—those casually incinerated bullets had to be prominent in her mind—for she didn't say anything.

"You have earned the hatred of all the magical beings in this part of this world." Zav walked toward me, his hands clasped behind his back, and then circled me, eyeing me up and down. It wasn't sexual—if he'd been affronted by the idea of an elf and a human mating, he'd wither up and die in horror at a dragon having relations with a human. It was more like that of an undefeated boxer sizing up a scrawny newcomer to the arena. "I can understand why, of course," he continued, "since you stomped into my way and killed the wyvern I was in the middle of arresting."

Why did I have a feeling this guy was making me his special project? Was it truly coincidence that he'd found criminals right next to me on two separate occasions, or was he stalking me for some reason? Running into each other at the seaside cave over the wyvern could have been chance, but what were the odds that his second arrest would bring him halfway across the state to the same mountainside where I was?

"The wyvern that killed humans and that I was charged by my authorities to kill," I stated. "I was on the case first, as I said. You weren't around when I executed the first two, and it's not my fault you came late to the third one."

"If there were others, they were not my concern. And you were *not* there first."

"I was already there when you walked in, asshole."

"Oh?"

Hell, hadn't he realized that? If not, I was an idiot for hinting at one of my advantages. If I had to fight him again, the cloaking charm might be the only thing that would save my life.

Zav stopped his circling at my side, his chest a hair's breadth from brushing my shoulder. He lifted a hand—I almost expected to see claws at the ends of his fingers, but he had normal, well-trimmed nails. As I watched that hand come closer, it was all I could do not to spring back and draw Chopper.

But the armed refugees behind me had inched closer, and Greemaw was watching me intently. I had the feeling this was a test. But if I annoyed him enough, he might break my neck. His hand was heading toward it. No, it was to my necklace, not my neck. He ran his finger along the charms and paused in front of the one that had camouflaged me that day in the wyvern cave.

"Yes, I see. I should take this from you, so you can't easily sneak up on the magical." His lip curled. "*Assassin.*"

I clenched my jaw but didn't allow myself to otherwise react. I could live without that charm, but what if he took Sindari from me?

At my side, the tiger crouched, his tail rigid as he watched this exchange. He looked like he wanted to attack, but even he would be no match for a dragon.

"But I am not a thief." Zav lowered his hand. "*I* am not a criminal."

"I'm not a criminal either," I growled. "You can't bring your laws to this world and expect people here to obey them."

"Of course I can. I am a dragon, sent by the Dragon Justice Court. That your puny people don't recognize our rule over the galaxy is laughable. It is only because nobody wishes to deal with your verminous infestation of this world that you've been allowed to run amok, breeding like *iyarku* and suffocating out almost all other life here." His lids drooped, leaving his violet eyes as mere slits. "You would be wise to respect dragons when they do visit."

"So sorry I didn't drag a throne and a red carpet into that cave as soon as you arrived."

"Someday," he continued, ignoring my outburst, "a dragon may decide to come and rule over this mess and straighten it out."

"You, perhaps? Just give me some notice. I'll put the word out on social media, so anyone who wants to appropriately worship you can show up at the portal."

"Not me." He curled his lip again. Maybe that was an involuntary tic. "I will spend no more time in this vile place than I must. I am no cowardly refugee."

A couple of the guys with guns glanced at each other at this insult, but nobody shifted their weapons from me to Zav. Too bad.

He prowled around behind me again, and my shoulder blades itched. The last thing I wanted was an enemy this powerful at my back.

He came around to my other side. "Because I think it could cut down on the length of time I'm forced to stay here, I am considering using you as bait."

"What?"

He smiled for the first time, and I decided that Amused Zav wasn't any more appealing than Pissed Zav. "They hate you, and they come out in droves when you're nearby. I've never had a pack of werewolves stand up to me in my life, but they wanted very badly to kill you, to receive credit among all the magical here for their great victory. Even when I was right before them, they thought that it would be worth it to sacrifice part of their pack to take you down."

"Nice of you to read their minds. That would be considered a violation of civil liberties here, but whatever. You've already said our laws don't apply to dragons."

"What liberties do your laws give to the magical?"

None, I admitted, thinking of the therapist. Maybe I'd call Mary later and let her know my acute stressors were at least as much of a problem as the chronic ones.

"I cannot read your mind," he remarked, watching me. "Which charm of yours protects you from that?"

"If you don't know, I'm not telling you. A girl doesn't lift her skirt for just any man."

He blinked and looked down. I almost laughed, realizing I'd confused him with the expression.

His surprise disappeared quickly, and he lifted his gaze and nodded. "Yes, bait. You could offend the magical with your tongue even if you hadn't alienated the whole community by slaying hundreds of them."

"Those weren't part of a community. They were rogues. And you're not dragging me off to dangle me above a cliff or whatever you have in mind. I'd kick my own ass before going anywhere with you."

"I wasn't going to give you a choice," he said dryly.

"I'm *not* being your pawn." I glared straight into those cocky violet eyes.

He stared back at me, indifferent, as far as I could tell, to my defiance.

"It is not wise to refuse a dragon," Greemaw said.

"People keep using that word," I said, "but I assure you it doesn't apply to me."

My mother rubbed her face. She had her Glock in hand again, but she didn't know what to do with it. I had a similar problem. I wanted to bash the pompous dragon on the head with Chopper, but I couldn't win, not here with all his allies around and probably not alone in a field with him either. Life was unfair.

"You are an honest mongrel," Zav said, "I'll grant you that."

"Thanks so much. You're not using me."

"We'll see." The violet glow to his eyes brightened, and he smiled again, then turned and walked into the stone wall.

Once again, his aura vanished from my senses far more abruptly than it should have. My legs almost buckled at the cessation of power. Mom came over and gripped my arm.

I wanted to wave her away, to say I was fine, but my muscles *were* rubbery and unreliable. I took a few deep breaths, refusing to fall or pass out in front of a lava golem and her entire clan of refugees.

"So, uh, Greemaw." I focused on her and tried to pretend nothing had happened, while hoping that Zav had taken off and I would never see him again. "I believe we were negotiating? For your assistance?"

She gripped her broad chin with one massive hand. "Zavryd came to check on us when he learned you were heading here. I have crossed paths with his family before, in another realm, another time."

"Are they all so delightful?"

She chuckled, the sound like rocks grating together. "He is young for a dragon, with much to prove to his family. Believe it or not, he would be considered polite and reasonable for one of their kind."

"Reasonable! He wants to dangle me as bait until some villain succeeds in killing me." I envisioned the black dragon version of Zav flying all over the West Coast with me tethered to one of his legs, hanging upside down thousands of feet in the air as wyverns and harpies and who knew what else flew at me with spears.

"Many dragons kill lesser beings—" Greemaw touched her own chest to include herself in the group, "—or keep them as slaves. Were I not too old for war, I would fight beside his family, to ensure they continue to hold majority power in the Dragon Ruling Council and Justice Court."

I had a headache and couldn't articulate how little I cared about dragon courts and councils.

"Even so," Greemaw said, extending her hand, palm upward, "I will admit it tickles me to see someone stand up to a dragon. That audacity will get you killed, but for today, I will help you if I can. Show me the vial."

My audacity had helped the situation? There was a first. I laid the vial on her palm, hoping she had a gentler touch than the size of her hand suggested.

"It takes heat to make the sigil visible," I said.

Mom cleared her throat and held up her lighter in offering.

"Not necessary." Greemaw focused on her palm, and the gray stone took on the orange color of a hot charcoal ember.

I could feel the heat from a couple of feet in front of her. Rather than trying to manipulate the vial with her large fingers, she used her power to levitate it into the air. It spun slowly, and she paused it to peer through the opening to the bottom. The elegant sigil was once again illuminated.

"I thought it might be elven, but my mother disagreed, and we didn't find it in any of her language books."

"That is because—" Greemaw allowed the vial to lower to her palm and extended it to me, "—that is a symbol from the special alchemical language of the dark elves."

"Dark elves? The ones that used to live underground and war with the light elves—or regular old elves, as we talk about them now—in Norse mythology?"

"They have warred with the sunlight elves for all of eternity and across many worlds," Greemaw said.

"Haven't they been gone from Earth for centuries and centuries?" Mom asked.

"As far as *I* know, that's the belief." I pulled out my phone, intending to text Willard and ask if she'd heard differently, but the magic that kept this place hidden also blocked cell signals. "I'll check with my boss later. If there are dark elves hanging out in Seattle, she would be the one to know."

But if she did know, wouldn't she have mentioned it in passing at some point? And would such beings, considered evil by the surface elves, have been able to fly under the radar for centuries?

Maybe it wasn't dark elves at all but someone who'd gotten ahold of one of the race's ancient alchemy books and learned to make a vial and a potion to get at Willard. That made more sense to me.

"Seattle," Greemaw said the name slowly, as if it weren't familiar. "What was that place called in past times?"

"I'm not sure what it would have been called when the last volcano erupted, if that's what you mean." I waved toward Paulina Peak again. "The Duwamish were the natives that occupied the land where the city now is."

"Ah, yes. It is a newer city, by your definition of that. If dark elves live there, they would have come relatively recently. They cannot stand the sunlight, so they can only be someplace with tunnels or caves."

"Maybe they were hanging out over in Forks with the vampires." I meant it as a joke, but Greemaw shook her head.

"Even a rainforest would not be dark enough for them to come out in the daylight. The sun burns them quickly, but they grow ill even under cloud cover. They will come out on a cloudy night, but never when the moon is present in the sky."

"Thank you for the information." I doubted I was dealing with real dark elves, but at least I had a starting point now for researching potions that could have hurt Willard. I didn't know any alchemists back in Seattle, but I was positive there had to be some in a city that big, and I would find them.

CHAPTER 12

"When you said your work—your life—is dangerous, I didn't fully grasp *how* dangerous." Mom looked at me from the passenger seat as we drove back to Bend.

"The dragon has taken it to a new level this week, but it's not uncommon for the magical to attack me. I've been killing their kind for almost twenty years, first as a soldier and now as a government contractor. They don't seem to realize that the ones I kill are horrible criminals and it would be best not to associate with them. They don't get it that I won't come after them unless they do something really, really wrong. It's frustrating."

As evinced by my white knuckles around the steering wheel. And the tightness in my chest again. I felt the need to grab the inhaler, but I didn't want to do it in front of Mom. In front of anyone. The only saving grace was that, so far, I'd been more prone to the lung constriction when I was in a quiet albeit stressful situation than when I was in battle. Maybe adrenaline helped keep the airways open. But could I count on that to last? I didn't know.

Rocket whapped his tail against the upholstery, wagging in sympathy. Or maybe he was showing relief that I'd dismissed Sindari.

I'd sent him back to his realm, wanting him to be fresh if that dragon showed up again and I needed him. I was still almost shaking with anger at Zav's audacity to want to use me as bait. If he showed up again to arrest someone I was in the middle of battling, I didn't know what I would do, but I would complain vehemently.

Maybe it was possible to lodge a protest with his vaunted Dragon Justice Court. I would just have to figure out how to mail letters through a temporary magical portal to another world. No biggie.

"If you did something to help them," Mom said, "the *good* ones, maybe your reputation would improve."

I almost said there weren't any good ones, but that wasn't fair. Greemaw had helped me, and it wasn't like the kids with the balls and pool toys had been oozing evil. Just because their families had fled their original worlds didn't mean they were all criminals. Even if that was what I'd been taught during my military training, I'd seen plenty of examples otherwise over the years, so I knew better.

"Help them, how? It's not like I'm rich enough to start a foundation."

"Maybe you could hunt the people that hunt them for sport."

I shot her a semi-confused look. "Is that a thing?"

"Greemaw said it was. That's why she's invited so many to her secure valley. Some of the beings we saw were there to visit and trade, but a lot of them are too weak to fight groups of people with guns, so they're hiding under her protection. They worry that if they defend themselves and kill a human, someone like you will come after them."

"I wouldn't. I research my contracts before I accept them." I did *now*. Now that I was an independent. Once, I hadn't had the choice, and there had been a few assignments that had been less than clearcut.

"I doubt they know that."

"I'll keep your suggestion in mind, but helping Colonel Willard is my priority right now."

"I understand." Mom removed her boots, plunking them down, along with her socks, and put her feet against the dashboard.

"Are you really seventy-one?"

"Do you ask because I'm far too healthy and spry to be so old or because you think retired people can't be quirky?"

"Yes."

She snorted. "I'm surprised you got the year right. You haven't been around for a birthday in a long time. Or invited me to visit for any of yours."

"I know." I didn't want to argue again, so I left it at that.

"Though now I understand a little better why," she admitted softly without looking at me. "That werewolf almost got me. My bullets didn't do anything against it."

Not sure what to say, I took the exit and headed toward her neighborhood.

"Should I get some silver bullets?" Mom asked. "I saw someone selling them in town and thought it was silly, but now I wonder. That's the correct course against werewolves, isn't it?"

"Silver is toxic to them, yes. You'd still have to plow one into their heart or brain to achieve a quick death. They're hard to kill."

"So I saw."

There were two black cars with government plates waiting in the gravel driveway as we approached. It had only been a matter of time.

I was tempted to keep driving, zip around the block, drop Mom off somewhere safe, and head back to Seattle, but two agents in gray suits were standing outside and waiting. They looked right at us. Not that I couldn't still run—I imagined the local news reporting on a high-speed chase through their quiet tourist town—but if I wanted my words to Zav to be true, that I wasn't a criminal, I couldn't flee.

Reluctantly, I pulled in behind their cars. Dimitri's van was in its usual spot, in the gravel beside the driveway, but I didn't see him around.

The agents' eyebrows arched when Mom exited the car and let Rocket out. There was a mixture of golden and silver fur all over the back seat. I hoped Lieutenant Sudo had to clean it.

"Hello, gents," I said once I got out. "If you're here for the car, I'm going to assume you brought another one that I can use. Did Lieutenant Sudo tell you about how my Jeep was wrecked in the line of duty?"

The two men, both clean-shaven except for bland mustaches, exchanged long looks with each other.

"Ms. Thorvald," one agent said, stepping forward. "We're taking you into custody under suspicion of colluding with Colonel Willard to embezzle tens of thousands of dollars from the U.S. Army Occult Research Department in Seattle. There's an additional charge for stealing a government car."

"It's not stolen. It's right there. You can have it." I buckled on my weapons, hiding the movement behind the open car door, while debating my options. I needed to get back to Seattle and find an alchemist to heal Willard. And it looked like I needed to clear her name—and mine, too, damn it. I couldn't get stuck in jail.

But if I beat the crap out of these guys and ran off, I might be labeled a criminal forever, never getting a chance to clear anybody's names. Worse, I'd end up with every cop in Seattle chasing me while I tried to figure out how to save Willard. I needed the government to work with me, or at least not oppose me.

"Will you come along without resisting arrest?" One agent eyed me warily.

He shouldn't have been able to see the magically camouflaged Chopper and Fezzik, but he looked like he suspected they were there. Too bad. I would rather have been eyed dismissively. If they knew all about me, it would be difficult to slip away from them. Maybe I would get an opportunity on the way back. So long as they didn't take my charms and I could still access Sindari...

Did they know about them? I had no idea how much Willard had recorded in my file.

"Yes," I replied. "I'm tired of driving. Do I get to ride in the back? We *are* going to Seattle, right?" If they meant to take me somewhere else, my willingness to cooperate would go downhill.

"Fort Lewis, for now. You're not in the military anymore, so you won't receive a military judgment, but it was deemed a safe place to hold you."

Safe. Meaning the army knew what they were dealing with and could handle me more effectively than a traditional civilian jail?

Well, at least Fort Lewis was in the right direction. The drive up there would give me five hours to contemplate my next steps.

"Remove your weapons." The man shifted his jacket aside to rest a hand on a handgun in his holster. "We know you have them."

I was tempted to rest my hand on the much *bigger* firearm in my thigh holster, but it was time to play nice and cooperate. Sighing, I removed Chopper and Fezzik and laid them on the gravel. The men stirred as I stepped back, and to them, the weapons appeared out of thin air.

One agent picked them up, and the other opened the door to the back seat of his car, gesturing for me to get in. There were two more men in the car in front of that one.

"Val," Mom said uncertainly. "Will you be all right?"

"I hope so. Will you keep taking care of the cat for now?"

"Of course."

"Thanks."

She headed for the front door, tugging Rocket along with her. The agents didn't try to stop her.

As I turned to get in the car, the man holding my weapons lifted his hand. "Give me your necklace too."

My gut dropped into my boots as he pointed straight at the Sindari charm.

"Pardon?" I plastered the most innocent expression on my face that I could manage. It probably came out as the most panicked expression.

"Remove it."

"Why? It's just jewelry."

"We know it's not."

I rethought my decision to cooperate. But there were four of them, and my mom hadn't made it inside yet. My mom and her dog. I couldn't risk a shootout here.

"Your necklace." He gestured firmly with his hand.

I reached for the tie in the back, as if meaning to comply, but my mind was scrambling. I spotted a wide-eyed Dimitri staring out from behind one of the curtained windows in the back of his van. So that's where he was. Had he been hiding in there because he thought the agents were here for him?

He saw me looking at him and pointed at something in the yard. One of the tacky metal statues. The bear facing the driveway and holding a giant fish. What did he want me to do with it?

"Take your time, Thorvald," the agent growled.

"I never take it off. It's a tough knot."

He pulled out a multi-tool, flicked open the pliers like a switchblade, then thumbed open an actual knife.

I should have let the dragon take me to dangle as bait. *He* wouldn't have made me take off my weapons and charms.

"I'm also not sure I can trust you not to hawk it on eBay," I added, stepping away from the knife, especially since he looked like he wanted to cut the leather thong for me, while it was around my throat. No way.

"I'm sure your faux ivory trinkets would bring a fortune."

Dimitri was still watching me, his eyebrows raised. A question on his blunt face. What?

I nodded once, though I had no idea what he was asking. Hoping for the best, I tapped my cloaking charm to activate the stealth ability.

The agent's eyes bulged as I seemed to disappear. I ducked, anticipating a snatch, and yanked Chopper and Fezzik out of his hands before he reacted. Soundlessly, I dropped and rolled away, evading a lunge and an attempt to grab me.

If Dimitri really could help, I didn't know, but I couldn't go back with these guys, not if they were taking all my stuff and my ability to fight, my ability to escape. Once I found a way to save Willard's life, *then* they could arrest me.

A buzz of magical energy ran up my spine as soft twangs reached my ears. Something whizzed over my head. *Several* somethings. Sharp hisses came from the cars in the driveway.

Careful not to make noise and give away my position, I low-crawled across the grass and scattered pine needles. The men cursed and ran to their cars.

"What was that?" someone barked. "Is someone shooting?"

More twangs sounded. This time, I glanced back quickly enough to see tiny metal darts shoot out of the bear's fish as the statue rotated back and forth, like a gardener spraying down a bed. Several darts pierced the glass windows of the cars with the power and authority of bullets. Others slammed into the tires. The hissing of air grew louder as it escaped through dozens of holes.

The roar of an engine sounded over the rush of the nearby river. The orange camper van, somehow spared the fate of the cars, spat gravel as it raced around them and turned toward the street. It paused, and Dimitri stuck his head out the window, peering into the yard.

Looking for me. I leaped up and checked to make sure Mom and Rocket had made it inside. They had, and she was peering out through the open front window.

"Stay safe!" I called in Elvish, one of only three phrases I remembered that she'd taught me.

I wanted to add for her to run out the back door and stay at a friend's house, at least until I was out of the state, but I couldn't say all that in Elvish. I had to trust that she would be able to take care of herself.

She disappeared from the window as I raced toward Dimitri. One of the agents dropped to his knees behind his vehicle—three out of four tires were deflated, still hissing weakly—and aimed his gun at the back of the van. His buddy grabbed his arm and said, "No shooting civilians."

"But she'll get away."

"She's not in the van. I think she went that way." He pointed toward the trees and the river.

Yes, keep thinking that...

I ran as soundlessly as I could, not stepping onto the gravel until the last minute. As the agents darted off into the trees to look for me, I opened the passenger-side door and pulled myself in.

"Go," I whispered, closing it as quietly as I could.

"That's creepy."

"What?"

"The door opening and closing by itself. I can't see you. It's straight out of *Ghostbusters*."

Dimitri peeled out. It was not quiet.

"You're too young to know that movie."

"They rebooted it."

"Without any guys in it. I didn't think anybody male watched the reboot."

"I'm not your typical male."

"Because of your dwarf blood?"

"Not exactly." Dimitri glanced in the side mirror as we rounded a bend and almost knocked over a garbage can.

"Well, you're helping me, so you can be as typical or atypical as you want. I don't care."

"Glad you're open-minded."

"That's me. Embracing diversity in all its shapes and forms." I grabbed the oh-shit handle as he roared around another curve fast enough to make the mailboxes cower. "Slow down, eh, Mario? You flattened all of their tires. They won't be after us. But the police might if we shoot through town doing eighty."

"Right." He slowed down as he drove toward the highway. "Where are we going now?"

"How far are you willing to go?"

"Depends on your destination. I'd have a hard time getting excited over Burns or Hood River. Also, I have to get gas if we're going more than fifty miles."

"I need to get to Seattle." I didn't expect him to drive me six hours to get there and was about to say so, but he smiled over at me—at my collarbone actually, reminding me that he couldn't see me.

"I love Seattle. Good club scene."

"I didn't know yard-art creators were big into clubbing."

"I'm only twenty-five. If you pay for gas, I'll drive."

I glanced at my side mirror, half expecting to find police barreling after us. Nothing but the city's ubiquitous SUVs were on the road behind us. Dare I hope we could make it all the way to Seattle without being pulled over?

"I suppose they saw your license plate," I murmured.

"Nah. The plumber statue by the mailbox squirted black oil all over it. It'll bleed off soon enough, but it should have kept them from getting the plate number if they didn't think to record it earlier." He grinned at me. "What do you think of my yard art? I admit when I was making it, I wasn't imagining a scenario quite so interesting. I just thought your mom might appreciate help defending against hoodlums."

"The hoodlums of Bend?"

"Yeah, they live in the seedy part of downtown."

"Where is that exactly? Between the yoga studio and the furniture store that sells ten-thousand-dollar couches?"

"No, two blocks south of that. And I think the couches there are twenty thousand dollars. The owner of that store turned her nose up at me when I tried to get them to carry my art."

"I'll bet."

I checked the mirror again, hoping my mom and Rocket would be all right. And hoping I could get to Seattle and find a cure for Willard before the government caught up to me.

CHAPTER 13

T wilight was falling by the time we neared Puget Sound, the city lights of Olympia off to the side. It was late enough that the traffic wasn't too bad. Soon, assuming the police didn't catch up to us in this last stretch, we would reach Seattle. I wished I had a better idea of where to go. I hoped Nin had more local magical contacts than I did and that she could point me to an alchemist—or someone who knew all the alchemists in the city.

Since Dimitri was still driving—I'd offered to take over, but he said he didn't let strange women hold his steering wheel—I pulled out my phone. I'd tried calling Willard earlier but had been shunted off to voice mail. This time, I texted her, asking if she'd heard anything about dark elves in Seattle.

After that, I called Mom's house again. Even though I doubted the government would harass her because of my actions, I couldn't help but worry. She was the kind of person who could wander off into the woods in one state and reappear three months later in another state, without having suffered any adversity along the way, but she was also law-abiding enough to hang out and wait to be questioned. And she would have felt obligated to watch Maggie. A burden I had imposed upon her. I grimaced.

All I got was the answering machine.

Shortly after I left another message, the phone rang. It was Willard's office number, not Mom's.

I made the mistake of answering before I realized it was unlikely Willard was in the office. "Hello?"

"Thorvald, where are you?" That sounded like Lieutenant Snotty. "Did you resist arrest? Your ass is dead meat. If you don't get back here and turn yourself in by dawn, I'll have—"

I made a hissing sputtering sound, my best imitation of static. "Hello? Sorry, I'm—*hiss*—having trouble hearing you. Driving through—*hiss*—tunnel. Is this—*hiss*—pizza guy? Just leave it at the door. Long tunnel, about to lose you." I hung up.

Dimitri glanced over at me.

"Wrong number," I told him.

"Darn, I was hoping for pizza."

"They don't chase you down to deliver it."

"No? I hear delivery drones are coming. They ought to be able to find you on the freeway." He braked in response to three lanes of brake lights ahead of us. We'd hit Tacoma. So much for the light traffic. "Especially when traffic is slow."

I glanced at the phone. No response to my text yet.

"Where in Seattle am I going?" Dimitri asked.

"Occidental Square."

"Oh, Trinity is near there. They have a dress code though. And might sneer at Bessy."

"Bessy?"

"Bessy." He waved a hand toward the interior of the yellow-carpeted van, the back seats replaced with a bed and boxes of clothing and personal items. The galaxy-colored curtains on the side windows were pulled, and an alien-head bobble doll on a crate wobbled as we started and stopped in the traffic. "Bessy would fit in more on Capitol Hill."

I doubted *Bessy* fit in anywhere. "I just need a few minutes to talk to a friend. She's got a food truck she usually parks there."

"She? That's a sketchy neighborhood at night, isn't it?"

"She sells a lot of her merchandise to the sketchy clientele."

"And they refrain from mugging her afterward?"

"She can take care of herself. Trust me."

Dimitri shrugged.

"Thanks for driving me up here, by the way." I should have said that five hours ago. "And helping me with the agents. I hope you won't get in trouble for that. I was a little surprised that you helped, given that you barely let me on the premises yesterday."

"They shoved their way in and were asking me questions before you got there. I asked them if they had a warrant to come into the house, and they got real pissy. Turned it into an interrogation. Like they already had me pegged as a criminal who'd broken probation."

I eyed his scarred, buzzcut head, pockmarked face, and black metalhead T-shirt. Even in a tutu, he would have looked like some mafia dude's bodyguard. All I said was, "Rude."

"That's what I told them. They found out I live in the van, not the house, and told me to go wait there and stay out of the way. I was tempted to knife their tires even before you and Sigrid showed up."

"So you helped me to spite them, not because you warmed to me as a person and a human being?"

"I'm mostly hoping to see your dank tiger again."

I assumed dank had evolved—or *devolved*—into slang, since Sindari was far from damp and musty. "Gotcha."

He looked hopefully over at me.

"I don't usually bring him out to sit in traffic. His time here is limited, so I save him for battles and when I need someone to vent to. He charges less than a therapist."

"Huh."

My phone buzzed as we rolled into Seattle proper, city lights glittering next to the dark waters of the Sound.

Get out of town if you aren't already, came in from Willard's number. *There's an investigation going on at the office, Sudo has brought in MPs and some brass, and I've got a guard outside of my hospital door. I don't know where they think I'm going while I've got all these monitors cabled to me, but there's someone there day and night. And I know Sudo is looking for you. And his car. What trouble are you getting yourself into, Thorvald?*

I stared at the screen, worried by the mention of monitors and cables. Had she gotten worse? How much time did I have to figure this out? Or was it already too late? Whatever she'd been given, it couldn't be some simple poison, not if it caused cancer.

I'm trying to figure out who dosed you and with what, I texted back, deciding there had to be a reason she hadn't accepted the call. Either she was too sick to speak, or the walls were thin, and she worried about that guard overhearing her. *You ever come across anything about dark elves? It looks like someone was in your apartment and spiked your coffee or something you drink regularly with a potion. There was a sigil on the bottom of the vial from the dark-elf alchemical language.* It took me three tries to get alchemical out without AutoCorrect inserting something stupid, and I growled at the phone. Maybe my mom wasn't missing anything by forgoing modern technology.

As I told you before, someone may have been in my apartment recently. By the way, is it true that the building burned?

Yes, sorry. I got your cat out. She's staying with my mom in Bend.

North Bend?

No. Bend, Oregon. It was a long drive.

I'll bet. Maggie can be vocal in the car.

You're a master of understatement, Colonel. FYI, she detests Sindari.

I'm sure. As far as dark elves... they're around. We've never sent you after them because they're too discreet to get caught kidnapping anyone, but the city morgue always has a few bodies in it that have been mutilated in ritualistic fashion. It's believed that a lot of the people who disappear in Seattle end up in their lair, but nobody's ever lived to talk about it. They hide the entrances very well. The police have looked and never found them.

Where's their lair? Do we know?

The Seattle Underground.

Uh, I went there on a field trip when I was a kid. It's a bunch of basements and a couple of spots where you can walk under the street downtown. I was underwhelmed.

That's only a tiny portion of what's down there. The whole city burned in the late 1800s. Today's Seattle is built on top of that. All of downtown, and some say there are tunnels that were added later and go under Lake Union and Portage Bay, all the way up into Fremont and the U-District. Every time someone's started exploring them, city workers die, and access points get cemented in real quick.

I rubbed my face. Why did this sound like a place I was going to end up having to visit?

But, Willard continued, *the dark elves have never given me trouble personally, and if you didn't know they existed, it seems unlikely that they would be behind this. Even if they had a reason to hate me, why would they come after me and risk bringing the light down into their tunnels?*

To get to me?

Willard was getting the brunt of all this, but I couldn't help but think someone might want to take both of us out of the picture. If she was gone and Sudo was in charge, I wouldn't have a job, and I wouldn't be going after the magical—or so someone might think. I would still kill murdering wyverns even if I wasn't on anyone's payroll.

They've spent over a hundred years convincing the city that they don't exist, Willard added. *They clearly like it that way. I think it's more likely that someone found one of their recipe books and made a potion.*

That's what I was thinking. I'll hope for that. A human dabbler should be easier to find and deal with. I didn't point out that creating the vial would have required more than a recipe book—that hadn't been some bauble picked up at Walmart. It had been handblown by an artist. And the glow-in-the-heat sigil was definitely magical.

Yes. I don't know where you would go to find an entrance into their portion of the Underground.

"We're here." Dimitri found street parking he could wedge his van into.

A homeless guy wearing five coats and pushing a shopping cart eyed Bessy, admiring the galaxy curtains, perhaps.

"Good. Thanks." I finished my conversation with Willard. *I'm going to talk to Nin, see if she has any suggestions on alchemists. I'm confident I'll be able to get to the bottom of this, so hang in there, all right? If there's an alchemical potion that did this, whoever concocted it can damn well come up with an antidote, and I'll bring it in personally. Along with your cat.*

I didn't share my concern that the cancer wouldn't be something that could be treated with a potion. I had to hope—had to believe—that if there had been a magical cause, there would be a magical solution.

I do miss my cat. Thank you for working on this for me, Thor— Val. But be careful. Our people were originally trying to find you and deal with you in-house, but Sudo got the police involved and said there's going to be a warrant for your arrest soon. If there isn't already. You better get a hood for that duster of yours if you're going to roam around downtown.

I'll look into it.

I grabbed the door handle. "You coming with me or hitting that nightclub?"

"What are the odds that you'll take your tiger out tonight?"

"His name is Sindari, and given my last two phone conversations, the odds are excellent."

"I'm going with you. Can I pet him?"

"If he lets you, sure."

"Will he let me?"

"Call him regal and noble, not a pet or a service animal, and he'll let you rub his ears."

We met on the sidewalk, and the homeless guy scooted away when he saw Dimitri's imposing height and brawn.

I lifted a hand to stop him. "How much for one of your jackets? That one with the hood."

He scratched a gray beard with gum stuck in it and eyed me up and down. "I'll give it to you for a kiss."

"I deal in cash only, friend." I pulled out a couple of twenties and rubbed them together.

"I'll trade it for your coat." He pointed at my duster.

"Another nope. This is part of my look. Werewolves would be distressed if I showed up to kill them without it."

"Shit, I hate werewolves." He spat on the street.

"Don't we all. Forty bucks. Deal?"

"Deal." As he pulled off the jacket, the streetlight caught a few dubious stains, making me regret my decision already.

We traded and I headed off down the street, putting on the jacket over my duster and pulling up the hood. The scent of pot and body odor almost made me gag.

"It'd be better to be arrested," I grumbled.

"What?" Dimitri was walking several steps to my side.

I had a feeling I wasn't the only one who could smell the jacket. "Nothing."

Nin's truck was still there when we walked into Occidental Square, but I doubted the three big men lined up by the side door were there for beef and rice. Two had some magical blood, my senses told me, and the third had a stronger aura, a purebred something. Not a mongrel, as Zav would have called the others—and me. Probably a shifter of some kind.

The men turned toward us, stepping apart from each other to give themselves elbow room in case of a fight. That wasn't the usual reaction I got from guys. Maybe Dimitri and his bruiser dwarf blood had them wary.

"Hey, girlie," one said, ogling my chest, though it couldn't have been that impressive under two coats. I had to be downwind from him, or he would have been gagging instead of leering. "Why don't you lose the arm tough and come over here and enjoy our company?"

"You sure you'd enjoy *her* company?" one of his buddies asked, pointing over my shoulder. "Her sword's bigger than yours."

My weapons' camouflage didn't work nearly as well on the magical.

The first speaker smirked. "I don't mind a challenge. And you might be surprised about what I keep in my pants."

"A sock ball, your mom says."

"You're supposed to be my wingman, not my buzzkill."

I hoped Nin was in the truck and would come out soon. If I had to make conversation with these Einsteins, I'd grind my teeth out of their sockets.

The third man, the shifter, eyed my sword with more than passing interest. "You get that from Nin? In the magical spectrum, it's lit up like the Space Needle."

"No." I stopped a few paces from them, so I would have time to react if needed. "I had to travel to Mordor, past the Dark Tower, up to Mount Doom, and do battle with the Lord of Barad-dûr for it."

"Sounds epic."

"I think they'll make a movie of it." Keeping my eyes on them, I pulled out Fezzik. "*This* I got from Nin."

This elicited a few oohs and ahhs. The gun looked pretty, but for those who could sense magic, its intricate web of integrated auras would be even surer to impress.

I let them step forward to admire it, though I watched them carefully in case anyone tried anything. Dimitri lurked nearby, not looking like he knew if he should threaten them on my behalf or stay out of the way. Fortunately, he opted for the latter.

It was possible the men would give me trouble, especially if I'd killed a friend, distant relative, or childhood schoolmate of theirs, but Nin's was considered neutral territory by most in the community. I hadn't seen many fights break out here. Muggings by mundanes, sure, but not battles among the magical. Nin sold guns to normal people who were afraid of the magical, but she also sold weapons *to* the magical, so they could settle their grudges with each other.

The side door opened, and Nin walked out, her blue hair swept up in two perky pigtails, and a unicorn on her pink T-shirt. A few smudges of grease and weapons-cleaning oil marred the hem, but it didn't keep her from looking ridiculously cute, especially standing next to the present company. She carried in her slender arms something that looked a lot like a Civil War Gatling gun complete with a crank handle. Everyone turned, their attention riveted to it. Even I, not a weapons enthusiast despite my armament, had to admit it looked awesome. I wanted to find someone to fire it at. A black dragon, perhaps.

The men listened with rapt attention as she described its dimensions and automatic function, demonstrating how to load and fire it. There was something ludicrous about someone who looked so sweet and with such a polite, earnest voice rattling off the morbid details.

"The bullets are in these packages." Nin grabbed paper wraps off the shelf of the food window that looked exactly like the ones she used to pass out her meals. "These are tipped with a paralysis poison." She handed the first wrap to the shifter. "These are incendiary and will blow shit up when they hit. And *these* will just kill the motherfucker."

"Perfect." The shifter handed over a wad of cash.

Nin carefully counted it, then slipped it into her jeans pocket, the seam lined with rhinestones. "A pleasure doing business with you gentlemen."

The shifter handed the big weapon to his sock-ball-owning buddy to carry and headed for the street. Sock Ball winked at me, hefting the machine gun. "Now whose weapon is bigger?"

"You win, buddy. Don't forget to lube it."

"Never." He winked again, and I was positive he believed we would inevitably get horizontal the next time we met.

"Nin," I said as the men left, "I like your lunch customers better."

"Yes, but my night customers pay so much better." She smiled and patted her pocket.

"You getting close to having enough to bring your family over yet?"

"Not yet, but one day. My family is very large, and I want to bring everyone to America. Now, there is Grandma and Mother and my seven sisters all living in a two-bedroom apartment. Only my brother has been able to afford to move out, but he does not make enough to help them. I want to be able to buy my family a house here, so they do not have to worry about working and paying rent right away, but it is very expensive. A house costs much more here than in Bangkok."

"Maybe you can set them up in the suburbs, and they can open a restaurant. Didn't you say your grandmother was the one to teach you to cook?"

"Yes, this is true. And my grandfather taught me to make magic guns." She smiled. "It is sad for my family that he disappeared, and everyone had to move into the city. There are so few opportunities there. Not like here. I am living the American dream."

"I'm not going to argue that. You make more than I do."

"An entrepreneur must be a marketer, Val. You should make clever videos and advertise on the socials. This is what I do for my food truck."

"I think they arrest you if you advertise assassin services online. But hey, with the way this week is going, it probably doesn't matter."

She tilted her head, one of her pigtails flopping onto her shoulder. "You are in trouble? Did you break Fezzik again?"

"No, Fezzik is good."

"You have acquired the services of a bodyguard?" She looked at Dimitri.

"No, a chauffeur. This is Dimitri. Listen, I'm trying to find out who's been tinkering with dark-elf alchemy to poison my boss. You have any dark elves for clients?"

"Oh, no. I have only heard rumors about them. They do not come up here." She waved to the street and the square. "And they do not purchase goods from outsiders. Have you spoken to Zoltan?"

"Isn't he the guy with the continuum transfunctioner?"

Her brow furrowed.

"Never mind. Who is he?"

"A vampire alchemist who lives in the basement of an old barn in Woodinville. Do you have any information about the poison? With a few ingredients, he may be able to identify it for you."

I leaned in, hope rising. If the alchemist could identify it, maybe he would also know how to nullify it.

"There are vampires in Woodinville?" Dimitri asked. "That's out in the suburbs, isn't it?"

"Vampires can't be suburban?" I asked as Nin pulled out her phone and looked up an address. "Maybe he's a fan of the wineries out there."

I would have to check the lore to see if vampires could drink anything but blood. I hadn't dealt with many in my line of work. Like these quasi-mythological dark elves, they stayed under the radar—and the surface of the earth.

"I suppose," Dimitri said. "He doesn't drive a minivan, does he?"

"You can't possibly have a prejudice against vans."

"Here." Nin texted me a link.

It wasn't the map address I expected but a real estate listing for a house that had been on the market for nine-hundred-some days.

"Do people not want to buy from a vampire?" I asked.

"Nobody outside of the magical community knows about the vampire. No, let me clarify that. Nobody knows where he lives. He is quite famous online. *He* knows how to use the socials." Nin gave me a stern look.

I lifted my hands in resignation. "If I manage to save my boss and clear my name, I will definitely look into social media marketing for my services."

"Excellent. I want to make sure my clients do well, so they can continue to afford *my* services."

"You're a savvy businesswoman."

"Yes." Nin smiled. "Wait one moment, please."

She hopped into the truck.

"My life has gotten very strange in the last thirty-six hours," Dimitri remarked.

"I've seen your yard art. Your life was already strange."

"Have we known each other long enough that it's appropriate for you to insult me?"

"I don't know. What if I buy you another tank of gas?"

"That'll make it okay then. Also, will you ask your friend if she teaches classes on business stuff? I don't know how to market my art. The people who come by the property only want to pay twenty dollars for it. But it takes me a long time to find the pieces that will work with my special touch." He wiggled his fingers to indicate the enchantments his dwarven blood had allowed him to learn.

Nin returned with a brochure and several business cards. "Please give these to Zoltan and let him know that if he needs any weapons made, or if any of his fellow vampires need them made, I can accommodate him. Also, I am thinking of branching out into magical armor."

"If he doesn't try to bite my neck the instant we meet, I'll give these to him."

"Of course he will try to bite your neck. You are the hated Mythic

Murderer. But please also give him my brochure as a favor to me. And then I will do a favor for you. This is how networking works."

"I'll see what I can do."

Nin kept me in guns and ammo. If she wanted me to hand out business cards to vampires, I would do it.

"Thank you." Nin waved to me and smiled shyly at Dimitri.

I wondered if he liked girls with blue hair. And if he was paying attention to her marketing tactics. Clearly, *he* needed to make brochures and hand them out.

"Mythic Murderer?" Dimitri asked as we walked back to the van.

"I hadn't encountered that one before. Lovely to hear that there are so many variations of my nickname."

"Are we driving to Woodinville tonight?"

"Yes." I imagined Willard hooked up to IVs with electrodes attached to her chest.

"Is night the best time to visit a vampire?" Dimitri climbed into the driver's seat.

"If you want him to be awake, probably."

"And we want that?"

"It's hard to question someone locked in a coffin."

Dimitri put the keys in the ignition as I buckled in next to him, but then held up a finger. "One second."

He ducked into the back and rummaged around in the crate under the bobblehead doll. He returned with…

"Why do you have a cervical collar?" I asked.

"My attempt to learn to snowboard last winter was problematic." He buckled it around his neck. All he needed was a backboard, and he would look like someone about to be carted out of a swimming pool for a diving-board injury. "There. My neck will be safe tonight."

As he drove off, I didn't point out that vampires could probably use *any* vein to suck blood. It wouldn't matter. Zoltan was sure to go for the Mythic Murderer first.

CHAPTER 14

"This is a nice neighborhood for a vampire," Dimitri remarked as we drove along winding roads that had once been out in the country but were now lined with well-lit McMansions with impeccable grassy lawns and immaculately trimmed hedges.

"Vampires are usually a few hundred years old. That's a long time to accumulate wealth. Though it sounds like the house is vacant and he may be a freeloader." I pointed to a driveway with a real-estate sign staked into the grass next to it. "That's it. Park anywhere. Nin said the vampire lives in the barn out back."

"You sure it's vacant? All the lights are on, and there are two cars in the driveway."

"I suppose just because it's for sale doesn't mean that it's vacant. Park over there. It looks like someone's having a party." I waved to the house across the street with cars filling the driveway and parked along the curb. "We'll do our best to avoid notice. Insomuch as we can in this van."

"What's wrong with Bessy?" Dimitri pulled up behind a Tesla.

"It's not part of the neighborhood's typical auto demographic."

I left the smelly hooded jacket in the car, doubting we'd run into the police out here, and crossed the street. Dimitri caught up with me as I headed up the long driveway. The grass was wet from an earlier rain, so I didn't want to walk on it and hoped for a path around the house farther up.

"You and your cervical collar don't have to come." I sensed the aura of someone magical in the distance, out back behind the house somewhere. The vampire was home.

"I'm still waiting to see the tiger. You'll have to bring him out if a vampire tries to bite your neck."

"True. I'm thinking of bringing him out right now." I reached for the figurine.

Once Dimitri rubbed Sindari's ears, I could send him back to the van. Even though he didn't look like the damsel-in-distress type, it would be stupid to take him to see a vampire. He wasn't even armed.

As I was about to call Sindari forth, the front door opened. Hell, we should have veered off across the lawn, wet grass regardless.

"Wonderful, wonderful," a woman said, walking out and guiding a couple to the parked cars. "No, no, I don't mind the late showing. I'm happy to work with people's busy schedules."

I shifted my hand to my cloaking charm but realized that would leave Dimitri standing alone in the driveway.

The woman spotted us before I finished debating if we could dart off across the lawn without being noticed.

"Uh, can I help you?" Somehow, she managed to smile and wave the couple into their Mercedes at the same time as she frowned at us.

"Yes." I spotted the RE/MAX logo on her SUV. "We saw that you were showing this house and wondered if we could also look around."

Her frown deepened as she looked at Dimitri and his metal T-shirt. "Did you see the price on the flyer out there?"

"Of course. We're pre-qualified." I smiled. "My fiancé works at Microsoft. Game designer."

"You injured your neck as a programmer?"

"Uh," Dimitri said.

"No, he did that while spring skiing up at Whistler. We have a condo up there. Vacation place, you know. We're looking to buy a new house down here, close to his work."

"Look, lady, my bullshit detector is spot-on." She pointed a finger at my chest. "There's nothing in there to steal. The owners moved all of their stuff out two years ago. You two get out of here right now, or I'll call the HOA security patrol."

Oh man, the HOA security patrol. That had me quivering in my boots. But I didn't really want to crack a real-estate agent on the head with the flat of my blade, so I led Dimitri back across the street. We found some dark, damp hedges to smoosh ourselves into while we waited for her to leave.

She called someone before getting in the car. The security patrol, no doubt.

"Sorry," Dimitri said. "I'm not that good at lying. There was never any point when I got caught doing something as a kid. Nobody believed I was innocent no matter what I said."

"Where'd you grow up?"

"South Bronx. My parents immigrated from Russia. Dad beat me up at home, and the big kids beat me up outside of it. Until I got big enough to take care of myself."

I opened my mouth, about to ask if that had been when he was seven or eight, but a few shadowy figures stepped out of hedges similar to ours farther up the street. Had they come from the party? They all had their hoods up and were wearing long dark jackets or maybe cloaks. Who the hell wore cloaks anymore?

Something twanged my senses, magic being used. Were they magical themselves? I couldn't tell. They seemed strangely blank to my perceptive elven blood.

"Who are they?" Dimitri muttered.

"Not the HOA security, I'm guessing."

A shadow rose up out of the street as the figures crossed, heading toward the vacant house, and it seemed to engulf them. They disappeared from my sight and the magic faded from my senses.

"Friends of Zoltan, maybe," I added.

The real-estate agent remotely turned off most of the house's interior lights, leaving on the driveway lights, then drove away. A few seconds later, a security car cruised through. It pulled into the driveway, and the patroller got out and walked up to the front door with his flashlight and night stick.

"This is taking forever." The house next door had all of its lights off, so I headed up the street for its driveway.

Dimitri stayed close. Once again, I was tempted to send him back to the van, but after seeing those hooded guys disappear, I worried he would be safer with me. Once I reached the next driveway, I summoned Sindari.

I sense a vampire, he informed me before he'd fully solidified.

That's Zoltan. Do you sense anyone else?

Hm, I smell many people about, across the street and walking around that domicile. His nose was pointed at the vacant house.

The security guard?

No, this is a group that's moving around the side of the house and heading to the back. I believe stealth charms are being used, but they are not as good as yours, since they do not camouflage scent.

I headed up the gravel driveway, the only gravel anywhere on the street, to a log rambler that must have been here long before the rest of the neighborhood was built. I wondered if the HOA trooper covered it, or if it was left out of the club.

The windows were dark, so I led the way around to the back, where the mowed grass stretched halfway back to a pond, with much taller, unkempt grass beyond it. Once we were back there, two structures were visible behind the vacant house. A horse barn and arena setup that alone had to have cost a million dollars and an out-of-place, dilapidated carriage house on the back corner of the lot. There were no lights there, but I could tell the wood siding was falling off and one door hung halfway off its rusty hinges.

I sensed the vampire's aura in that direction.

Are the hidden people heading there? I pointed at the old carriage house.

No. They're lurking behind what I perceive is a children's playhouse there beside the patio.

The playhouse was bigger than my apartment in Ballard.

And looking in this direction, Sindari added. *You may wish to activate your cloaking charm.*

The security guard walked into view, shining his flashlight around the side and back of the property.

I don't suppose you'd like to lead everyone away? I didn't want to see the guard get jumped by the vampire or the mystery pack of magical people.

That didn't go well with the dragon.

He's not here. The vampire is the most dangerous thing we should encounter tonight.

Very well, but if something flies out of the sky and tries to light me on fire again, I'll have cross words to share with you.

Thank you, Sindari.

Before heading off, Sindari paused, his tail swishing as he looked at Dimitri. He had shifted closer and had a hand out toward the tiger's back.

"Uhm, can I pet him now?"

Pet him? Sindari asked. *What is petting? A thing you do to a pet, yes? Should I be insulted?*

No. Out loud, I said, "You forgot to point out how regal he is."

"He's *magnificent*," Dimitri breathed.

He just wants to feel your fur. Maybe it'll give him good luck.

If a tiger could sigh, Sindari did. *Very well. I shall permit it.*

"Go ahead," I said.

Dimitri slid his hand down Sindari's back several times with appreciative enthusiasm. "He's so soft."

"But regal, don't forget." I checked on the vampire. My senses told me he hadn't moved.

"Regal and soft and magnificent." There was no sarcasm in Dimitri's voice. Sindari had a new admirer.

His tail swished, and he let out a few chuffs.

"What does that noise mean?" Dimitri asked.

"Tigers can't purr, but it means he's pleased."

This man has good hands.

Of course. He makes that yard art.

You should claim him for a mate.

He's a little young for me. Maybe I'll try to set him up with Nin.

Sindari crouched and faced the playhouse. *I should go before the security officer stumbles across them and gets himself killed.*

Good idea.

Sindari sprang over the fence and roared. He sailed around the back yard, running right past the playhouse. Unfortunately, my nose wasn't as good as his, so I couldn't tell if the stealthed group moved. The security guard issued a high-pitched shriek and ran back toward the front of the house.

As Sindari raced around the big yard again, automatic sprinkler heads popped up.

"Uh oh," I muttered.

They came on with a hiss and water sprayed everywhere, including at Sindari. His roar turned into the tiger equivalent of a curse, and he sprang over the far fence and into the next yard to escape.

The stealthed strangers are chasing me, Sindari informed me. *And I shall ruthlessly chew off your arm later for that trick.*

I didn't know about the sprinklers.

Lies.

I promise. Thank you for leading them away. Keep them busy for twenty minutes if you can, and then come by to see if I need to be rescued from the vampire.

May I slay them if they pester me overmuch?

Not unless they've slain innocent humans and are on one of the lists that came out of Willard's office.

I'm chewing someone's arm off tonight. I'm soaked.

How is this different from when you jumped in the river to bathe? I jogged to the wooden rail fence, hopped over, and ran to the carriage house.

It's extremely different. The sun was out then, and I jumped in by choice. I wasn't attacked by spring-loaded waterspouts.

Waterspouts? Really, Sindari. I had no idea you were so melodramatic.

Rivulets of water are assailing my ear canals.

Dimitri stopped beside me in front of the broken door of the carriage house. "I don't see a doorbell."

"I think this thing predates electricity."

Now that we were closer, I could tell the vampire was down below somewhere. But I assumed he could come up quickly if he wished.

I left the noisy Fezzik in its holster and drew Chopper. When I stepped inside, an ancient floorboard creaked underfoot. So much for silence.

Piles of junk rose everywhere, enough to bring every garage-sale shopper and picker in droves, and the scents of dampness and moldy straw filled the air. A loft overhead sagged under the weight of more junk, and built-in shelves along the walls held even more. I had a feeling it had all been here long before the people selling the house had moved in. And long before most of the houses on this street had been built.

A breeze swept in through a boarded-up window, shattered glass on the floor underneath it. Creepy creaks emanated from several directions. I stopped moving. The creaks continued.

"Did the real-estate listing mention a haunted barn?" Dimitri wasn't moving either. The creaks and groans came from all around us.

"I don't think such features go in the MLS. Not everybody would see it as a selling point."

Something broke free from the loft and clattered onto a pile of rusty metal.

"I'm surprised nobody ever tore this place down," I added.

"I bet some of this stuff is cool. I'm tempted to turn on my flashlight app and look for materials for my new projects."

"If you want to stay up here and do that, you can. I didn't mention it earlier, but your fancy neckwear isn't going to save you if the vampire is hungry."

My senses told me the vampire was still lower than we were, but he wasn't directly under us. He was farther back, behind the carriage house. Was there a root cellar or something back there?

I wandered toward the rear wall, looking for a trapdoor.

"You're making me consider it..." Dimitri tapped on the flashlight app and pointed the beam toward the piles. "But in all the horror movies, doesn't the guy who gets separated from the person with the gun and the sword usually end up eaten?"

"You're thinking of the dumb blonde girl who hears a sound in the basement and goes to explore by herself."

He looked at my hair.

"Don't say it."

"Who, me?" His roving flashlight beam paused on some shelves full of boxes. "Oh, man, is that an old Lionel train set? It's the box, at least. I gotta see if there's anything in there."

Using my own flashlight app, I kept looking for the trapdoor while he clambered over tarp-covered piles to get to those shelves. There had to be an entrance to a lower level somewhere. The vampire had to go out to find blood now and then.

The creaks and groans continued, the whole structure sounding like it could collapse at any moment. As I rounded a pile of junk in the back, my light played over the seams of a trapdoor. It was made from the same old wood boards as the rest of the floor, but the seam was clear, as was a pull-out handle tucked into a groove.

Expecting a tight space, I traded Chopper for Fezzik, put my phone away, and activated my night-vision charm. Dimitri's nearby flashlight beam made me wince with its brightness, but I kept my back to him.

When I opened it, the trapdoor creaked even louder than the rest of the carriage house. I might as well have rung a doorbell. There was no way the vampire didn't know I was coming.

Nothing so grandiose as stairs awaited me. The dusty rungs of a ladder led down to a tiny bricked-in room. I didn't see a door, but I assumed there had to be one. All the dust made me frown with doubt. Maybe this wasn't the way the vampire came and went. Even the undead disturbed dust.

I dragged a rusty ship's anchor over and used it to prop open the trapdoor, then climbed down the ladder with one hand. With the other, I pointed Fezzik downward, in case someone popped out or I triggered a trap.

The carriage house groaned and creaked again, followed by a noise that sounded like branches scraping against a back window. When we'd walked up, I hadn't seen any trees around the building.

A puff of dust rose when my boots hit the bottom. This definitely wasn't the way anyone went. I almost headed straight back up, thinking to check for root cellar doors around the back of the carriage house, but ran my fingers along the walls for a quick search.

A thunderous scrape came from above, and I looked up in time to see the anchor shift aside and the trapdoor thump down. I almost yelled to Dimitri that his joke wasn't funny, but magic plucked at my senses. And it wasn't dwarf-yard-art-enchantment magic.

Wrought-iron bars slid out of holes I hadn't noticed and clanged into place inches under the trapdoor. I sighed, debating if Chopper could cut through them or the brick walls surrounding me. With enough time, I was sure I could do it, but I sensed the vampire heading in this direction. Somehow, I doubted he would stand patiently by while I hacked at his security system.

I glanced at the time on my phone. I still had fifteen minutes left of the twenty I'd asked Sindari for. He wouldn't be coming to rescue me any time soon.

CHAPTER 15

A rumble came from behind me, and I whirled, Fezzik pointing at the hidden door before it opened.

"Oh dear," the male figure standing in the tunnel said, eyeing the barrel. "Are you here to rob me? Do I need to raise my hands? What's the protocol here?"

He was strikingly handsome if also strikingly pale, with black hair pulled back in a bun and a neatly trimmed mustache and goatee. He shifted from eyeing my gun to eyeing my neck—maybe I should have borrowed Dimitri's cervical collar—but his gaze didn't linger long. He met my eyes, his brows rising in inquiry.

"I brought you some brochures," I said.

"Really? I so rarely get old-fashioned mail anymore. It all comes from the interwebs. Would you like to see my laboratory? You're not one of my fan-girls, are you? They're usually younger. An astonishing number of teenage girls are interested in making potions and aren't put off by my fangs." He flashed those fangs.

I tried not to take his interest in teenage girls as creepy. It was hard.

"I'll take a tour if you're offering." Fourteen minutes until Sindari came looking for me. I didn't trust Mr. Sexy with his Hungarian accent.

"Certainly. This way, please." Zoltan bowed and extended an arm toward the tunnel. "Pardon the dust. You came in the back way. This used to be a meat locker." He glanced up at the bars and made a hook motion with his finger. "Naturally, I have no use for a meat locker."

"Just a refrigerator for your blood?"

"Chilled blood? What a dreadful thought. I can't imagine the vampire who would accept such an off-putting thing. The nutrients are most superior, the flavors most nuanced, when the blood is warm and straight from the vein."

"Uh huh. Do you drink wine?"

"Certainly not."

"Guess that answers that." I pointed the gun down the tunnel. "You go first, friend."

"Ah, yes, the robbery. I forgot. Will you need me to show you to my valuables? I didn't bring that many with me when I left Europe. It was a tumultuous time back then." He led me through unlit tunnels, and I was glad for my night-vision charm.

"I'm not robbing you. I'm hoping you can answer a couple of questions. I'll pay. Also, the brochures are from Nin Chattrakulrak in Seattle." Sadly, my pronunciation of her last name was even more execrable than my pronunciation of her signature dish. "She makes magical weapons and is branching out into armor and thought you might be interested. Or maybe she thought you'd mention her shop to the teenage girls. I'm not quite sure."

"Armor? Interesting. I do have various security systems around the premises, which you'll discover if you shoot me and attempt to take my wealth, but I rarely feel the need to secure my person. Usually, I find that my superior strength serves sufficiently in confrontations." He looked over his shoulder as he swung open a door and entered a surprisingly well-lit room. "Unless I'm facing someone with a gun full of magical ammunition. Here we are. Welcome to my laboratory."

Laboratory *and* video studio, I decided as I stepped inside, eyeing a three-monitor computer, mic, and sound-engineering setup that any internet video star would admire. The bright red lights appeared to be infrared rather than LED or fluorescent. Maybe infrared was safe for sensitive vampire flesh.

The red light gleamed off a huge metal barn door on the wall to the right of us. Was that where he kept his coffin? If so, it was a touch grandiose.

Opposite the computer setup were counters full of condensers, test tubes, flasks, and lots of other chemistry equipment I couldn't name. Was that a centrifuge? When Nin had said Zoltan was a vampire alchemist, I'd been imagining bags of herbs and mortars and pestles. The lab rats in cages lining one wall were closer to what I'd envisioned. I decided not to ask if they were for experiments or dinner.

As I walked deeper into the lab, I stepped on a floor tile that was identical to the others but that shifted underfoot, depressing a half an inch. A fluke of an old floor? No, Zoltan turned, leaned his hip against a counter, and smiled at me.

The big metal door ground as it shifted along its slider to reveal a dark room. A dark room with two glowing red eyes inside. A sweet earthy smell wafted out, as something made a skittering sound.

"Food, Luca!" Zoltan clapped his hands.

A tarantula as tall as I was and much wider hustled out and sped straight toward me. I fired four times before it got close, the bullets sinking into its brown furred torso, and it didn't slow down. It was probably hopped up on some alchemy potion.

Swearing, I jumped back into the tunnel, a tunnel that was large enough for the tarantula to fit into. At least it couldn't get at my sides.

I fired twice more as it chased me back into the passageway. A thick green ichor that did not look natural oozed out of the six wounds. This time, the great tarantula let out a loud, angry hiss, but it kept coming.

As I retreated, my heel bumped against something that hadn't been there before. A wall. Damn it, I'd walked into a trap.

The tarantula raised its forelegs high and opened a huge mouth, fangs dripping saliva. And venom, I realized, the sickly-sweet scent of its breath washing over me.

I fired one more time, then yanked out Chopper. The fanged mouth darted toward me. I whipped my blade across, cutting off one of those fangs.

Something hot spattered my arm and face. The torso reared up, and I shifted my grip, jamming my longsword up under its jaws before it could bring its fangs close again. A normal weapon might not have pierced the exoskeleton, but my magical blade crunched deep. The tarantula hissed again, battering my eardrums.

It tried to shake my sword loose. I shoved it deeper, hoping to reach its brain. The tarantula charged forward, shoving me against the wall with its body, and pain blasted my torso. I almost lost my grip on

Chopper, but I hung on with determination, twisting and driving the blade deeper.

The tarantula backed up, only to ram forward again. My breath whooshed out as it crunched into me. I couldn't take much more of that.

As the tarantula backed up again, I yanked my sword free. Hot blood and ichor poured out onto me. When the tarantula rushed forward to ram me again, I dropped to the ground and scrambled under it.

The forest of hairy black legs trampled down all around me, trying to smash me. I rolled and twisted, found my feet, and lunged upward, my shoulder against its abdomen as I rammed Chopper through its exoskeleton again and again.

Nasty, sticky blood poured down, but the legs kept thrashing. I drove the blade deeper. The entire body trembled, and at the last second, I realized the tarantula was going to collapse. I tugged out Chopper and dove out an instant before the heavy body hit the tunnel floor.

I flattened my back to the wall nearby, not sure yet if I'd killed my enemy, but not wanting Zoltan behind me. He stood in the tunnel entrance, watching. I pointed Chopper at the tarantula's backside and Fezzik at Zoltan. He didn't appear to be armed, but that didn't mean he couldn't throw more attacks at me.

Fortunately, the tarantula didn't move again. I lifted a sleeve to wipe disgusting gore off my face.

"One of your lab critters got out," I said in as bland and unperturbed a voice as I could manage. As if I weren't breathing hard, a faint wheeze to my exhalations. Stupid asthma. My fingers twitched toward the pocket with my inhaler, but I didn't want to use it in front of the vampire.

"Ah, do forgive me." Zoltan bowed grandly, sweeping his long coat out wide. "I forgot to warn you about my pet."

"Forgot. Right." Pointing the gun at him, I walked closer to the lab again.

Zoltan backed away. I wasn't sure if it was because he found me threatening or he was disgusted by the globs of tarantula ichor falling off my clothes and spattering onto the floor.

"I hear you wheezing. Were your lungs punctured by the fangs of the tarantula?" When most men looked at my chest, they were ogling my boobs, but Zoltan had to be hoping to find fresh blood dripping from a wound. That was just as bad.

"No, and don't sound so hopeful. I'm fine." I tried to will away the tightness and breathe more quietly.

Vampires were probably among the magical with excellent hearing.

"An aerosol made from venom from the spiked tail of a manticore and mixed with liquid magnesium sulfate will clear the lungs right up. Perhaps you'd like to trade a small taste of your blood for such a concoction." He licked his lips. The only thing worse than a vampire was a hungry vampire. "I have the ingredients here."

"No, thanks. Listen, Zoltan." I stepped back into his lab and lowered the gun but didn't put it away. "I need a few minutes of your time, and I'll be happy to pay your hourly rate. Then you can go buy someone else's blood."

"Hourly rate? Madam, do I look like a prostitute?"

"Lawyers, plumbers, and consultants all have hourly rates."

"Do they? I must get out more in the world. What can I do for you? If I'm able to assist you, perhaps you can owe me a favor, eh?"

"No favors." I pulled out a wad of cash and smacked it down on the nearest counter. To think Sudo wondered why I needed my combat bonuses delivered in hard currency. Was I supposed to PayPal a vampire? "Two hundred dollars for your time. Do you agree?"

"Is that what plumbers charge?"

"Yes." As if I knew. I had a landlord that called the plumbers.

"Very well. I will assume this is reasonable. What is your question?"

"First off, do you know who made this?" I carefully withdrew and unwrapped the vial. "And is there any way you can tell what potion it was holding? If so, and if you can give me an antidote that will magically heal the friend of mine that was made sick by it, I'll pay more."

"All this money you're throwing around, as if I'm going to take off on a holiday to Hawaii with it."

"Maybe you need another computer monitor."

"Hm, yes. My equipment is expensive." Zoltan took the vial from me, his hand cold when it brushed mine.

He went to a Bunsen burner and heated the bottom. I leaned forward, encouraged that he'd known about the heat-activation without me saying anything. I wished I'd thought to ask Nin for alchemist recommendations in the first place. Then I could have avoided that trip to Bend and the run-in with the government agents—and the dragon.

"Mm hmm," he murmured, and walked to a bookcase full of thick tomes with yellowed pages. Few had titles printed in English. He pulled out one so old that the binding creaked. "Mmm."

Val? came Sindari's voice through our link. *I cannot find you.*

I'm under the carriage house in the vampire's laboratory. I don't think the door I used is the best one. Look around back for something.

Are you in danger?

Not at the moment. Will you check on Dimitri? We got separated, and I don't know his phone number. Nor did I know if I had reception down here. Was Zoltan's computer setup using a cell signal for internet access? Or had he somehow gotten cables run underground out here? Obviously, he had electricity.

I'll check on him. I think those people I led around are elves—or dark elves—and I think they realized I was deliberately leading them away from their prey. I expect them to return to this property.

Am I their prey?

Probably. I think you were the target at your colonel's apartment.

Then I'm glad their aim has been lousy.

Has it? That room you were in burned down, with the roof collapsing on it. If you'd been a little slower to get out...

I take your point. Keep me updated, please.

"Here, you can see this sigil." Zoltan laid the book on the counter, open to a back page.

Though my instincts warned me about getting too close, I came over, keeping Fezzik between him and me. Zoltan beamed an admiring smile at my neck. I must have caught him on a hungry night.

The familiar symbol was one of four drawn on the page in faded brown ink—or was that blood? The smaller text written around each symbol was in black ink.

"What's it say about it?" I couldn't read anything, but the flowing script was in the same stylistic vein as the symbol. "And what language is this book in?"

"The particular alchemical language of the dark elves. They have four different tongues, one for alchemy, one for religious purposes, one for teaching, and one for everyday use. Even in their heyday here on Earth, few people knew the alchemical language."

"Are you one of those people?"

"You called me a people. I'm honored." There was that smile again and a slight bow.

"Weren't you one once?"

"Indeed, indeed. Not so long ago that I can't remember it. But these days, I merely stay in my dark hole and research and teach, and occasionally contemplate summoning my followers to this place so that I might feast on their blood while turning them into young vampires. I could raise up an army to do my bidding."

"Followers?"

"Yes. To my channels." He extended his hand toward the computer setup. "There are *millions*." His dead black eyes managed to gleam.

"Oh, the teenage girls."

"And some boys. Also, my demographics studies have shown that housewives between the ages of thirty-four and fifty-three find me quite the tiger's meow."

I squinted at him, suspecting that was to let me know that he knew Sindari was prowling around up there. "Tigers don't meow."

"No?"

"What would you do with an army?"

"That's the question, isn't it? Perhaps I could find a way to rule this nation—your political system seems fraught with strife, so it's clear that a superior option is needed—but my difficulties with sunlight would pose a challenge. And I'm certain your government would field someone like you to come slay me. Which would be tedious."

"No doubt."

"And besides, my followers are terribly valuable where they are. My sponsors value them a great deal. Their funds pay for me to have my alchemical supplies delivered. The world has become a fascinating place."

"Yes. Can you read that?" I tapped the page.

A light warning zap ran up my finger.

Zoltan lifted a hand, shooing mine away. "Only one versed in the language and suitably respectful to the dark elf way may read this book."

"Does that mean it's unlikely that some kid—such as one of your followers—found another book like it and taught himself or herself to make the potion that was used against my boss?"

"They're called formulas, my dear, and no mere mortal alive today could have mastered this language and learned enough to interact with a tome such as this. As you felt, it's warded against simpletons turning its pages, and I do not teach the dangerous arts to my followers. Only enough for them to poison a brutal lover or abusive parent if they wish. Self-defense, if you will."

"Noble of you."

"Yes."

I had about given up on him getting to the point and offering me useful information when he touched the sigil. "For your two hundred dollars there, I'll tell you that this formula was created as a way to kill people slowly so that suspicion would be drawn neither to the deliverer of the formula nor the alchemist who created it."

"How much time does it take for the victim to die?" I whispered.

"Oh, four to six weeks for most people."

I swallowed. How long had it already been since Willard had been dosed?

"This is the list of ingredients. A few of them would be challenging to acquire, at least for this landlocked vampire."

"Do you know who made the pot—formula and if there's an antidote? Something that will cure the illness or at least remove the magical component of it so that modern medicine can do its job?" I worried that the disease might have progressed too far for modern medicine, but I refused to give up hope.

"If the formula was made and delivered in this part of the world, I can most certainly tell you who crafted it. But let me take a closer look, eh."

Zoltan picked up the vial and walked to a microscope, a fancy modern one hooked up to a computer. He prepared something resembling a drugstore cotton swab, moistening the end with liquid from a dark bottle, and prodded around in the vial. How much residue would he find in there after it had spent weeks in Willard's coffee-ground-strewn garbage disposal and then been carted around in my pocket?

I kept myself from pacing as he prepared a slide and examined it. *Sindari, any update?*

I haven't been able to find Dimitri.

What? My fist clenched. If bringing him here got him killed, I'd have more blood on my hands—more guilt. Why hadn't I ordered him to go back to the van and wait inside with the curtains drawn and the doors locked? *Did he leave the carriage house?*

I don't believe so. His scent lingers here, but he is not in this loft or anywhere in this main room.

There was a trapdoor. Maybe he found it, went down, and got stuck like I did. I will check.

"I can verify that the formula that existed in this vial is what the sigil says it should be." Zoltan pointed at the open book. "I can also verify that a drop of the alchemist's blood was used in the making, per the recipe. There are two types of DNA present in the sample."

It was strange hearing a long-dead vampire talking about DNA. "Whose?" was all I asked.

"One belongs to a kraken, the other to a dark elf."

"A kraken? Where does one find kraken blood, and aren't krakens poisonous?"

"Venomous and very much so, yes. But not their blood. Their venom comes from their bite, from a venom gland in their mouths, the same as with a squid. Kraken venom is an excellent ingredient to work with. But exceedingly rare. If you come by any, do let me know. I will purchase it at market rate plus ten percent."

My only familiarity with krakens came from mythology, so this notion that they not only existed but had a market rate was disturbing.

"Kraken blood also cannot be ordered online. It's likely one has taken up residence nearby, and the blood was collected fresh." Zoltan stepped away from the microscope.

"I hear Lake Washington is nice. All those fat harbor seals down by the Arboretum to munch on."

He nodded. "A possible location, or out in Puget Sound. They traditionally prefer deep-sea waters to tumultuous surface waters, and saltwater to fresh, but they can exist for periods of time in fresh water."

"Thank you for looking up the formula. Is there an antidote? And you said only one person around could have made it. Who?"

"A reversal of the formula *could* be constructed, something that would essentially clean out the residue in the afflicted person's system.

After that, you would also need a long-acting healing elixir to reverse the cellular damage. I could not guarantee that would be effective. If the disease is far along, it would be too late. One *could* make the elixir more potent with a drop of the victim's blood."

A return visit to the hospital, check.

"And to make the reversal formula, it would require the blood of the same kraken and of the dark-elf alchemist who made it."

Ugh, I would need more than a visit to the hospital to find those.

"You would also need a highly trained and exceptional alchemist willing to create all this for you." He smiled.

"Any chance that's you? Or am I going to have to find this dark-elf alchemist—does he have a name?—and force him to do it at gunpoint?"

"I wouldn't trust any formula that was made under duress. As to if I can do it, I am capable, but I would not wish to incur the wrath of the dark-elf clan living in the area. My simple home would be easy for them to breach, and I could not fight off many of their mages. Their magic is very strong."

An entire clan? Great.

"But I would possibly risk their wrath if the price were right and if the alchemist—Synaru-van is her name—never learned of my involvement."

"What's your price?" My skin crawled as I imagined him demanding my blood—or for me to bring some of his followers here so he could enjoy *their* blood.

"You have lingering about you the aura of a dragon."

The unexpected statement startled me. "He left his aura on me? Nasty."

"Many of my ancient formulas require a drop of dragon blood. This has been hard to come by. For the longest time, there were no dragons left on Earth, not even as visitors. It seems that has changed." He beamed his smile at me, not at my neck this time but at me. Or maybe at that crusty dragon aura lingering about me.

I vowed to take a bath later and scrub with my loofah and that high-powered pumice hand-cleaner that mechanics liked. I used it whenever I got an assignment's blood on me, and I would slather myself from head-to-toe to get a dragon aura off.

"To sum up," Zoltan said, "I will create both the reversal formula and the healing elixir for you, but I require a drop of Synaru-van's blood, a drop of the blood of the kraken that she used, and, for my own payment, a vial of dragon blood."

"A *vial?* Not just a drop?"

"I have *many* formulas that require a drop of dragon blood. Thus I need many drops." He rubbed his cold hands together with hot glee.

"These aren't the formulas that would allow you to take over the White House, are they?"

"Oh, no. I could do that simply by making followers. Please be honored that I'm not asking you to become one."

"My neck and I are pleased. Is it because the dragon aura clinging to my skin makes my blood undesirable?"

"Not at all. The dragon aura would enhance the flavor and perhaps even give me increased vitality."

I was *definitely* using the loofah later.

"It's the powerful magical gun you haven't stopped pointing at me that's problematic."

"I'm glad I brought it then." I looked at his shelves. "Do you have some empty vials I can borrow? And, uh, syringes. I assume you don't want the bloods to mingle."

"Certainly not. I'll prepare you a sample kit."

"Do you have any idea where I can find this dark-elf alchemist?"

"In the tunnels beneath Seattle."

I could have guessed that from what Willard had told me. "Is there a favorite entrance she uses when she goes out to shop for groceries and human sacrifices?"

"I doubt Synaru-van goes out. I do not know where their entrances are, but she didn't find the kraken blood in a puddle under the freeway."

I scratched my jaw. Meaning there was likely access somewhere near a large body of water? Unfortunately, that didn't narrow things down much. Most of Seattle was within a mile or two of one significant body of water or another.

He's not in the little room under the trapdoor, Sindari told me. *And if you've ever tried to open a door with only paws and claws, you'll thank me for my effort.*

Where else could he have gone? Back to the van?

No. He's still here. I smell him close. As if he's under the floorboards.

"Zoltan, did you capture my chauffeur?"

"Your what?"

"A large man with some dwarfish blood in him."

"Hm, not I. I was focused on you. It's possible this house captured him. You may have noticed it's haunted."

I rubbed my face. "What?"

"Why do you think I chose this for my domicile? Its tenacity and will to continue existing have kept the human bulldozers away. I've watched all the large houses be installed around it."

"The noise and progress haven't bothered you?"

"Not at all. It's made it easy to find sustenance. Though it's unfortunate that a new family hasn't moved into the nearest building yet." He waved in the direction of the vacant house. "It was so handy to have warm blood so close at hand."

"Shocking that they put the house up for sale."

"My touch is light and comes in the dark of night. Nobody ever has anything but suspicions. Though I'm not so subtle with enemies." He smiled at me, and I had a feeling it truly was only the gun that had kept him cooperative tonight. "Here are your vials and syringes."

"Thanks. How do I get my friend out of the carriage house?" I pointed upward.

"Leave it an appropriate sacrifice."

"Is that how all the junk got up there?"

"It is. The house has eclectic tastes."

If Dimitri had tried to take that box of trains he'd seen, that might explain why the house had captured him. How did I get it to *un*-capture him? I didn't have any valuable junk I could leave.

Are you almost done? Sindari asked. *I smell the dark elves. They're returning, and they've acquired larger weapons.*

Fantastic.

CHAPTER 16

Zoltan showed me a way out—he seemed pleased that I would leave without robbing him, and even believed I might be able to bring him some dragon blood. Before I could contemplate how that might occur, I had to find Dimitri and deal with these dark elves. Or find Dimitri and run before the dark elves got to us.

I wasn't itching for a fight, and I highly doubted the alchemist I needed was one of the dark elves out harassing suburban neighborhoods. These were probably some lowly minions sent to hassle me. Bonus points if they killed me.

As soon as Zoltan was gone, I used my inhaler. If this new development—I glared down at my faulty lungs—was going to interfere with jobs, I would have to cave to the doctor's suggestion to get the steroid inhaler. Either that or take a more serious stab at figuring out how to de-stress and lower inflammation. It probably involved drinking mai tais on a beach somewhere and not battling giant spiders. How boring.

The inside of the carriage house was just as junk-filled as I'd left it, but there was no Dimitri. Sindari trotted soundlessly through the door as I was peering behind tarp-covered piles.

You're sure he's not outside? I asked silently, not sure how far away the dark elves were.

No. I smell him and sense him in here.

Where?

The house creaked and groaned, as if it were talking to us. Or threatening us.

Sindari padded uncertainly around. I remembered the toy train box that had caught Dimitri's eye and found the shelves he'd been looking at. My night-vision charm wasn't designed for reading or making out fine details in the dark, so I turned it off and shined my phone's flashlight at the area. The shelves were *full* of boxes. I didn't see a train kit, but it was hard to tell what lay under all the dust.

You're close to him.

I shined the light upward, but this section wasn't under the loft. Only the ceiling lay above, a hole in one spot showing clouds scudding across the starry night sky. He wasn't up there. I tilted the light down, thinking there might be another trapdoor.

Behind you, Sindari warned.

I whirled, hand on my gun.

A faded image of Dimitri floated in the air, more like a holographic projection than a flesh-and-blood person. He glowed with a faint yellow light. His feet floated above the floor, and ethereal vines wrapped around him, also glowing. In the image, he was blindfolded and gagged.

Sindari? Is he…

Not really there. It's a projection from somewhere else. But this place is muddling my senses.

The vampire said it's haunted.

It's definitely magical, a very old enchantment, I believe. I couldn't tell you what species of magical being created it.

The dangling and bound Dimitri was clutching a box in his hand—the dusty train box.

Zoltan said all the junk here is stuff that people brought for the house, like sacrifices to a god.

A god who loves junk?

Apparently. Maybe if I give it something it deems worthy, it'll let him go. Let us all go. I glanced toward the front door and wondered if I would be allowed to simply walk outside, or if the floor or some portal to another dimension would open up and swallow me.

What will you offer? Sindari asked warily. *The most valuable thing you have is me.*

I'm not giving it your figurine. Also, you have a high opinion of your self-worth.

I simply know my self-worth. You cannot deny that I'm far superior to your other charms.

That's possibly true, but Fezzik and Chopper have gotten me out of a lot of scrapes.

Have they ever flung themselves off a cliff and into the ocean to lure a dragon away?

No. I concede your point. You're infinitely valuable.

I ran a finger along the other charms on my necklace. Even if they weren't as valuable as Sindari, they were all irreplaceable, and almost every one represented a quest and a battle I'd undertaken to acquire it. But what else did I have that might tempt the house into releasing Dimitri? Was it even truly responsible or was this some other trick of Zoltan's? A component of his *security* system?

But the piles of dusty valuables on the shelves did seem to hint of a presence—a sentience?—with tastes differing from the vampire's. It was hard to imagine Zoltan pushing toy trains around his laboratory.

What could I offer the house that it would want? I shouldn't offer up the most valuable things I had as an opening move. That was no way to bargain. Besides, not everything on those shelves looked that valuable. More quirky.

"I have an idea," I blurted. "Stay here, Sindari. So it doesn't think we're leaving. I'll be right back."

Don't let the dark elves see you, Sindari said as I trotted for the front door.

Normally, that would have been difficult, since nothing but the lawn and the vacant house stood between me and the street, but I touched my cloaking charm and activated its camouflage. The house didn't try to keep me from leaving. Maybe it only kidnapped one trespasser a night. Or maybe it had only been irked at Dimitri because he had presumed to touch one of its boxes.

Even with a few stars visible between clouds, the night was very dark, save for the street lights out front. One shined on Dimitri's van, my destination.

Trying not to stir the wet grass much, I skirted the house. I started toward the driveway, but that security car was still there. Why had the patroller lingered so long? I'd thought he'd been scared off.

The driver side door was open. Maybe he was ordering a pizza.

But as I drew closer and caught the scent of recently butchered meat,

I realized the truth. Blood pooled on the driveway under the open door, and the man was slumped in his seat, hanging over the center console. The dark elves must have killed him—I'd been with Zoltan the whole time, so I doubted he was responsible. Besides, a vampire would simply bite his victim, not cut his throat or whatever had been done to make that mess.

I didn't go closer to investigate—with all the trouble I was in, I didn't need to risk getting my fingerprints all over a crime scene—but I couldn't help feeling guilty. This guy had only been called in because of me, because I'd been in a hurry and hadn't been more careful coming up to the house.

Why the dark elves had bothered him, I didn't know, but I was starting to hate them for more than poisoning Willard and burning her building. I vowed to find their leader and make him or her pay for all this.

Angry, I threw open the van door with more force than necessary, and the clunk echoed up and down the street. As the inside light came on, I cursed my carelessness. My cloaking charm couldn't hide all this.

Well, maybe it would lure the dark elves back out here. Then I could circle around, get Dimitri, and escape the carriage house without an encounter. Even if I wouldn't mind sinking my sword into their chests right now, we'd seen five of them initially, and that was more than a sane person would fight, especially when I was stiff and bruised from the tarantula fight.

I snatched the alien bobblehead doll off Dimitri's crate, closed the van door, and turned back for the house. A bush in the beauty bark on one side shivered even though there was no breeze. Yes, the dark elves were coming to investigate.

Careful not to make any more noise, I hurried around the opposite side of the house. With luck, they wouldn't expect me to go back.

I made it to the carriage house without encountering any of them and slipped inside. The projection of Dimitri had disappeared. Sindari sat waiting by the door.

That's the bribe you're going to leave? he asked skeptically.

I'm going to try.

Does it have any value?

You'd have to ask Dimitri. I'm not a collector of, uh…

Useless junk? Sindari suggested.

Movie paraphernalia.

Useless junk. He sniffed disdainfully.

I took the bobblehead to the box-filled shelves and, in case the house was watching in judgment, hugged it and patted its head, as if its loss would grieve me greatly. Then I set it on a dusty box and backed away. If this didn't work, Sindari and I would have to start tearing up floorboards.

A moan came from all around us, and a wind came up out of nowhere to batter at the roof. Chains I hadn't seen rattled in the corners, and the sound of something heavy being dragged across the floor of the loft above filtered down.

This dwelling is melodramatic, Sindari informed me.

Are there no haunted houses in your realm?

No.

A green light started glowing in the center of the carriage house, and I glanced at the boarded-up windows. There were plenty of cracks between them, so if some of the dark elves were still in the back yard, they would see this. The light grew brighter. I was starting to hate this place. If I saw Zoltan again, I'd tell him to be like a normal vampire and get a nice basement apartment in the city.

The light flared so bright that I had to turn away. A loud thud came from the center of it, and I whirled back, Fezzik at the ready.

Abruptly, the light vanished, leaving me blinking away spots in my vision. And staring through them to where Dimitri groaned on the floor, grabbing his arm and looking like he'd fallen twenty feet instead of two.

I jogged forward and knelt beside him as I pointed Fezzik toward the door. "Are you all right?"

Sindari stood near the exit, gazing out into the yard, his ears twitching and his tail rigid.

"I think so." Dimitri winced and grabbed his head. "I'm not sure what happened. I was checking out that toy train, and then it went all dark, and I felt this stabbing pain and this sense of being lifted and... I'm not sure after that. Until I dropped out of, uhm." He looked up at the ceiling.

"I'll explain it later. Or maybe I won't. It's time to go. Can you stand up?"

"I think so."

They're in the yard out there, Sindari told me. *All five of them. Looking toward us. Your charm can't hide anyone else, right? They'll see Dimitri. I don't think we'll be able to get back to the van without a fight.*

Thinking of the dead security guard, I replied, *I wouldn't mind a fight.*

Dark elves are strong and agile. And what about Dimitri? He has no magical weapons with which to defend himself.

That was the problem. Belatedly, it occurred to me that we should have fought the dark elves and *then* gotten Dimitri out of the house's weird alter dimension.

I almost called 911 to report the dead security guard—that ought to have police milling all over the property, and if the dark elves were as dedicated to not being seen as Willard had said, they would disappear. But I was a wanted woman. Calling the police would get me in more trouble than the dark elves.

They're by the playhouse again, Sindari reported. *I can hear them talking. They feel the magic of this carriage house, and that's the only reason they haven't made their move, but they're thinking about charging in to look for us.*

I eyed a handful of lawn-maintenance tools inside the door. I doubted a weed whacker and a leaf blower would scare the elves away, but perhaps they could be deterred by another distraction. Or a threat.

A rusty five-gallon can tucked behind the yard tools caught my eye— was that gasoline for the weed whacker?

"Dimitri," I whispered. "Do you have a lighter?"

"No."

"I should have brought Mom."

"Hey, I'm useful. I can make things with my hands and imbue them with magic."

"Yeah?" I grabbed the canister, opened it, and sniffed, confirming that it was gasoline. Possibly gasoline that had been there for decades—I hadn't seen a tin like that for ages. "Can you turn this gas can into a Molotov cocktail?"

I was being sarcastic, but he shrugged and said, "Easy. Are we burning down the carriage house?"

"No." I pointed toward the dark elves—I couldn't see them, but I trusted Sindari's senses.

"The *main* house?" Dimitri threw me a shocked looked. Perhaps for an obvious reason, he hadn't sounded disagreeable about burning the haunted carriage house, but someone's estate was another matter.

"Just the playhouse. We'll be doing the next owners a favor. You wouldn't want your kids playing next to this evil carriage house, would you?" I shoved the gas can toward him. "Also, the playhouse is full of dark elves getting ready to storm in and slay us."

His grunt didn't sound that agreeable, but he went hunting for a rag and went to work.

Something clanked onto the roof. I leaned out the door, ready to shoot if the dark elves were charging us. Something cylindrical—a homemade grenade?—bounced off the roof. *Far* off. As if it had been launched from a trampoline rather than simply hitting wood boards. Was the house defending itself?

The grenade flew up more than a hundred feet before exploding with a fiery orange boom. If anyone in the neighborhood had been asleep, they were awake now.

A faint twang reached my ears, and I ducked back inside. A crossbow quarrel slammed into the door where my head had been.

"I don't think we have much time," I muttered.

"This won't take long," Dimitri said.

What's behind this property, Sindari? Do you know? On the way to the carriage house, I'd seen the back fence, tall grass beyond it, and houselights in the distance, but they'd been a good hundred yards away. *Is there another way to get to the road if we sneak out the back?*

There is an equestrian trail behind this property. It smells strongly of their droppings. I do not know where it goes.

I'm sure we can loop back through someone's yard.

"Ready." Dimitri hefted the can, his fingers gripping the end of the fuse he'd made.

He'd done more than that, I realized, now sensing magic emanating from the rag and the can.

"Can you throw it all the way to the playhouse? And time it so it'll blow up as it lands? All while not being shot by dark elves with crossbows?"

"Uh." He peeked out the doorway. "Maybe."

Another faint twang sounded, and I yanked him back inside. A crossbow quarrel quivered from the edge of the door, inches from where the first one had struck.

Dimitri looked grimly at it. "I'll find a way. Hang on." He closed his eyes and ran a hand along the bottom of the rusty can.

He's a natural maker, Sindari noted.

You've seen his yard art.

He appears to have only one-quarter dwarven blood. Whoever his magical ancestor was, he must have been very powerful.

"I'm ready," Dimitri said. "I can throw it that far now, but I could use some cover."

I pulled out Fezzik. "Are they behind the playhouse or *in* it, Sindari?"

Normally, I wouldn't fire rounds in the middle of a residential neighborhood, but since they'd already thrown an explosive, it hardly seemed to matter. Besides, if someone else called the police, it would probably get rid of the dark elves.

In it, Sindari said. *One is standing on the right side of it and pointing his crossbow in our direction.*

I jogged over to one of the boarded-up windows that faced toward the playhouse. I found a gap large enough for Fezzik's barrel and fired. As far as my eyes could tell, I was firing at the playhouse and empty air, but a grunt of pain reached my ears, so I'd at least grazed one of them.

For a few seconds, only I was firing, as the dark elves took cover. Shards of the wood from the playhouse flew all over the patio. Then crossbows fired from inside and behind the structure, quarrels zipping across the yard to thud into the window boards. One skidded through the same gap as I was using, and I jerked back as the fletching grazed my knuckles.

Were those quarrels poison-tipped? I had to be more careful.

Dimitri leaned out and grunted as he heaved the gas canister. I resumed firing, not wanting the dark elves to notice him—or it. Sirens wailed as distant police cars sped into the neighborhood.

Whatever magic Dimitri had applied to the five-gallon can helped it sail farther than anyone should have been able to throw it. Fire danced on the end of the fuse. The can landed with enough velocity to crash through the roof of the playhouse.

Two seconds after the can disappeared inside the playhouse, it exploded. Flames shot in all directions as the walls of the structure blew outward.

I sprinted for the carriage house door, pushing Dimitri ahead of me. "Go, go!"

We rushed out, turning toward the trail Sindari had promised. I fired back over my shoulder in the general direction of the explosion, hoping to get lucky—and hoping I didn't run out of ammo I might yet need that night.

Sindari started after us, but he paused, silver head rotating around. Then he raced toward the burning playhouse. He only made it halfway across the yard before springing at something.

The dark elf that he hit was still invisible to me, but from Sindari's movements, I could tell he'd slammed into the chest of his target. He bit down with a snarl, shook something in his powerful teeth, then jerked away as something slashed into his side.

"Does he need our help?" Dimitri stumbled—he was also glancing back.

"No." I pushed him through the tall grass, dew dampening our pants as we ran. "He's buying time for us."

I didn't point out that I would have gone back to help if Dimitri weren't there. I owed it to him to get him to safety. He'd already gotten in far more trouble than he'd bargained for when he offered me a ride.

A roar rang out over the sounds of battle and the wailing of the approaching sirens.

You're a wonderful companion, Sindari.

It is good that you recognize this truth as self-evident.

As we clambered over a wood fence and came out on the promised trail, which turned out to be a well-maintained dirt road, the police pulled into the driveway of the vacant house. Their lights flashed off the walls of the neighboring houses and cars in the streets. Hopefully, all the activity—and light—would make the dark elves flee.

Dimitri and I ran down the dirt road, passed through a gate, and came to a spot where it crossed a paved street. We turned onto it, and I pulled out my phone for the map. I was fairly certain we'd been on the popular Tolt Pipeline Trail, but the streets back here were a maze.

"It's a circuitous route back to your van," I reported, "but maybe that's for the best."

"So the police and dark elves are gone by the time we get there?"

"Yes." I envisioned returning to a tape-covered crime scene and hoped we would be able to slip away.

The sound of claws on the pavement came from behind, and I turned as Sindari trotted up. He was limping, and when I reached to pet him, my hand came away wet with blood.

"Poor boy." Even though he would repair quickly once he returned to his own realm, that didn't keep him from feeling the pain of injuries while he was here. "Thank you for your help. Go rest now."

I will, but I wanted to warn you… They are very fast and very strong, and I think those were lowly minions among their kind. Do your best to avoid them, Val.

When I thought of Zoltan's list of requirements and the sample kit in my pocket, I shook my head sadly. *I don't think I can.*

CHAPTER 17

"Tell me again why your apartment has a parking garage and we can't use it?" Dimitri yawned noisily as he circled the nearby blocks.

Parking was always tight this close to Old Ballard, with apartment buildings rising up behind the popular restaurants and bars, some of which were still open, even though it was long after midnight. I pointed toward an alley where visitors could usually get a spot.

"Because Sudo probably has someone watching my apartment, and the main way in is through the parking garage."

"Should we avoid it altogether?"

"Yes, but I have a date with a loofah."

He threw me a startled look.

"Apparently, there's a dragon aura clinging to me that I need to scrub off. Tarantula blood too. I'm decidedly grimy."

"You don't think it would be better to go to a hotel?"

"Maybe, but I need some ammo and a change of clothes too." I poked at the tarantula ichor that had hardened all over my duster and the shirt I'd been wearing for two days. Or was it three now? "And some time on the computer to figure out where I can find an entrance to this secret underground."

My jaw cracked under the influence of a giant yawn. I would need to collect a few drops of blood from Colonel Willard, too, but I'd been up for ages, and I was exhausted. Her blood ought to be the easiest to get, even allowing for the guard she'd mentioned outside of her hospital room door, so I could do it last. Finding the dark-elf alchemist would be a challenge, and I had no idea how to convince a kraken to come to shore so I could get some of its blood. And then there was Zav. How would I convince him to give me a vial from his veins? Was he still in Oregon? The idea of driving all the way back to Bend made me even wearier.

"Do you have a guest room or do I get to sleep in my van?" Dimitri found a spot in front of a dumpster and parked.

"I have a guest… couch."

"Am I allowed to use it?"

"After driving me all over the state? Yes. I've been told it's moderately comfortable. Assuming there isn't a government agent sleeping on it now." I had numerous deadbolts on my door, but Sudo could have gotten permission to force them open.

I put on my borrowed jacket and kept the hood up while leading Dimitri in a circuitous route toward my apartment building. The organic grocery store on the first floor was closed up for the night, but the parking garage was open, as always. I walked past it, glancing in, and spotted a black car with government plates parked near the elevator.

"Yup," I muttered, continuing on to an alley around the corner. "They've got someone here."

Dimitri didn't try to convince me to leave. He kept yawning, too, so maybe he was fantasizing about my couch.

I used my lock-pick charm on the fire-escape door in the alley, checked inside, and didn't spot anyone. We headed up to the fourth floor, out into the empty hallway, and I slowed again when we reached the corner. I peeked around, already assuming someone would be there and that I'd have to climb out the window and over to my little balcony. But the hallway was empty. There *was* something on my door, some kind of electronic device. It had been mounted right above the knob.

"Hm." I leaned back around the corner.

Dimitri arched his eyebrows.

Whatever that thing was, I had a feeling it would alert someone if it was touched or the door opened.

"Back door." I pointed to the window next to the fire-escape stairs.

"That's a window."

"It leads to the back door."

I passed him, used my charm again to unlock it, and looked down before climbing out. The alley was still empty. The brick wall was flat with no ledges, but we were on the top floor, and the gutter along the edge of the roof looked sturdy.

"You can go back to your van if you don't want to follow." I hopped onto the sill, leaned out, and stood, fingers brushing the gutter. It was a reinforced metal one, so I wasn't too worried about it holding my weight. I hopped up, caught the lip, and scooted along the side of the building.

Dimitri leaned out and watched. "How often have you done this?"

"First time. I usually use the front door."

"How far is your apartment?" He pointed hopefully at the first balcony.

I kept scooting past it. "Third one over."

My fingers ached from holding up my body weight, and my forearms were quivering by the time I reached my balcony, but I hopped down successfully. Dimitri waited until I nodded and gave him a thumbs-up. He must have found the gutter too flimsy for his greater weight, for he pulled himself all the way up on the roof. He crawled over on his hands and knees, then plopped down with a grunt.

"There's a rooftop deck up there," he said. "This is a cool place."

"Especially for the fancy apartments that have access to it." I pointed toward the other side of the building. "They have views of the water." I gestured at my own view of the brick wall across the alley, including a neighbor's bathroom window, which he unfortunately didn't have curtains for. Nonetheless, I'd been happy to get an apartment with a balcony, especially one with room for the little table and chair.

"This balcony is larger than my van. It's still nice."

"I'm not positive that's true, but thank you." I tried the sliding door, even though I'd locked it before I left last time.

It was unlocked, so I wasn't surprised when I opened it, pushed aside the curtains, and stepped on something. A lot of somethings. Books. Clothes. A couple of canvas grocery bags from the store downstairs… My belongings were strewn all over the combination living room, dining room, kitchen.

"Maybe a hotel would have been better after all," I muttered.

"Did you leave it like this?" Dimitri stepped in after me.

"I'm not a neat-freak, but I'm not this much of a slob." I pulled the curtains closed behind him before picking up a small lamp that had been knocked on the floor and turning it on. In case one of the agents watching the place wandered down the alley, I didn't turn on any brighter lighting that would give us away. "The question is whether the government guys did this or someone else has been here."

"What would the government have been looking for besides you?"

"Lieutenant Sudo is doing an investigation. Maybe he had some agents come in to see if I have enormous wads of cash stashed anywhere."

"Do you?"

I lifted the big glass wine jug by the door that held several years' worth of change. Amusingly, it was still sitting in its spot on the bookcase, probably because it had been too heavy to knock off without effort. Copper was the dominant color inside, and I doubted there was more than a hundred dollars in coins.

"Enough for a few pizzas, eh?"

"Soft drinks too." I checked the bedroom and found it in a similar state of disarray, with the top mattress flipped and all the bedding on the carpet.

"Sindari," I whispered, touching my charm. "Will you come back for a bit?"

I wasn't sure he could so soon, not after I'd had him out for hours, including a fight and a chase, but I wanted his assessment—his keen nose. Also, I wouldn't mind having him guarding the door if I was going to get naked and take a shower. Assuming I could find my loofah and soap.

When the mist coalesced into the familiar silver tiger, Sindari was on his back with his paws in the air and his eyes closed. By luck or design, he'd ended up in the middle of the comforter on the floor with his head on a pillow.

"Is that your way of telling me it's bedtime where you are?" I asked.

Yes. I am healing from the wounds those vile dark elves gave me.

I'm sorry. I shouldn't have called you so soon, but as you can see, someone ransacked my apartment.

He opened an eye and rotated his head, taking in the comforter. *You did not prepare this bed for me?*

Sorry, no. Would you sniff around and see if you can figure out who was here?

He yawned, displaying his fangs, and his nostrils twitched. No, they *sniffed.* He was taking my request literally.

I assume you know about Dimitri. Older lingering scents that I detect... someone was chewing cinnamon gum. Odious. There's also the faint odor of a pine-scented shampoo or soap. Coffee—you don't drink that, do you?

No. And I doubt dark elves do either. These sounded like the scents of a government agent, or at least a human.

I know little of their culinary preferences, but I do believe the two intruders were human and came at least twelve hours ago.

I glanced at the clock radio currently dangling off the bedside table. It was almost four in the morning. *So, after we peeled out of Bend. There's at least one agent keeping an eye on this building tonight. Will you stand—or lie—guard while I take a shower? Then I'll let you go back to your realm for a nice long nap.*

Very well. Eyes closed, Sindari looked like he would do precisely as asked. Lie guard.

I leaned into the living room to tell Dimitri I'd be busy for long enough to scrub off a dragon aura but found him snoring on the couch already. It didn't look that comfortable. Someone had thrown the cushions across the room, and he hadn't bothered to retrieve them.

The bathroom was the least destroyed room in the apartment, so I found my soap bottles—I took all three containers and both kinds of shampoo into the shower with me—and my back scrubber and loofah. The hot water felt amazing after the long day, and I put together a mental to-do list while I thoroughly washed everything.

I would start out studying a map and scribbling down ideas for places to look for entrances to the Underground. I would scour the internet too. In a city this populous, *someone* had to have stumbled across the dark elves' doorways before—and lived to tell about.

As I was re-braiding my hair and putting on clean clothing, a growl emanated from the bedroom.

"Sindari?" I grabbed Fezzik—yes, I'd brought my weapons into the bathroom, and no, that wasn't weird. I also hadn't opted for pajamas, since, with the government car in the garage, I might have to flee out the balcony door at any moment.

I sense trouble, he informed me.

Heading our way?

Yes.

No... No more trouble. *It's after 4 am. Trouble isn't supposed to visit after midnight or before dawn. Those are discourteous hours for visitors.*

It's the dragon.

My first instinct was to be pissed and affronted—what was he doing in my state and in my neighborhood like a creepy scaled stalker?—but then I remembered my new task. His blood. I needed it. And I was going to get it.

I strapped on my belt and jammed Fezzik in the thigh holster, then slung Chopper's scabbard across my back. As soon as I shoved my feet back into my boots, I grabbed the vampire's sample kit.

I assume he's on his way here? There's no way he's coincidentally flying through the same place as me for a third time.

Even as I finished the thought, I sensed his big powerful dragon aura. The aura I'd so assiduously scrubbed off. If he gave me a vial of his blood, I'd forgive him for oozing it all over me again. Maybe.

He's landing on the roof. Sindari rolled to his feet.

Mongrel human, a telepathic voice that was nothing like Sindari's boomed in my head like a wrecking ball slamming into a gong. *Come to me. I will speak with you.*

"Is that arrogant blowhard kidding?"

Sindari gazed blandly at me. Dimitri snored from the living room, his head half hanging off the couch.

He won't fit through the balcony door, Sindari remarked. *He squashed two patio chairs when he landed.*

So you're saying he has a big ass?

All of him is big. You may want to go up there. If you hope to ask him for a favor, you won't want to irritate him. Further.

Can't I just find a soft spot on his hide and stab him with a syringe when he's not looking?

Dragons don't have soft spots.

That figures. I slipped out the door onto the balcony and climbed onto the railing so I could grab the gutter and pull my chin over the edge of the roof.

A pair of large violet eyes glowed at me from the darkness. It took my own eyes a moment to adjust to the darkness and pick out his black scaled form from the rest of the roof. He *was* big. Seeing him in the wilderness hadn't prepared me for how large he would be on the rooftop of my apartment building.

Come up here, mongrel.

My hands and forearms already ached from holding my bodyweight from my fingers. I wasn't sure I could pull myself up again after my earlier climbing feat.

"It's Val, and humans don't clamber around on rooftops." Never mind that I'd done so a half hour ago. "If you want to talk to me, change into something small enough to fit through my door, and come visit me like a civilized person."

I dropped back down to the balcony, less to be contrary and more because my fingers were cramping up.

Remember how we discussed not irritating him? Sindari asked as I walked back inside, leaving the door open.

I'm not going to drop to my knees in front of him and kiss his slippered toes.

Not even for a vial of blood?

A strong breeze gusted through the door, knocking the curtains about, and Zav strode inside, once again in human form. He wore his usual black robe and slippers. Apparently, shapeshifters didn't need to change clothes. I supposed I should be relieved he didn't appear naked, like those werewolves.

"Thank you," I forced myself to say, and smiled politely. It was possible I bared a lot of teeth during my polite smile. "What are you doing here?"

Nose in the air, Zav looked at the snoring Dimitri and the disarray of my apartment. Maybe inviting him in hadn't been a great idea.

"Wondering why you brought me into this disheveled kobold hovel."

"Sorry my apartment isn't up to your standards. Some goons broke in and tore it apart."

"Did you slay them?"

"No, I'm saving that until after breakfast."

He gazed impassively at me, but I had a feeling he couldn't tell if I was joking or not. Maybe dragons didn't have sarcasm. Or maybe *mongrels* weren't usually sarcastic with them.

"I am progressing through my list of criminals that I must capture and return to the Dragon Justice Court. It is a tediously long list. This world has been neglected for centuries."

"You know what they say. The reward for a job well done is another job."

"Do not interrupt me, mongrel."

"You paused. I thought it was my turn to talk."

"I paused to gather my thoughts."

"That is important. Carry on."

Val... Sindari's gaze was less impassive as he looked at me. *Don't goad the dragon.*

He won't kill me. He wants something from me or he wouldn't be here gathering his thoughts.

A dragon can easily lose his temper and inadvertently kill someone he's talking to. He would have no regrets. He would find someone else to gather thoughts with.

The arrogant prick rubs my fur the wrong way.

Have you composed a will? If you die, will my figurine go to Dimitri?

Is that what you want? He won you over with ten seconds of petting?

He rubbed my fur the right way.

I'll keep your request in mind. Right now, my fourteen-year-old daughter is the heir to my estate. I flicked a finger to indicate the trashed apartment and all its vast wealth. Maybe she would get some use from the coin jug.

"There are two dark elves on my list," Zav said.

"So?" I focused on him and ignored Sindari's mental sputtering about being lumped in as part of an estate—and going to a teenager.

"I have learned that you will soon hunt dark elves."

"Just one."

"You will enter into their lair."

"I have to find it first."

His violet eyes narrowed, and he stepped closer to me. "Do you *never* stop interrupting when greater beings speak to you?"

"I don't think you know how conversations work." I rested my hand on Fezzik, though I hadn't forgotten that he could incinerate bullets. Would he do so as easily with magical ammo?

He flicked a finger, and Fezzik flew out of its holster and across the room. I jumped as it smacked into the wall, almost hitting my change jug, and clunked to the floor.

"Do not threaten me, mongrel," Zav growled, his eyes slits as they bored into me. "In my realm, you would be slain for presuming to carry a weapon in a dragon's presence."

"No wonder everybody there flees to Earth." I folded my arms over my chest, refusing to admit that I was shaken by his presence—by him. Even though I'd encountered plenty of enemies who could knock my weapons aside if I wasn't fast enough, I could feel his aura crackling in the air like electricity on a high-voltage line. I knew Sindari was right, that he could kill me by accident, and that I wasn't strong enough to fight him.

"Only criminals flee," he said softly, dangerously. "As the two dark elves I seek did. They recently joined the horde of them living under your city like ants under a rotten log. When you enter the dark-elf lair, you may encounter a high priestess, Yemeli-lor, and her odious mate, a warrior named Baklinor-ten."

Though numerous sarcastic comments popped into my head, I managed to keep my mouth shut and listen.

"The two I seek stole from a prominent dragon family an artifact of cultural and historical significance," Zav continued, "and they are using it in their foul sacrifices to their bloodthirsty goddess. If you see them, you will bring them to me. If you see the artifact, you will retrieve it for me."

"Uh." I lifted a finger to protest further, but he reached for me.

Startled, I tried to leap back, but some invisible power immobilized me, and I couldn't move. He pressed the heel of his palm against my forehead, his fingers resting against my hair. What the hell?

"It looks like this."

An image surged into my mind on a wave of power that would have dropped me to my knees if his magic hadn't been holding me. I saw a thick platter carved from some purple and blue swirling stone or gem that I didn't recognize, and on it lay a great gilded eggshell cracked into two pieces and adhered to the surface. The interior of the broken egg glowed with a soft blue light.

Zav removed his hand, and the power gripping me disappeared. I locked my knees before they could buckle and did my best to hide the shakiness of my breath.

He watched me for several long seconds.

"Is it my turn to speak now?" I asked.

"It would be appropriate for you to obediently say you'll do my bidding."

"Uh huh. I don't know how you know I'm looking for a dark elf—maybe you're a fan of Zoltan's internet alchemy channel—but the ones you named aren't the one I'm looking for. I need a cure for my boss, not a weird dragon artifact."

His eyes narrowed again. Sindari stood next to me and bumped his hip against my side. Possibly, it was a show of support, but more likely, he was reminding me not to irk the dragon.

"I *may* be willing to help you," I continued, though I was already daunted by my own quest, "in exchange for a small vial of your blood for Zoltan."

"*Nobody* takes a dragon's blood to use for magical debauchery. Or for any other reason. I have already told that alchemist that he will get himself killed—further—if he attempts to collect such a thing."

"That's probably why he wants *me* to collect it."

"No doubt he sees you as expendable."

"What were you doing talking to him, and why can't you get your own dark elves?"

"I sensed that several dark elves were above the surface and easily accessible. I went to see if any of them were the two I sought. They were not, but I am no longer surprised when you are found in the presence of the magical. Whether you accept the honor or not, you *are* my perfect bait. And I will continue to use you as such."

He looked so smugly pleased at having discovered my secret utility. I wanted to punch him in the nose. It was a straight, strong handsome nose, so it would feel particularly satisfying to smash it, but even if he looked like a human, I doubted he was as fragile as a human.

"When you aren't sending me in to do your work for you," I said.

Fresh irritation—or maybe that was indignation—rose to his eyes. "Find the criminals and the artifact, and I will reward you."

"By *not* using me as bait?"

"No. I *will* use you as bait. The sooner I complete my task, the sooner I may leave this vermin-infested world. What other reward would you wish?"

"A vial of your blood."

"Not that."

"A cure for my boss."

"I am not an alchemist."

"Then I need a vial of your blood. What's the big deal? I saw how humongous you are. It's not like you're going to miss it."

Most guys would be delighted to be called humongous, but Zav stepped back, tension snapping into his body. It was only then that I realized he'd been speaking to me normally, almost pleasantly. Until I'd pissed him off again.

"No dragon would allow his blood to be experimented on, not by another dragon, and definitely not by some vampire vermin."

I had a feeling he considered everyone who wasn't a dragon to be vermin. "That's my price. Why can't you find their lair and get your own dark elves, anyway?"

"I can. I choose to delegate."

"I didn't sign up to be your assistant. I have my own mission, someone's life to save. Sorry, but that's more important to me than your to-do list." I waved to the open balcony door. "You can see yourself out."

He strode toward me, not away, his eyes darkening with his anger. Sindari growled and crouched. I reached for Chopper.

I was fast enough that I managed to get the sword halfway out of its scabbard before his power locked on to me again, but that only made me feel like an idiot with my arm stuck over my head. Sindari growled again, but he appeared as frozen as I was as Zav stepped in close.

Again, he reached for my head. This time, he laid his hand on the side of it and stared into my eyes in some parody of a lover's gaze. But there was no love in his expression. He didn't hurt me or dig his fingers into my scalp, but his eyes were as haughty as always as he stared into mine, and the power that crackled around him skittered over my skin and made my nerves tingle with something closer to pain than pleasure.

"It is an honor to serve a dragon, to be selected as a personal minion," he said softly, "and you *will* serve me. Bring me the dark elves, and bring me the artifact, and do not question me further."

A new type of power gripped me, something more subversive than his raw strength. It altered my thoughts, and I envisioned myself doing as he wished, dragging his enemies out of some tunnel to lay before him, then dropping at his feet and lifting the egg-relic up over my head to him, so eager to do his bidding, eager to please, hoping for a pat on the head like a dog...

I couldn't voice the words "Fuck you," but I was pleased that I managed to think them. Unfortunately, that didn't drive the eagerness to please him out of my mind. And he only smirked as he stepped back, releasing me again. Weirdly, my body missed that power crackling all around me and through me.

Without another word, he walked toward the balcony door, the curtains swirling on a gust of air again. He looked back over his shoulder as he strode out, but I couldn't read his expression. Then he was gone, springing off the balcony railing and shifting in the air back to his dragon form.

I released my grip on Chopper, the sword sliding back into its scabbard, and sank to my knees. A new level of exhaustion came over me, and I dropped my hands to the floor, needing the support. As I stared at the rug, two things sank in. First, I'd made a mistake in not negotiating until I'd found a reward that he would give me—a dragon could make a charm or something even more useful that would help me. Second… even though he'd left, and his aura was fading as he flew farther away, he'd imparted an urge in me that I couldn't deny.

I *did* want to bring his enemies out to lay at his feet. I longed to please him, to have him touch my head again and tell me what a good girl I was.

Snarling, I balled my hands into fists and thumped them against the floor. I was going to *deny* that urge. His dark elves could stay in their lair, having orgies all over his precious artifact. I'd die before I helped the smug bastard.

CHAPTER 18

When the waiter at Bitterroot BBQ brought my tray of brisket, ribs, beans, and collard greens, I dug in with enthusiasm, wishing I could eat Dimitri's share too. He sat across from me, looking cheerful and perky as he grabbed his cornbread. I couldn't believe he'd slept through the entire dragon encounter, snoring in oblivion while I was getting my mind diddled.

I also couldn't believe that, once I'd finally fallen asleep, I'd spent the night dreaming of riding a black dragon over the city, over the mountains, and across the Sound—and loving it. Laughing as we dipped and soared, looking down at a passenger ferry from high above and startling sea lions sunning themselves on a beach. Either my mind was messing with me or Zav had left the notion in there, along with the one of me eagerly doing his bidding. Maybe that was the reward he thought I would want, though I had a hard time imagining him deigning to let a mongrel ride on his back. More likely, my sleep-deprived brain had come up with the dream all by itself.

I shoved a rib in my mouth, gnawing on the bone far harder than pleasure would have demanded. At least my stomach was happy. We hadn't eaten since driving back from Bend the day before, and I'd woken up at noon, ravenous and with no food in the apartment that hadn't been thrown on the floor and trampled.

"You all right?" Dimitri asked.

"I'm just trying to figure out how I'm going to collect everything

I need to get when I don't even know how to get down there." The restaurant was busy with people eating at tables close to ours, so I refrained from mentioning dark elves and secret underground tunnels. "Did you really not wake up at any point last night when Zav was in my apartment?"

"Nope. I was passed out." He'd woken up even later than I had. I'd had to prod him off my couch with the promise of food.

"He really asked you to fetch some, uh, bad guys for him?" Dimitri glanced at one of the side tables where the couple was cheerfully chatting about their plans to visit the Chihuly Museum and go to a Mariners game. What must it be like to have such a normal life?

"Yes. I don't get it." I leaned closer and lowered my voice. "Couldn't he smash through the building or street or whatever is on top of the tunnels and reach in and pluck them out? You didn't see him on the rooftop. He's huge."

"Maybe he's not supposed to destroy cities to do his job."

"Even if that's true—and I have a hard time imagining his justice court caring about lowly vermin cities—then why couldn't he walk down there as a human and get them? Why send me? A puny little mongrel."

He lowered his voice. "I'm sure you know more about dragon shifters than I do—"

"Not *much* more. This is my first one."

Dimitri raised his eyebrows. Maybe I did have a problem with interrupting.

"I wonder if he's less powerful in that form and worries that an entire clan of dark elves—how many live down there?—might overpower him."

"He incinerated bullets and froze me in my tracks while in human form. He froze Sindari, too, and he's at least moderately resistant to magical attacks." I didn't want to contemplate the possibility that Zav was afraid to go down there, not when I had no choice but to go in.

"I said *less* powerful, not a wimp."

"I don't know." I scraped collard greens onto my fork and shoveled them into my mouth while I considered. "He's so arrogant that even if he *was* less powerful, I think he'd still believe he could kick all of their asses."

"Maybe he's just busy then. Long list of criminals to catch."

I snorted. "He does sound aggrieved by that. And pissed that it's forcing him to visit our lowly world. Who gave him this task, do you think?"

"Someone higher up on the totem pole?"

"His mom?" My snort turned to a snigger as I imagined Lord Cocky getting taken by the ear—the horn—and being given the to-do list as punishment.

Dimitri's mouth twisted with skepticism.

"He did mention that female dragons are powerful and run the show. Maybe that's why the males, embittered by their pitiful status in society, take their aggressions out on smaller species."

"Maybe you can run that hypothesis by him next time he lands on your roof. If he kills you, at least you'll die at home."

"Flattened like those poor deck chairs." I set down my fork as a new unpleasant thought surfaced. "What if he's still pissed at me for interfering with his arrest of the wyvern, and he's trying to get me killed? By giving me an impossible task?"

"Couldn't he have killed you last night in your apartment if he wanted you dead?"

"Or any of the times we've met, yes, but maybe that's against the laws he's upholding. I don't think he killed any of the werewolves, though the ones that caught fire might have eventually died." I grabbed another rib. "You know what I should have done? Told him he'd have to come with me down into that lair and that I'd help him get his dark elves, but only if he and his bullet-incinerating body stood in front of me while I hunted down the alchemist."

The baseball couple glanced at me. Maybe I hadn't lowered my voice enough. The waiter brought their check, which they hurried to pay without waiting for change and then hustled away from the table with a few backward glances toward me.

I waved a rib at them.

"He would be a powerful ally," Dimitri said, "but can you really imagine a dragon working with anyone but another dragon?"

I didn't want him for an ally anyway. I worked alone. That wasn't going to change. It was bad enough I'd let Dimitri go see the vampire with me. It had almost gotten him eaten by a haunted house.

"Until I figure out how to find this lair, it's a moot point." I dug out my phone and tapped open the map application again, thinking of Zoltan's implication that the alchemist would have to have access to a body of water large enough to hold a kraken.

I'd been attacked twice by dark elves in hoodies, so it wasn't as if they *couldn't* travel outside, at least at night, but it would certainly be convenient for the alchemist if she didn't have to go far to collect blood from sea life. Maybe there was a tunnel exit right by the water.

Puget Sound would be the most obvious bet for housing something as large as a kraken. It connected to the Pacific Ocean, and, as a quick search told me, was a lot deeper than Lake Union or Lake Washington.

But how would someone on land or a boat get close to a kraken? Weren't they supposed to be hundreds if not thousands of pounds? Could a kraken be lured up to shore? And trapped for long enough to give a vial of its blood? Or its venom. Zoltan had gotten an excited gleam in his eyes when he'd spoken of that. Even if it had nothing to do with the potion—formula—that had taken down Willard, maybe a dark-elf alchemist would be just as excited by kraken venom and try to collect it regularly.

I closed the social media application I'd had open, checking on a status update from my daughter's latest swim meet, and did some searches for Puget Sound plus sea monsters, giant squids, and krakens, to see if anything came up. Nothing within the past decade. Hm. More on a whim than because I thought I'd get lucky, I did the same search with Lake Union and the ship canal. Willard's words about the Underground tunnels extending under the lake came to mind. A ship could pass from the Sound through the ship canal, Lake Union, and Portage Bay into Lake Washington, so wasn't it conceivable that a kraken could too? The idea of it correctly timing its passage through the locks was a little amusing, but maybe they were smart.

"Ah, what's this?" I murmured.

"Leftovers?" Dimitri pointed to my plate. "Are you going to eat that cornbread?"

"Go ahead. I'm reading about a recent sighting of the Loch Ness monster in Lake Union. Several of them. From residents living in the houseboats there. How *interesting*."

"Does that have something to do with dark elves?"

"It may. Look at the dates." I showed him my phone screen. "There was a flurry of sightings about eight weeks ago, then nothing, and then more sightings last month. Could my alchemist be luring the kraken into Lake Union for easy access? And then maybe coming up from some subterranean tunnel to trap it or stab it with something that gives her a vial of blood?"

"I don't know what you're talking about, but since you're letting me eat your food, I won't object."

I finished off my brisket while explaining what Zoltan had said about kraken blood being necessary for the formula that had taken down Willard.

"Something must be happening once a month to make that the ideal time for her to lure in the kraken and take her samples. Eight weeks ago probably would have been about the time she was collecting ingredients for the potion that waylaid Willard." I still didn't know why the dark elves wanted to kill Willard, but I would be sure to ask the alchemist while I was wringing her neck.

"If there were sightings eight weeks ago and four weeks ago, maybe we're due for another one."

"If she still needs ingredients, that could be. Maybe she's making lots of these formulas to take out lots of enemies, but she can only bring the kraken in to get fresh blood once a month. It was dark last night, wasn't it? Even without the clouds, I don't think there was a moon." I snapped my fingers and tapped in a new search. "Hah, that's it. There was a new moon eight weeks ago, the night the first sightings were reported. The sky would have been extra dark that night."

"Safe enough for a dark elf to pop out of its hole?"

"*Her* hole. Dark elves must be able to come out any night if they properly protect themselves, but maybe darker nights are preferable. Or maybe the *kraken* only shows up on the darkest of nights." Dread and anticipation mingled to create a weird sensation in my gut as I scrolled further down the page and checked the date. "There's a new moon tonight."

"So if we hang out on a houseboat tonight, we might see a kraken?"

"If the alchemist is following the pattern and luring it in again." I couldn't know for certain that the dark elves were responsible for these Loch Ness monster sightings, but this was the best lead I had. Besides, who but someone with a use for kraken blood, and a need for it to be delivered close to the dark-elf tunnel system, would invite such a creature into Lake Union? "If she's already got all the blood she needs, she might not be. But it's either investigate this or sneak into the Underground tour and knock on the walls, hoping to find a hollow one that could be knocked down, and that would lead into the rest of the tunnel network. But you'd have to think there's some separation between the tunnel systems for the dark elves to have avoided notice for all this time."

"It sounds like we've got until dark to figure out what we need to invade a dark-elf lair."

"We need? Dimitri, I appreciate you driving me around yesterday, but it's too dangerous for you to go. The *dragon* didn't even want to go."

"Maybe he just hasn't figured out where the door is."

That was a possibility. The dark elves might have some enchantment in place to keep people, magical and mundane, from stumbling onto the entrances they use. And as powerful as a dragon was, some magic *did* work to camouflage things from them—I'd seen that with my own cloaking charm. Weaker beings throughout history had probably made an art of hiding from dragons.

"We haven't exactly figured it out either." I leaned back in my seat as the waiter took our trays. "Is the tunnel entrance just near the lake or… is it possible it's *in* the lake? There has to be a reason the alchemist chose that spot to lure the kraken to. Maybe I need to shop for SCUBA gear today."

Except that I didn't know *how* to SCUBA dive, and the impression I'd always gotten was that it took instruction and some practice. Maybe I could free dive. I was a good swimmer and could hold my breath for a while.

According to my searches, Lake Union was only fifty feet deep at its deepest point. Lots of spots were shallower. Swimming with my boots and weapons would be a pain in the ass, but it could be doable if I knew exactly where to go. Maybe I could find some bathymetry maps and make some guesses about where a tunnel entrance might be. There would have to be an airlock to keep water from flooding the tunnels, and the door would be magically hidden to keep mundane humans from noticing it. Would I be able to find it?

I scratched my jaw. Was all this likely, or was I following a hunch down a rabbit hole? Maybe the alchemist simply came out on the beach at Gas Works Park and summoned the kraken from there.

"Do people do that here?" Dimitri asked. "The water is really cold, isn't it?"

"Yes, it is, and yes, they do. In cozy warm wetsuits."

Out of curiosity, I searched for SCUBA rental outfits. There were a couple right by the lake. "Interesting. Wreck diving in Lake Union is a popular hobby. I didn't know that. This says there are a whole bunch of old ships down on the bottom. Maybe one of them is on top of my theoretical entrance to the dark-elf lair."

My phone rang, and I jumped. It was Mom, so I hurried to answer. I'd tried calling her as soon as I'd woken up earlier but had gotten her machine again.

"Hello?" I answered warily, afraid one of those agents might have gone back to her cabin and was using her phone.

"It's me. Are you all right?"

"I'm fine, Mom. Are *you* okay?"

"Yes. I hung out behind the trees on the top of the cliff, and I think they thought I'd disappeared for good. They left once they got their tires fixed. They did come back this morning, so I took off for a few hours, but they're gone now, hopefully for good."

"They should all be up here chasing me now."

"Care to explain why?"

"It's a long story. Willard is being investigated too. I'm going to clear our names though. Is her cat all right?"

Mom hesitated, but she decided not to question me further. "Maggie is doing fine. She's claimed the loft and keeps knocking things over up there. Rocket can't get up the ladder, so he barks at her to let her know how naughty she is. The last time he did, she pushed a book over the side and it almost whacked him on the nose. I'm positive that book was on a shelf in a bookcase, not on the floor. This cat isn't magical, is it?"

"No. Just obstreperous, from what I gather."

"Hm. She's eating and doing fine, if you want to tell your boss."

An unexpected lump formed in my throat at the thought of the cat possibly not seeing her owner again. And of Willard possibly not seeing her cat again. I wished I'd brought Maggie by the hospital before I left town. I had no idea if that was allowed—probably not—but I should have done it anyway.

"Thank you. Stay safe, Mom."

"I think I'm supposed to say that to you. Stay safe, and don't let my roommate get in trouble either. He owes me his three hundred dollars next week."

I imagined government agents outside my apartment, police competing with dark elves to find me, and killer krakens swimming around in Lake Union. Somehow, I doubted staying safe was going to be a possibility for me. But I said, "I'll try," before hanging up.

"Mom's okay," I said to Dimitri's inquiring expression. "And you better drive back and sell some yard art. Your rent is due next week."

"I have the money for it. You've been kind enough to pay for all my gas." The waiter dropped off the bill, and Dimitri pushed it toward me, adding, "And food."

I took it. He deserved more than gas money for hauling me from one state to the next and around the city in the middle of the night. But I didn't want him following me again tonight.

"You can't come with me to find the kraken and the dark elves," I said.

He frowned. "Look, I'm not saying that I'm some epic war hero, but don't you at least want someone nearby with a ride? In case you need to run?"

"I thought you came up here to club, not to man my getaway car."

"It's a getaway van, now missing a bobblehead."

"I'm sure you can find another one at a garage sale."

"Not vintage. Maybe if I come with you, I'll find one stashed in the dark-elf lair."

I leaned my elbow on the table and rested my forehead in my hand. I didn't usually have this much trouble getting rid of men—they all said something about the package not being worth fencing with my sharp tongue and my surly disposition. Dimitri had touched my tiger. What else did he want?

"I think your mom would be super pissed if I let you get killed," Dimitri admitted.

"You can't keep that from happening."

"You never know. The getaway van can do zero to sixty in under thirty seconds."

"That's acceleration that NASCAR drivers fantasize about." I leaned back and dropped my hand. "All right, how does this sound? You hang out at Nin's tonight, and I'll text you if I need help." I mentally put waterproof baggies on my shopping list for the night's activities. Chopper and Fezzik would survive getting wet, but my ammunition and my phone were another matter. "Maybe you can get some business tips from her. She's smart. She's only been in the U.S. for a few years, and she came with something like a suitcase and fifty dollars."

Dimitri's face shifted through a number of expressions as he seemed to war with wanting to go along with me and this new enticement. "I guess that's not that far from Lake Union," he finally said.

Depending on the traffic, it wasn't. I only nodded encouragingly. Then started doing more research. Right now, I had a fancy hunch and not much more. Before I went for a midnight swim, I wanted to be reasonably certain that the tunnel entrance was *in* the lake. I didn't want to miss the dark elves because the entrance was three blocks away in somebody's wine cellar. I was positive that Willard didn't have until the next new moon.

CHAPTER 19

As twilight dwindled and I sat between a planter and two kayaks on the dark deck of a houseboat with nobody home, I found myself missing Dimitri's company. He'd dropped me off and promised he would head to Nin's food truck but said I should call or text or email or all three if I needed help. I'd left my apartment keys with him, so I wouldn't lose them in the water.

My phone was zipped away in a plastic baggy with my extra ammunition, everything stuffed into a buttoned pocket. I'd also grabbed a few magical grenades that Nin had once sold me, promising they were waterproof, and food, water, a first-aid kit, a lighter, goggles, and a waterproof flashlight. My mother would be proud.

Whether or not I would go for a swim remained to be seen. It would depend on if the kraken showed up and I sensed a dark elf in the lake.

Hours of research hadn't revealed anything definitive about underwater doorways, but it had lent more credence to my hunch that one existed. There was a history of strange things occurring at night in Lake Union, not just the supposed Loch Ness visits. People had reported everything from glowing lights under the water to inexplicable high-pitched keens that woke up residents but that nobody could pinpoint.

I was tempted to call out Sindari for company, and because he would sense magical beings much sooner than I, but if I did end up in a dark-elf lair, fighting for my life, I would need him at my side then. The longest I'd ever managed to keep him in our world was six hours, and if we engaged in a lot of battles, his ability to stay here would dwindle further. I had to save him for when I needed him.

Gradually, it grew darker, as much as it would with street lamps and lit houseboats all around the lake, and the headlights of cars brightening the freeway high overhead as they whizzed past. I touched a charm I hadn't used since I visited the wyvern's cave, making sure there was life down there before I committed to climbing down. That seemed like weeks ago instead of days ago.

As I held the heart-shaped charm and murmured the activation word, the lake came alive to me, thousands of fish that I could now sense swimming around under the surface. A few larger turtles and seals also plucked at my senses, along with hundreds of people in the rows of nearby houseboats.

I'd never used the charm in the middle of the city, and feeling so much life in all directions was overwhelming. It took me a few minutes to sort through it and verify that there wasn't anything giant in the lake. No krakens. Not yet. Just a few thousand fish. A lot of them were swimming around the bottom of the lake not far from my spot. That much interest had to indicate food. Maybe the Parks and Recreation people tossed munchies into the lake so people would have something to catch when they fished.

Cars honked up on the freeway as traffic backed up. Those people from lunch probably weren't the only ones heading into the city for the baseball game. What if the dark elves were fans and, instead of luring krakens in for their blood, they were all sitting around a subterranean TV watching the warmup?

"Sure, Val," I muttered.

I leaned against one of the wood planters, the fragrant flowers of whatever bush it held competing with the dank fishy smells of the lake.

Chances were it would be hours until something happened—if anything happened at all. Doubts filled my mind as I waited, gazing around at all the city lights. Would they be visible from under the surface? Maybe this was still too much light for a dark elf. Was it more likely that the alchemist would choose the darker shores of the Arboretum or the Union Bay Natural Area to lure the kraken to?

But their tunnels were over here. Or so Willard had said. Did she truly know? Or had she been repeating unsubstantiated rumors?

I drummed my fingers, tempted to leave and look for a darker spot along the waterway, but I made myself stay put. If I caught a ride somewhere else, I might miss the kraken. I might—

An awareness came within range of my senses. The kraken? No, it was the *dragon*.

He was in the sky, not the water, flying over the city, his black body and wings invisible against the clouds. If not for my ability to sense the magical, I wouldn't have known he was there. But I looked right toward him as he flew over the lake, and glimpsed two glowing violet eyes looking back down toward me.

"What a stalker," I grumbled.

Zav continued flying north, toward Green Lake. Maybe he was simply out looking for bad guys. Or maybe he was looking for his own entrance into the dark-elf tunnels. Or maybe—

I sucked in a breath as I sensed another large presence. This time, it wasn't the dragon, and it wasn't with my innate senses. It was through the charm. A huge life form was swimming this way from the Ship Canal.

The kraken.

The charm didn't identify life forms—it only gave me an idea of how large they were—but I knew with certainty that this was it. Tonight, there would be reports of a Loch Ness monster again.

I rose to my feet and re-checked my gear, making sure everything was buttoned, zipped, or buckled in. The kraken swam into the far side of Lake Union. Would it continue through and on toward the quieter and darker waters on the way to Lake Washington? Or would it dive down, lured to one of those wrecks?

It was heading toward the same area where so many of those fish were hanging out. I lurched to my feet. What if the dark-elf alchemist was the one feeding the fish? What if this was her bait? Something so yummy that the fish were coming in droves and the kraken had been lured in from miles away.

Something magical? I strained my senses, wishing they were stronger. Again, I was tempted to pull Sindari out, but I didn't want to waste his time here.

My gaze fell upon the kayaks. "Let's take a little ride out there, shall we?"

If I was right over that spot, I ought to be able to sense something magical. Magical fish bait? Who knew?

I found a paddle and eased the kayak off the deck, my weapons clunking the sides as I slid in. As I shoved off, I took note of what the house looked like from the water, so I could find it again and return the kayak.

The lake was calm without much of a breeze, so I didn't have trouble paddling toward the fish meeting spot. The dragon's aura plucked at my senses again. I paused and glared upward. If he came close, I would wave my paddle at him and tell him to get his scaly butt down here to help me.

But as I frowned up into the cloudy sky, I picked out two auras, not one. The dragon and a smaller but still magical creature. Another wyvern?

A distant roar floated to my ears, almost drowned out by the surrounding traffic noise. Whatever it was, they were fighting. I could just make out the smaller winged figure, a tail whipping in the air as it faced Zav. It wasn't a wyvern. It was a manticore. It dipped as Zav arrowed toward it, then flew upward, using its talons to slash at the dragon's underbelly.

I sucked in a concerned breath before I caught myself—there was no way I was concerned about that big arrogant jerk. If I was, it was only because of whatever spell he'd cast on me.

He didn't need my concern anyway. A blast of raw power slammed into the manticore before the talons raked Zav's belly. It hurled the smaller foe all the way down to slam into the rooftop of a tall building. The dragon streaked down after him, probably smashing deck chairs when he landed. The walls around the rooftop were high, so I couldn't see what happened after that. I didn't know whether to feel sorry for the manticore or glad that Zav was stealing away some magical criminal for judgment in another realm. Either way, he wasn't here to stalk me, after all. And he would be too busy to help if I got into trouble.

Not that I'd expected or wanted his help.

I slowed the kayak, bobbing gently in the waves as I peered over the side. A faint yellow glow was visible, and I was close enough now to sense a hint of magic. Whatever bait was luring the fish—and the kraken—it wasn't natural.

"So now what?" I murmured.

The bait and the kraken were interesting, but neither was what I wanted. I closed my eyes, trying to sense other magical beings in the area.

The dragon and the manticore were far enough away to have faded from my limited range. But there was something else…

I held my breath. A magical person similar to the dark elves that had shown up in Woodinville had come onto my radar. He or she wasn't straight down but over toward the bank, maybe fifteen feet below a row of houseboats. I was positive the dark elf hadn't been there long. He or she had popped up on my senses as if from behind an insulated door.

I paddled slowly in that direction. The dark elf hadn't moved yet. Lights were on in several of the houseboats, and a couple was out on their deck in a hot tub. Possibly naked. Wonderful. The dark elf was almost right under them. Still not moving. Waiting for… what? The kraken to get full before trying to collect its blood?

If I swam down there, could I surprise the dark elf? Maybe knock him or her out and get into the tunnels?

The people in the hot tub were looking at me. They probably thought I was a creeper peering into windows at night. Like it was my fault that they were naked in their hot tub above a dark-elf lair.

I waved a paddle and continued past, pretending I lived in one of the houseboats nearby. I turned down an aisle between two rows of them, trying not to get too far from the dark elf.

Even as I tried to find a spot to slip out of the kayak, the dark elf moved. I couldn't see anything with my eyes, but I could sense the magical aura moving away from the side of the lake. Swimming? Something about a dark elf in SCUBA gear made my brain hurt, but he or she was moving quickly out toward the kraken.

I almost followed in the kayak, but I wanted to get into the tunnels, not necessarily waylay whichever dark elf had come out. Unless it was the alchemist. But would it be? Or would she have sent a minion?

A light went on in a nearby house, and I made my decision. I pulled my goggles over my face and eased over the side of the kayak, almost gasping as the cold water engulfed my body. I sucked in a huge breath, sank down, and swam toward the area where the dark elf had seemed to emerge from the side of the lake.

Not surprisingly, it was as dark as it was cold under there. I activated my night-vision charm in time to avoid cracking my head on the log float under a houseboat and swam under several more houseboats to get to the spot. I tried not to think about them above me—and how I'd have to navigate a maze to get back up to take a breath.

The lumpy sides of the lake came into view, along with debris buried in silt. But I also saw a square hole in the slope, barely visible amid tendrils of seaweed waving in the currents. My lungs were already starting to crave air, but I swam toward it. My senses told me the dark elf was close to the kraken now. If I could slip in without anyone noticing…

Just as I reached the square hole—it was larger than I'd realized, big enough to drive a car through—a door that looked like the seaweed-covered side of the lake itself started to grind shut. Before I could reconsider it, I yanked Chopper out and lunged in, jamming the blade into the door's path. It slid shut on the blade, sending a jarring reverberation up my arm and making me wince. This was *not* the proper use for a sword. But Chopper successfully kept the door from shutting.

Using the hilt to pull myself down, I tried to use the blade for leverage. I pushed at the door, hoping to force it open, but I worried about breaking my sword. Even though Chopper was magical, I was sure it wasn't indestructible.

Precious air bubbles escaped my lips as I shoved. The door opened an inch. A few more inches, and I could slip through.

But I needed air. I glanced up, thinking of releasing Chopper and going up for a quick breath, but the bottom of a huge houseboat blocked me from the surface.

Frustrated, I shoved harder. The door inched open further. I squeezed into the gap and almost thrust myself all the way through before I thought wiser of it. What if I got trapped somewhere without any air?

Though I worried I'd run out of time and the dark elf would come back, I wedged Chopper in the long way and swam out from under the houseboat and up to the surface. I sucked in air, confused for a moment by the nearby rumble of a motor and bubbling water. Then I remembered the hot tub. Hopefully, the nude bathers couldn't see me or hear me sucking in deep breaths of air right beside their deck.

I sensed the dark elf on the move again, heading back toward the door.

Out of time, I inhaled one more deep breath and swam back down to my sword. Poor Chopper, being used as a doorstop.

I swam through the opening, careful not to dislodge the sword, and found my earlier guess to be correct. This appeared to be some kind of airlock. On the far side, about eight feet away, was another door, this one made from simple metal. Next to it, a grimy wall slick with algae held two levers.

I paddled through the water and pulled one at random. Even if there had been a sign with directions, I wouldn't have been able to read it.

Gurgling not dissimilar to the hot tub started up. Water draining? Yes, there was an air pocket overhead now. I swam back to grab Chopper and cursed silently. The dark elf had almost made it back. I rubbed my cloaking charm, hoping I wasn't too late in activating it, and tugged my sword free. The door closed.

The dark elf had to have a remote way of opening it—I hadn't seen a lever on the outside.

As the water drained out of the chamber, I swam to the inner door. There wasn't a handle or a knob. I tried pulling the other lever, but that only made the water stop draining. I pushed it back up, and it resumed.

Fingers wrapping around my lock-picking charm, I rested a hand on the cold wet door and willed it to open. A thunk emanated from within the metal. The door rumbled open too slowly for my tastes.

A faint scratch came from the outer door. I sensed the dark elf on the other side. I hoped he or she couldn't sense me through my charm. If the dragon couldn't, an elf shouldn't be able to... I hoped.

As soon as the inner door was open wide enough, I stepped inside, Fezzik out now and leading the way. I tugged my goggles down to my throat. The long tunnel that stretched before me, reminding me of some railroad passage through a mountain, was empty.

Good, but what about the dark elf that had to be on the way in right behind me? I shoved the door behind me shut.

Seconds later, water surged into the airlock chamber, the sound penetrating the door. Should I run and hope to disappear into the complex? Or try to capture the dark elf and ask for directions to the alchemist?

If this person was the alchemist's assistant or even the alchemist herself... it would be foolish not to interrogate her. Maybe she even had a fresh vial of kraken blood, and I could get it, and a sample of her blood, without going into the complex at all.

Water drained out of the chamber. The dark elf would come out soon. My heart filled with anticipation at the thought that my mission might be so close to being over.

But where could I hide for an ambush? The tunnel was stark without alcoves or side passages.

A *thump-scrape* came from the other side of the door. I only had seconds.

There was a tiny ledge, maybe three inches wide, formed by the top of the door frame. The ceiling was several feet above that.

"It'll have to do," I muttered.

As much through desperation as athletic ability, I gripped the narrow ledge and pulled myself up while walking my feet up the wall of the tunnel. Half leaning against the wall and half balancing on the tiny perch, I stood above the door. Water dripped from my clothes, and I groaned. My cloaking charm wouldn't matter. The dark elf wouldn't miss that.

Before I could change my mind and jump down, the door rumbled open.

CHAPTER 20

I held my breath as the hooded dark elf walked through the doorway beneath me. She—and I could tell from my elevated perch that a woman's curves lay beneath her surprisingly dry, dark, flowing garb—glanced back the way she had come. Checking to make sure the kraken hadn't followed her back?

I wished it had, so she would be distracted, but I doubted the giant squid would fit into that airlock chamber.

As I balanced precariously above the door, all I could do was hope she didn't notice the puddle on the floor and the drips falling from my boots. If she didn't, maybe she would lead me straight to the alchemy lab, where I could get a sample of the alchemist's blood. I couldn't tell if she had samples from the kraken in a pocket.

The dark elf turned, reaching for a lever to close the door, but she glanced down and paused. My puddle. Another drop of water fell off my boot. She was going to figure it out. There was no hope of avoiding notice now.

As I dropped down, trying to flatten her, I yanked a dagger free. I wanted to hold it to her throat and convince her to talk, but she reacted too quickly. With all the preternatural elven agility that the legends spoke of, she danced away from me, and I barely bumped her arm. She spun to face me and attacked with a kick. Clearly, she was close enough to see through the magical camouflage my charm gave me.

I knocked the kick aside with my knee and slashed at her leg as she retracted it. My blade sliced through her pants but didn't draw blood. Again, she was too fast at springing away. I should have drawn Chopper.

The dark elf reached for something at her belt. I threw the knife at her to buy a second, and she had to spring to the side. By the time she recovered, I had Fezzik out, the barrel aimed at her chest.

"Stop right there."

She froze. Did she understand English? Or only that a weapon was pointed at her? I didn't want to fire and alert everyone in the underground lair that I was there, but I would to defend myself.

She curled her lip and scowled. I'd expected dark skin from a dark elf, the first one I'd seen up close, but she was more of an albino with matching white hair, her features elegant but frostier than a glacier.

"Are you Synaru-van?" I asked. "The alchemist?"

She looked too young to be a well-known professional in her field, but who knew with elves. I looked young for my age, too, and I only had half-elven blood.

A stream of lilting, musical words came out of her mouth. They sounded beautiful; I was positive they were a curse, probably accompanied by disparaging remarks about my ancestry.

Without letting my gun waver, I risked lifting a hand to tap my translation charm.

"…and Synaru-van will flay you for presuming to attack one of The Chosen. Then she will take you to be sacrificed at midnight with the other, you blasphemous mongrel bastard."

"So you're not Synaru-van. Good to know. Take me to her."

"Goddess take you!"

The dark elf lunged again for her belt, yanking a vial out of a pouch. This time, I was faster. As she hefted the vial to throw it, I fired.

The round slammed into the glass, knocking it out of her hand and against the wall behind her head. The vial shattered, and red liquid darkened the wall as a puff of crimson vapor oozed out.

She swore, eyes bulging as she glanced at the mess and skittered away from it. Her reaction told me all I needed to know: that was some dangerous stuff.

Holding my breath so I didn't inhale the vapor, I slammed a side kick into her torso. Even though she hadn't been looking, she almost managed to dodge. But my boot clipped her ribs. She tumbled into the wall, the back of her hand cracking against the red stain. She shrieked and grabbed her knuckles, then shrieked again and let go.

Though I hated to kick someone when they were down—or crying out in pain—I'd already made a mess of this. Between the screaming and the gunfire, someone was sure to hear and come to investigate.

I lunged in, ramming a palm strike into her chest. Her head jerked back, clunking against the wall. I tore the pouch that had held that vial off her belt and flung it away.

She snarled and clawed at my eyes. I ducked and dove in, driving my elbow into her solar plexus.

The dark elf pitched forward, gasping for breath. I backed away, pointing Fezzik at her again, ears straining as I listened for noise that would indicate someone else was coming.

"Take me to the alchemist," I ordered as she struggled to recover from the blow. Since I'd been hit in the solar plexus often, I could sympathize, but I didn't have time to wait.

Surprisingly, she dropped to her knees, her hands flexing in pain. Her palm and knuckles were burned, as if that stuff had been fire—or acid. She pitched onto her side, wheezing now, and I backed farther from that stained wall. The crimson vapor had dissipated, but had she inhaled a lungful? Was it poisonous? Or deadly?

Her yellow eyes rolled back in her head, her pale hair spread out like a mop around her.

A distant clang echoed down the tunnel. Like a door or hatch opening and hitting a wall. It was far off, but I was sure I'd have company soon.

Not knowing if the dark elf was alive or dead, I summoned Sindari. It was definitely time for his help.

As the mist formed, I patted down the dark elf. She didn't move. I found two vials of blood in her pocket and two that were clearer. The kraken's blood and venom, I hoped.

I jammed them into my collection kit as I glanced through the still-open door. Surprisingly, a tiny one-person submarine rested in a pool of water in the chamber. So that was how she'd gotten out to the kraken—and not been soaking wet when she came back.

You are supposed to bring me into this realm before you slay the enemy, Sindari remarked.

Another clang sounded, closer this time. My throat was starting to burn, and my nostrils itched. Despite holding my breath, I must have caught a whiff of that vapor before it evaporated.

There'll be enemies aplenty soon. We have to find the alchemy lab.

Do you know where that is?

No. I started to leave, but the clear dome-shaped lid was up on the submarine, and a voice spoke from a speaker inside.

"As soon as you complete the task, hurry to the lab. I'm mixing the charcoal and blood now for the midnight ritual. Priestess Yena is eager to thank Yemeli-lor and Baklinor-ten for their gift by officially bringing them into the cult."

"If that's the alchemist, that means she'll be waiting for us. Let's hope we can get a sample of her blood and get out quickly."

Sindari was facing the tunnel. *We'll first have to deal with two dark elves that are heading this way.*

Nobody was in sight yet, but I trusted his ears. *Not if they don't see us.*

I tapped my cloaking charm again to make sure it was still active and checked the ground for wet footprints. My clothes weren't anywhere near dry, but I'd stopped dripping.

I shall do my best to hide myself, but if we must walk right past them, they may see through both of our magics. Sindari faded even to my eyes, appearing more like a silver apparition than the usual solid tiger.

As we headed down the tunnel, I listened for the thud of footfalls. Then I remembered these were elves. They would move lightly, perhaps without a sound.

When we reached a bend, my night-vision charm allowed me to pick out movement in the pitch blackness ahead. Two cloaked and hooded figures.

With Fezzik in hand, I plastered my back to the wall and held my breath. Would elven ears be keen enough to pick up the sound of my heart beating?

Sindari melted against the opposite wall, and I lost sight of him.

The dark elves ran closer, aware that something was up, but they didn't look at me. One's step faltered, and he reached for a gun at his belt as his gaze searched the opposite wall. Did he sense Sindari?

As soon as they reached the bend, his buddy hit him in the arm and pointed. They'd spotted the female dark elf crumpled on the floor, the door open to the submarine chamber. The one who'd sensed Sindari forgot about him or was distracted. Their jogs turned to sprints, and they ran past us.

I waited, reminded that they might hear my steps if they were close, until they were almost to her, then ran in the opposite direction. Sindari trotted at my side. We passed through an open hatchway.

Distant thuds and clangs reverberated from walls that had changed from uniform gray cement near the lake to a mix of ancient brick, stone, and cracked cement. At one point, a giant pipe made up one of the sides of the tunnel, and we also passed the missing door and cracked glass window of some old storefront. The whole place smelled dank and wet.

I sense a great deal of magic ahead, both powerful people and powerful artifacts, Sindari reported.

Ideally, we'll avoid all of that and detour to the alchemy lab. I led the way through a second hatchway, and then things got complicated. A four-way intersection offered three options. *Any idea which way? Can you smell chemicals?*

Wouldn't chemicals be locked away in containers?

I don't know, but isn't your sense of smell amazing?

All of me is amazing. But I still don't smell chemicals.

What about blood? She's mixing blood and charcoal for some ceremony to welcome new evil minions into the cult. I was fairly certain the names the speaker had mentioned were the same names Zav had shared, the criminals he wanted me to retrieve along with his broken-egg platter. Later, I'd happily let him know they were down here, but I was just here for blood. There would be no side trips to run errands for dragons.

An inner emotion that didn't seem to be my own oozed disapproval at this line of thinking. I gritted my teeth, annoyed that Zav had imprinted some compulsion on me, that stupid eagerness to please him.

I smell much blood. Sindari twitched his tail.

Can you lead me to it?

I shall try.

It was a testament to how strange my life was that I wanted to be taken *toward* the copious amounts of blood and not away from them.

Sindari headed right, took a left at another intersection, and then opted for a sloping ramp heading upward instead of stairs leading deeper underground where a moist mildewy odor wafted up from below. The idea of this place having multiple levels daunted me. Seattle was at sea level, so it was hard to imagine that the dark elves could have dug many extra tunnels down here without water creeping in.

My lungs did not like that mildew scent, so I took a puff from my inhaler. Better to use it preemptively now than need it in a fight later.

New noises joined the clangs and thuds, a clanking and grinding. It sounded like machinery—did they have pumping equipment running down here?

As the ramp led us higher, the rumble of cars driving somewhere above us also seeped down through the layers. Lastly, I heard the chanting of voices. A lot of voices.

They rose and fell in a creepy cadence. If they were speaking a language, it was one my charm didn't know how to translate. Maybe it was nonsense. It had the repetitive nature of some ancient mantra.

I slowed my pace. *I don't think this is the way to the alchemy lab. Not unless it's a popular place.*

What if the lab was where this ritual would take place? Surely not. Who sacrificed goats or virgins or whatever in a science lab?

Sindari glanced back. *We are still going toward the smell of blood.*

This place probably smells like blood all over.

That is not untrue, but it is stronger up ahead. I also detect charcoal. You mentioned that, yes?

Yes. Reluctantly, I kept going. After all I'd faced in my life, I shouldn't be afraid of a little blood and chanting, but something about this place gave me the creeps.

For the first time, we reached a series of doors along the sides of the tunnel. Some were open, some closed. Some were made of sturdy metal full of rivets, some of old rotting wood.

I peeked inside the open doors, hoping for the lab, but they appeared to be personal quarters, meeting rooms, and storage areas. One of the latter was full of shelves of knives, skulls, and human body parts in jars. Torture implements, some I could name and far more that I couldn't, hung on racks.

My stomach lurched queasily, and I reached for the pouch of grenades I'd brought, but I thought better of it. As much as I'd like to blow up all of their evil torture stuff, that would only draw the dark elves down on me. As it was, we likely had only minutes before the two who'd found the female reported back. That would put an end to the chanting and a beginning to hunt-Val time.

We rounded a bend, traffic still audible rumbling by overhead, and for the first time since I'd left the surface, light reached my eyes. Infrared light, similar to what Zoltan had brightened his laboratory with.

The tunnel ended at a wide balcony lined with a metal railing and overlooking a chamber below. The source of the red light was over on the far side of the chamber, a huge two-story statue of a multi-limbed, insectoid figure with four heads. If that represented their goddess, she was hideous. The statue was made entirely from bones, some human, others from larger animals. The four heads were the fossilized skulls of dinosaurs. The bones appeared to be more recent.

As I crept closer, drawn by curiosity—or maybe it was the dragon's influence—the backs of the heads of dozens, maybe hundreds, of dark elves came into view. Some were hooded, and some had their hoods back, their white hair tumbling to their shoulders. The dark elves stood chanting as they faced the massive sculpture and dais. Nobody stood on the dais yet, but a vat of a dark liquid gurgled over a fire pit where a pulpit in a church might have been. Was it blood? *Whose?* On a table next to the vat rested Zav's cracked-eggshell artifact and a paintbrush.

The urge to fling myself over the railing to sprint up and snatch it surged into me, and my legs carried me three running steps before I slammed an anchor down on that urge. I planted my hand against the wall, bracing myself before Zav's compulsion could force me onto the balcony and into a suicidal act.

Val? Sindari spoke into my mind. *Back here. This is where I smell the charcoal. There is also blood inside, though not as much as is in that vat.*

Though I had to struggle against my will—against Zav's will—I stepped back. But after only one step, a squirming girl with red hair was brought out, bundled in a blanket and toted on two male elves' shoulders.

From the balcony, I could only see part of her face, but it was enough to read the terror in her eyes. How had she ended up down here? She was my daughter's age, maybe a little younger.

I stared in horror. Was she their sacrifice for the night?

CHAPTER 21

V *al?* Sindari prompted again. He faced a metal door, the alchemist's lab.

Gulping, I forced myself to step back from the balcony and join him. Maybe once we got a sample of the alchemist's blood, I could find a way to rescue the girl. I had grenades. If I threw them all, was it possible I could slip in through the chaos and reach her? And then somehow find a way back out of that chamber? With so many dark elves down there, it was a daunting prospect, but I wouldn't let myself give up on the idea. Hopefully, the girl had some time.

I joined Sindari, determination and anger making me shake.

The tunnels were cool, but sweat beaded on my forehead. My throat burned, as if the crimson vapor from that vial had seared off all the cilia and some of the flesh. My lungs were tight, too, affected by the vapor or maybe just unhappy with the mildewy undertone of this place. I was tempted to use my inhaler again, but I was only supposed to do that every few hours, not every twenty minutes. Besides, its soft puff might be loud enough for those keen elven ears to pick up.

I tried to ease the door aside, but it didn't budge. Once again, my lock-picking charm came to the rescue. After applying it, I slid the door aside easily.

Sindari charged in, almost bumping me out of the way. He flew through the air and smashed into the startled female dark elf turning toward us. Synaru-van? It had to be.

I jumped inside, glimpsing counters full of vials and equipment in a lab twice as large as Zoltan's as I rushed to close the door, hoping it was soundproof. Especially when the alchemist shrieked a curse and dropped two glass flasks as Sindari plowed into her. They shattered on the cement floor.

Wincing, I threw a deadbolt on the door, though I doubted it would keep out the rest of the dark elves for long, and pulled out Chopper and Fezzik.

Sindari had caught Synaru-van off-guard, and she lay on her back under him, arms and legs pinned under his paws. She struggled and spat in his face, but he was strong enough to keep her down. Numerous tools and pouches were attached to her belt, and I rushed forward to yank them off.

"Sorry to intrude," I said as she glared daggers at me, "but I'm in need of a sample of your blood and also to know why you and your people poisoned my boss. Oh, and if you already have an antidote handy, that would be great. I doubt that dragon is going to give me any of his blood. He's super uptight about it."

She spat at me. I jerked my head back to avoid the phlegmy wad, then patted down the slick oddly-textured black robe she wore to make sure she didn't have pockets full of weapons.

"You are the Ruin Bringer," Synaru-van said in realization. "You have delivered yourself to us?" She lost her ire and frustration and cackled.

I liked it better when she'd been spitting mad.

"You were the only one in that organization that my people thought would get in the way of our plans, but we weren't sure if we could kill you. If we killed your employer, and bribed someone to close your office, we thought you would quit."

Great, confirmation that Willard had only been targeted because of me.

"But now you're here in our lair. You'll never escape." She laughed so hard that tears came to her creepy yellow eyes.

Someone pounded at the door.

Do you want me to bite her head off? Sindari asked.

Yes, but I didn't say that. I gripped the mad elf's shoulder. "If there's an antidote, tell me, and I'll keep my tiger from eating you."

Someone pounded again and tried to shove the door aside. Synaru-van kept laughing. What a nut.

Keep holding her down. I dug a syringe out of Zoltan's sample kit.

Synaru-van spotted it, and her humor shifted to rage. "You think I'll let you take my blood?"

"I sure hope so." I shoved her sleeve up as she renewed her bucking and thrashing against Sindari.

As I struggled to hold her arm down and find a vein, I expected her to fling a magical attack at him—or me—any second. It took three stabs to get the needle into her vein, and she shrieked at the indignation.

"What are your plans anyway? Our office wasn't even bothering your people." I hadn't even known they'd existed two days ago…

She calmed, focusing on Sindari, and I sensed a psionic blast targeting him. There was the attack I'd expected. He shook his head and growled without releasing her.

Shouts came from the tunnel. I only had a half a syringe of blood, but I pulled out the needle and capped it. It would have to be enough.

Synaru-van's mad yellow eyes turned toward me, and I knew she would launch her next psionic attack my way. I stuffed my syringe in the kit and pocketed it.

The wave of power came not from her but from behind. The deadbolt snapped as the door flew open, banging against the wall.

Sindari lowered his fangs toward the alchemist's throat, but another wave of pure energy came crashing into the lab. It struck hard, flattening me to the floor and hurling Sindari across the lab. He smashed into a cabinet, breaking open the doors, beakers and flasks tumbling out and shattering all around him.

Mages stood in the doorway.

I swore and shoved myself to my feet, swinging my gun toward them as two dark elves charged in. When I fired, my bullets bounced off invisible barriers around them, ricocheting into the ceiling and nearby cabinets. I switched Fezzik to my left hand and pulled out Chopper, hoping the magical blade would cut through their shields.

A few feet away, Synaru-van reached into the bosom of her robe—why hadn't I checked there for weapons?—and pulled out a vial. Before I could stop her, she flung it to the floor at my feet.

Holding my breath again, I sprang backward and scrambled as far from the cracked glass as I could. Synaru-van was too far away to reach with Chopper. I fired at her, hoping she wasn't shielded, as blue smoke writhed from the floor, its tendrils stretching toward me.

One of my bullets sank into her shoulder, and she shrieked, but my victory was short-lived. Invisible energy slapped against my wrist with bone-crunching force, and I couldn't keep from crying out and dropping Fezzik. One of the dark elves rushed to protect Synaru-van as the other sprang for me.

I still had Chopper in my other hand, and I stabbed like a fencer to keep him back. The blade pierced his shield, and his eyes bulged as the point dug into his chest. For the first time, one of them retreated, scrambling madly back out of reach.

Taking advantage, I reached into my pocket to pull out a grenade. I had the blood. It was time to blow my way out of here. Maybe the ceiling would collapse, and I could climb out.

But even as I slashed and cut my foe, slicing into flesh three more times as I kept him between me and the others, another mage by the door flung a hand up. He had no trouble targeting me around his buddy, and that same invisible power struck me again. It hurled me back against a counter.

Sindari was pinned by magic, one of the mages completely focused on him, but he kept trying to break free. He shook his head, roared, and waded forward, as if against a stiff wind. But two more dark elves ran inside, fingers splayed as they added their power to that of the others. Sindari was knocked back again. His muscles strained under his sleek fur, but even he wasn't strong enough to fight that much power.

Outside, the chanting had stopped. Would the entire assembly swarm up here to use those torture implements on me? Or would one of them simply shoot me and end it?

My grip tightened on Chopper as two dark elves approached. I vowed to go down swinging.

My chest was as tight as my grip, and I grimaced, embarrassed and furious at the wheezes coming from my own throat. I was a warrior, damn it, not some cripple.

"Do we kill her, Synaru-van?"

The alchemist stood back, a hand gripping her bleeding shoulder, and looked like she wanted to nod vigorously. But she said, "Not yet. I will question her first. We must know how she found a way in and if others know about our entrances. If so, we will have to cave them in and make others. Just tie her up for now. And someone get rid of that slavering tiger."

Sindari was still straining against the magic, trying his best to get to the dark elves, to protect me from them.

I swung Chopper as one of the uninjured dark elves tried to get close. Before the blade could connect, he twitched a finger, and I flew all the way back to the corner. My face caught the edge of a counter as I crashed down. Blood flooded my mouth as I accidentally bit my tongue, and I crashed to my knees.

The chanting of a spell, not some religious fervor, came from the doorway. My charm didn't translate the words, but Sindari's head bowed.

I'm sorry, Val. He knows how to force me back into the figurine.

It's all right.

I don't want to leave you. You need me.

I know, but I'll figure something out. I'll call you again as soon as I can.

The figurine grew warm against my chest, and Sindari turned to silver mist, then disappeared.

I hoped I hadn't lied. I hoped I would get a chance to call him again.

An entire pack of dark elves strode toward me. More milled in the tunnel, peering in.

I couldn't win, not right now. Maybe Synaru-van would question me alone. But they would take all of my belongings before tying me up, and I was nothing without my magical tools, nothing that could defeat mages and alchemists.

One of the dark elves reached down for me. I rose on my knees enough to slam a side kick into his stomach.

I smiled grimly around the blood dripping out of my mouth. Maybe not quite *nothing*.

But with so many more dark elves behind him, it was a futile effort. They fell over me, using their magic to pin me down. I turned my back to them and wrenched an arm free long enough to tug two of my charms off my leather thong, their tiny metal hoops snapping. I shoved them into my underwear an instant before both of my arms were pulled behind my back. I wished I'd dared pull the cat figurine off, but they had seen Sindari and would know to look for his charm.

They spun me around, shoved me against the wall, and proceeded to search me and steal all my stuff. Chopper, my phone, the sample kit, my dagger, my grenades, and even my inhaler—shit, I wheezed as I saw that go, worse than a heroin junkie watching her stash get confiscated.

One dark elf untied my necklace and took the rest of my charms, leaving me defenseless. He knew those were valuable, and he stroked the cat figurine, then tied the thong around his own neck. I wished I could shoot bullets out of my eyeballs at him.

He puzzled over the inhaler, then tossed it to the alchemist. Synaru-van smiled vilely at me as magical bonds similar to what Zav had created wrapped around me, holding me against the wall, keeping me from moving my arms or legs. The dark elves hadn't stuck their hands into my pants and found the charms I'd snagged, the lock-picker and the one that let me see in the dark. But it probably didn't matter. Seeing my end wouldn't be helpful, and I doubted the other charm could unlock magical bonds.

Murmurs came from the corridor, the dark elves out there looking back toward the ramp. I imagined the two males I'd sneaked past charging up to report on the alchemist's dead assistant. That would only make Synaru-van more furious.

She strode toward me, holding the inhaler up, and said something in her language.

"Your thugs took my charms. I can't understand you."

So much for the questioning.

"The Ruin Bringer needs drugs to breathe?" she asked in English.

"I was holding it for a friend."

"I hear the rasp in your voice."

"Because your buddy threw some deadly red crap in the air, and I caught a whiff." Maybe I shouldn't have mentioned her assistant. Maybe she hadn't known about her yet.

Voices rose in agitation in the tunnel. Yes, they had to have found the body.

Synaru-van squinted at me. "Then I will let you breathe something else for a while before I question you." She smiled. "If you survive to be questioned."

She plucked a container off the shelf, opened it, and dumped beads on the floor. They looked like bath beads, but I knew they weren't. When they shattered, a hazy green smoke wafted into the air, immediately stinging my nostrils. I tried to hold my breath, but there was no point. I couldn't do that forever.

Synaru-van smiled and backed away, leaving before she was affected by her own poison. Tears were already streaking from my stinging eyes.

I watched bleakly as she stepped into the hall, where she would soon find out I'd inadvertently killed her assistant. She didn't shut the door, but she turned her back. I was screwed, and just as bad, Sindari was now in the hands of assholes who sacrificed children.

CHAPTER 22

The acidic smoke wafted up, tearing my eyes and making my nose run. Worse, it was making me wheeze. I'd never had a serious asthma attack, nothing I had to go to the hospital for, but I'd also never had an alchemist dump toxic bath beads at my feet.

A shout came from the tunnel, and Synaru-van stepped out of sight. For a moment, I couldn't see any of the dark elves.

I closed my eyes and concentrated on the lump of the lock-pick charm against my skin, then mentally willed it to deactivate the bonds. I didn't truly believe it would work, but I had to try.

The charm grew warm against my skin, as if it was doing its best to help me. But the bonds remained intact, crackling bars of energy wrapped around me, stealing my ability to move. I focused harder, seeing the charm in my mind's eye even as I imagined the magical bonds breaking.

"Work," I rasped, voice as raw as my breaths. "*Work.*"

The charm grew even hotter, almost burning me. I imagined smoke wafting up and my underwear catching fire. What a way to go.

"No, *focus.*" I poured all my mental energy into the charm, imagining the bonds breaking. Snapping like breadsticks.

A surge of energy seemed to pour from me. Not from the charm but from *me.*

The magical bonds pinning me against the wall disappeared so quickly that my knees almost buckled as my weight settled onto them again. I lunged and caught the counter for support.

Confusion washed over me as I shook the feeling back into my legs. Had the charm done that or had I?

Beyond my innate abilities to sense magic and heal, I'd never been able to summon a lick of magic in my life. My ragged breaths echoed in my ears, reminding me that my healing ability wasn't helping now. I had to figure something else out.

As quietly and quickly as I could, I scrambled away from the vapors wafting from those beads. But getting away didn't improve my breathing. I struggled to get enough air into my lungs, and panic made my hands shake. The dark elf had taken my sword, my gun, my sample kit, Sindari, and even my cursed inhaler. How was I supposed to get out of this mess?

Maybe I should have accepted Zoltan's offer to make me a lung-clearing concoction. Not that the dark elves wouldn't have taken it when they searched me.

Wait, what had he said would work? An aerosol of manticore venom mixed with… what had it been? Magnesium sulfate. That was Epsom salt, wasn't it? Maybe there was some in the alchemy lab. Would there be manticore venom? And had Zoltan been messing with me, or had he been earnest? The vampire *had* sent a giant tarantula after me. Manticore venom sounded like something that would kill me, not save me.

But if I couldn't fix my lungs, I might die anyway.

I scrambled to the cabinets and started flinging open doors, hoping I'd be able to identify whatever ingredients I found. If everything was in the dark-elf language, I was screwed.

More shouts came from the tunnel, and the floor quaked. Startled, I gripped the counter. Whatever was going on, it was more than two scouts warning their people of an intruder in the complex.

Two cloaked dark elves ran past the alchemy lab, their hoods down and their white hair streaming behind them. They didn't glance my way. I didn't know what was happening, but if it bought me a few minutes, I'd gladly take them.

I spotted and lunged for a giant bag of Epsom salt. Not only was it not labeled with obfuscating dark-elf symbols, but it looked like it had come from Walgreens. Or maybe Amazon. Did they two-day ship to subterranean dark-elf lairs?

With my breaths growing wheezier and more ragged by the moment,

I verified on the label that it *was* magnesium sulfate—thankfully enough of that infrared light filtered back from the chamber for me to read. I tore open the bag and dumped some out. The tiny crystals that spilled onto the counter didn't look like anything that one could inhale easily, but the stuff dissolved in liquid, didn't it? People *bathed* in Epsom salt.

Leaving it, I went in search of manticore venom. Sadly, that wouldn't be in a drugstore bag.

I saw an atomizer bottle and set it over by the magnesium sulfate. A mortar and pestle followed. A pen and a small notebook open and face-down on the counter caught my eye. I turned it over and spotted fresh ink in a foreign language and what looked like a list of ingredients, then shoved it in a pocket. It wouldn't help me breathe, but maybe it had information about the formula the alchemist had used on Willard.

After checking a dozen more cabinets and not seeing anything venom-like, I tugged open a refrigerator door. Vials and vials of blood, ichor, and unidentifiable strangely colored liquids I couldn't guess at hung in racks.

A boom rocked the tunnels, and the floor heaved again, the vials rattling. My senses were alive enough to tingle with awareness—someone was throwing magic around. A lot of magic.

Between the magic of the dark elves themselves and all the artifacts in the place, I couldn't begin to sort out individual auras. And at that moment, I didn't care who was giving them trouble. I felt faint, and the tips of my shaking fingers were numb. I wasn't getting enough oxygen into my body.

With fumbling hands, I pulled out racks, scanning the labels on the vials. These had all been labeled with sigils reminiscent of the one from Willard's apartment. There were three vials with symbols *identical* to that one—were these more of the same potion? They had to be. I snatched one in case it would help Zoltan create an antidote, and stuffed it in a pocket.

In a rack in the refrigerator door, there were vials of dark red liquid—blood—mingled with clearer vials. The labels held drawings as well as sigils. They were of animals, lizards, and even fish. There was the kraken. I grabbed it for Zoltan in case I didn't get my sample kit back and kept scanning. An elephant, a wyvern, a toad. I didn't see any dragons. But there—my heart lurched. Lion head, wings, barbed tail. A manticore.

There were two of them. One vial held blood and the one next to it was filled with a clearer liquid—it had to be venom. I *hoped* it was venom.

As a female voice screamed nearby, more power was unleashed, back in the direction of the ramp. It was closer than it had been before, as if the dark elves were fighting off some intruder.

I dumped some of the Epsom salt into the mortar, then stared at the little vial of venom. There wasn't nearly enough to fill an atomizer bottle or even mix with more than a few crystals. Maybe I was supposed to dilute it? That seemed logical. Breathing straight venom sounded suicidal, but maybe a smaller dose stimulated the airways into expanding without killing a person.

I stuck the mortar under a sink faucet. But how much water to add? Even if I'd had my phone, it wasn't like an internet search would have given me this recipe.

It was going to be a miracle if I survived the next ten minutes. With no other choice, I guessed amounts and dumped water, venom, and more Epsom salt into the mortar. As carefully as I could with trembling hands, I ground everything together. My eyes stung from the vapors. That venom was more potent than onions.

After everything dissolved, I dumped the concoction into the atomizer bottle, shook it up, and stared at it. It looked like a way to spray perfume, not inhale something. How was I supposed to do this?

Silence fell in the tunnel outside, no hint of the chanting or even anyone talking. That was more ominous than the shouts had been. It might mean the dark elves had dealt with the intruder and would return to deal with me next. The silence made the sound of my own wheezing distressingly noticeable.

I closed my eyes, squirted some of the concoction into the air, and leaned in to inhale. Faint moisture touched my skin, and an even fainter vile taste hit my mouth, but I doubted I'd gotten anything down into my lungs.

An ominous growl sounded in the tunnel. That didn't sound like one of the dark elves.

My tongue tingled. I sprayed the air again, decided that wasn't working, and grabbed a cloth. I doused it with the liquid, pressed it against my mouth, and inhaled through the moist fabric. Some of the concoction seemed to swirl down my air pipe, but it could have been my imagination. My throat tingled. I hoped I wasn't about to die from inhaling this.

Despite the terrifying thought, I kept the cloth to my mouth and inhaled several more times as the growling sound drew nearer. A familiar aura lit up my senses. I would have groaned if I hadn't been busy breathing.

The owner of the aura strode past the open door in his black robe and slippers with a glowing yellow sword in his hand. He glanced my way and twitched an eyebrow when he saw me but continued past without a word.

That explained the commotion. He must have come for his egg platter.

Shouts arose again, this time from the chamber below the balcony. I realized that I was breathing more easily. My heart was pounding as if I'd injected myself with straight adrenaline, but that was fine. I would need adrenaline to get out of here.

I stuck the cloth in my pocket in case I needed it again, then looked around for something I could use as a weapon. Those awful bath beads. They probably made *anyone's* lungs close up, asthma regardless. I snatched up the container, ran to the doorway, and peeked out.

To the left, dark elves lay unconscious or dead on the floor. To the right, Zav stood at the railing of that balcony with the sword raised. Crossbow bolts and fireballs slammed into an invisible barrier that he had created around himself. The items incinerated when they hit it. It made for a startling fireworks show.

My belongings had been dumped in a pile by the door. Relieved, I dove for them and belted on the sword scabbard and gun holster, then dug out my phone, the sample case, and my inhaler, and stuffed them in a pocket. My grenades were there too. Good. I snatched them up, tucking them under my arm with the toxic bath beads. Now, where was the dark elf who'd put on my charm necklace? If I could find that, I could get out of this hell.

A scared cry came from the front of the chamber, and with a guilty lurch, I remembered the girl. I couldn't leave her here.

I crept toward the balcony, staying low in case Zav let his barrier down and that barrage of attacks got through. At first, I thought he was indifferent to the assault as he gazed down at the chamber floor—

there were still a hundred or more dark elves down there, half of them throwing some attack or another at him—but his face was tight with concentration. Dimitri's hypothesis that he wasn't as powerful in human form came to mind.

Crouching, I peered through the railing. The girl was still wrapped in that blanket—it looked more like some massive spider's webbing—and lay on the dais next to an angry female dark elf with a bone knife in her hand. If she hadn't been glaring at Zav, she might have already plunged it into the girl's chest. The blood in the vat bubbled, filling the air with a disgusting salty metallic scent.

"If you want to go ahead and mow them all down with your power," I told Zav, "I'll scramble down there, get the girl, my necklace, and even your platter if I have time."

"My *what?*" He didn't look at me.

I was surprised he'd responded at all. "Whatever you called it. Your artifact."

"I must have it, but I must also capture the two criminals to return to the court."

"I can't help you there. These guys all look the same to me. Are you going to attack them?"

"When they have worn themselves out, I will turn my power to knocking them out of my path." He sounded as arrogant as always, but his voice was definitely strained. There was a frantic edge to his eyes as his gaze swept back and forth in a searching way.

On the dais, the female hefted the girl up and pressed her bone dagger to her throat. "Leave our home, dragon," she called, "or I will slay this child before the ritual time is upon us."

I was surprised I understood her—maybe my translation charm was somewhere nearby.

"I care nothing for that vermin girl or your infantile ritual," Zav called down, his voice ringing with power. "Bring Yemeli-lor and Baklinor-ten, or I will drop the ceiling on your heads and bring the human automobile-way through your ritual chamber."

Fearing for the girl, I was tempted to spring over the railing and run through the dark elves, but they were all armed and powerful. There was no chance I'd make it even halfway to the dais.

But there was a door in the wall beside the looming statue of bones and skulls. There had to be a back way to it. I remembered the stairs that had led downward at the same intersection the ramp had led upward.

"Here." I set the container of bath beads down beside Zav's foot. "Throw some of those down when you get a chance." I backed away slowly, not wanting the dark elves to notice. "And try to keep them distracted. Keep saying arrogant things."

Zav looked over his shoulder, pinning me with his glare. "I do not take orders from law-breaking mongrels who do not acknowledge the supremacy of dragons."

"Yeah, say stuff like that." I gave him a sarcastic thumbs-up. "You're a natural."

With that, I sped back the way I'd come, pausing only to check the fallen dark elves in case one of them wore my necklace. No such luck.

My lungs were inflating fully with blood soaring through my veins as I raced down the ramp, skidded around the edge, and ran down the stairs. My rapid heartbeats hammered my ribcage so hard that I could feel them as I ran. That manticore venom had either turned me into Wonder Woman, or I was about to keel over from a heart attack.

I came face to face with a dark elf running up the stairs and reacted a split second before he did, my reflexes faster than usual. Chopper's hilt bashed down on the top of his head, bone crunching. I yanked his crossbow from his hand and readied my sword for another strike. He collapsed. Apparently, I was stronger than usual too.

"Definitely going to have a heart attack," I muttered, racing off, though I had no idea where I was going, and Sindari wasn't here to lead me this time.

I passed through several intersections, continuing straight and hoping for the best as I tried to gauge how far I'd come. Was I under the chamber now?

Booms and thuds echoed down from above me. The dark elves fighting Zav?

The ceiling quaked. He must have gotten his opportunity to throw an attack. Bits of rock and brick tumbled free all around me, pelting me on the shoulders. Fear drove my legs even faster as I envisioned the tunnel collapsing on top of me. I almost raced past a narrow set of stairs heading upward to my left.

Human and animal skulls lined the walls, and the handrail was made from femur bones. A velvet cord hung across the entrance, as if to deny access to the reserved seating area at a pretentious theater. I slashed through it with Chopper and ran up the stairs. This *had* to go to that dais.

As I charged up two levels, another whomp of power emanated from somewhere above. The stone stair treads lurched so hard that I tumbled into the wall. The femur railing jabbed into my waist, and a human skull tumbled from its mount and shattered next to my feet. Chunks of brick and ancient mortar fell all around me, bouncing off my head, and I wished for some old-fashioned plate armor.

The ground continued to quake, but I propelled myself upward. Red light came into view as I burst onto the last landing. The shouts and clangs of a battle floated to me, and, like the insane person I was, I rushed toward it.

With Chopper leading, I burst out of the tunnel right beside the dais.

Smoke and dust filled the red-tinged air of the great chamber. Zav stood on the railing now, conjuring fiery yellow spears and hurling them down like meteorites upon the dark elves below.

They kept shooting back at him, but the spears somehow zigzagged and incinerated crossbow quarrels before striking down to the floor—or hitting an enemy. Some of the dark elves had the power to create invisible shields and repel the magical projectiles. Others burst into flames and ran out of the chamber like ambulatory torches.

A fireball slammed into Zav, almost knocking him from the railing. Rage and pain burned in his eyes as he steadied himself. With sudden certainty, I knew he couldn't attack and keep a magical shield around himself at the same time. He could probably only concentrate on one or the other.

I almost chucked one of my grenades toward a knot of dark elves responsible for most of the attacks heading Zav's way, but right now, everyone's focus was on him. Nobody knew I was there.

I peered around the bone statue and toward the dais, hoping it wasn't too late to rescue the girl. The old dark-elf female—the priestess responsible for the ritual—had moved, and horror rushed through my veins. Was I too late?

No, there she was. On the other side of the dais and the bone statue, her back to the wall. She still held the dagger to the terrified girl's throat, was still using her for a shield.

"Dragon! This is your last chance. Leave this place or—" The priestess's gaze scoured the chamber and the dais, then locked on to the egg-platter artifact. Understanding lit fire in her yellow eyes. "Or I destroy what you came for."

The priestess tossed aside the girl, who was too wrapped up to use her legs and tumbled to the floor, and charged toward the artifact. Zav spotted her and pointed his sword at her. A beam of liquid fire shot across the chamber, over the heads of the dark elves and straight toward her heart.

She halted in front of the artifact and raised her hands. An invisible barrier formed a foot in front of her, and Zav's beam deflected into the ceiling. It started boring a hole into the stone above the chamber.

I could only sense the invisible barrier, not see it, but I could tell from the way the beam bounced off that it was flat, rather than convex. Off to the side of the priestess, I drew Fezzik, lined up the shot, and fired without remorse. If she'd been about to sacrifice one girl, I was positive she had slain countless others.

Because she looked hard to kill, I held down the trigger for automatic firing. She wasn't looking at me, and the bullets tore into the side of her head. She toppled sideways, knocking over the vat of boiling blood. It fell on top of her, and my gorge rose as the steaming stuff flowed out all over the dais.

Zav's hard gaze turned toward me. I thought I'd been helping him, but I had the distinct impression from the anger still marking his face that he didn't appreciate me butting in.

Movement to my side drew my attention. The alchemist and the bastard who was wearing my necklace were charging at me.

I whipped Fezzik toward them, but I was too late. One of them hurled a wave of magical power that catapulted me over the dais.

Pain slammed into my back as I landed on the other side next to the crying girl. The male dark elf lifted a hatchet to throw at me. I would have rolled to the side, but I was afraid the weapon would hit the girl. I aimed my gun, knowing I was too late.

But as the hatchet left his hand, an orange fiery beam incinerated it. Zav.

His beam moved across and sliced through the throats of the alchemist and her assistant like a chainsaw downing saplings. For a second, I gaped in horror as their heads thudded to the stone floor, their bodies following soon after.

When a dozen voices cried out with curses and orders to *get the human*, I jumped to my feet. Before grabbing the girl, I dug out my grenades as quickly as I could. I pulled the tabs and threw them at the dark elves advancing toward me like a tidal wave.

Then I slung the girl over my shoulder in a fireman's carry and ran across the dais toward the door. I grabbed the dragon's artifact on the way past, ducking when the twang of crossbow bolts reached my ear. Quarrels skipped off the bone statue in all directions, one piercing my side. I gasped, wobbling with pain, but caught my balance and ran on, using the platter as a partial shield.

The first grenade went off with a resounding boom that shook the chamber every bit as much as the magical attacks had. Maybe more. The others went off in a chain reaction that hurled me against the wall again. I glimpsed the balcony tumbling down with Zav still standing on the railing. A huge cloud of dust hid his landing from my view, but I heard the great crash, and his roar of fury. Or was that pain?

There was nothing I could do to help from so far away. With the floor shaking under me, I grabbed my charm necklace from the floor by the headless dark elf. I rushed through the back exit and into the tunnel as massive cracks emanated from the chamber's ceiling.

Huge slabs of brick and stone tumbled down, and I caught a whiff of fresh night air as I raced away. Everything was quaking now, like the largest earthquake Seattle had ever seen.

As I raced toward the only way out I knew about, I feared there was no way I could make it before the entire tunnel system collapsed.

CHAPTER 23

Bricks pounded down all around me as I ran through the quaking tunnel, with the girl whose name I didn't know draped over my shoulder, my necklace back around my neck, and the dragon's artifact under my arm. Had Zav survived falling into the middle of those dark elves with half the ceiling tumbling onto him? I had no idea.

I passed all the intersections I'd run through on the way in without encountering anything but dead dark elves. No, make that unconscious dark elves. One groaned when I stepped on his arm as I ran past.

Zav hadn't come to kill anyone, it seemed. Except those two dark elves who'd been about to kill *me*. I owed him one now, and I hated that. If he made it out of that rockfall in the chamber, I hoped he wouldn't mention it, but I was sure he would. While calling me vermin and a mongrel.

The first of the two hatchways came into view. As I jumped through, the girl squirmed on my shoulder. I felt her weight keenly. The boost of energy I'd gotten from the manticore concoction was wearing off.

"Almost there," I panted, exhausted but too terrified to slow down.

Rubble littered the tunnel floor, and I'd heard more than one massive crash behind us. Any minute, we might run into—

I skidded to a halt. The way ahead was caved in. *Completely* caved in.

I swore and lowered the girl, needing a break and to figure out how to get away. I'd already used all my grenades.

The girl couldn't stand with that weird webbing wrapped all around her, so I propped her against the wall.

"We're going to have to find another way out." I needed to cut that webbing off her, but it looked like a chore, so I touched my cat figurine, wanting Sindari to watch my back.

The charm was oddly cool to the touch, as if Sindari were far more distant than usual. That dark elf better not have done something to him.

"Sindari," I whispered, "come back to Earth."

The mist was slow to form, as if it was trying to coalesce but something held it back. While I waited, I tried to cut off the webbing with my knife. It looked like fabric, but it was more like armor. I switched to Chopper, hoping the magical blade would have more luck.

The girl's eyes had been glazed, as if she was in shock, but when I brushed her with the hilt of the weapon, she tried to hop away. It wasn't until that moment that I remembered she wouldn't be able to see anything down here. She didn't have a night-vision charm. She might not even know I was human. Half-human, anyway.

"I'm going to cut these bindings off you. Then you can run, and we'll get out of here." I glanced toward the pile of rocks blocking our way. "Some way. What's your name? I'm Val."

She shook her head slowly and didn't answer. Yes, she was definitely in shock. I shuddered to think about how long she'd been a prisoner and what that vile priestess might have already done to her.

"Where do you live, Silent One? As soon as we get out of here, I have a friend who can pick us up and take you home."

"Shoreline," she whispered, naming a suburb to the north.

I shuddered again. My daughter only lived a few miles away from there. Had this girl been taken from there or during a trip into Seattle?

Sindari finally formed in the mist. I paused to hug him.

Valmeyjar, he spoke into my mind far more formally than usual. *I did not think it would be you. I thought you would be dead.*

I started to reply, but I sensed a powerful magical aura approaching from behind us. Sindari faced it. I recognized the owner of the aura before he came into sight, but I still debated on drawing Fezzik. It wasn't as if Zav had officially said we were working together, and he might be pissed that I'd killed the priestess. And that I had his artifact.

It was hideous, and I definitely didn't want it. Maybe if I threw it at him, he would be appeased, like some volcano god accepting a virgin hurled into his caldera.

Zav was limping when he came into view, blood streaming from cuts on his bruised face, but as soon as he spotted me, he hid the limp. Or gritted his teeth through it. His black robe and dark hair were coated in dust. I never would have guessed he could appear so disheveled.

He still carried that sword, and he raised it and pointed it at me. I swore and lunged to the side, trying to protect the girl even as I drew Fezzik.

This time, an entire roiling wave of fiery orange power sprang from its tip, not a single beam, and it nearly blinded me. I turned my back as the power passed me, somehow not stirring a hair on my head, and pounded into the caved-in rocks. They blew backward with the thunderous boom of dynamite exploding, the power pulverizing them to ashes before they hit the ground again.

Just as the power hadn't struck me, the shrapnel from the exploding rocks didn't touch me. I sensed a magical shield protecting me and the girl.

Zav grabbed the artifact from my hand as he passed and kept going.

"You're welcome," I called.

"I advise you to leave," he said without looking back. "The tunnels are unstable."

"No shit. You made them that way." The way was clear so I took the girl's arm and led her after Zav.

"It was not until *you* threw explosives that the ceiling collapsed and my perch crumbled," Zav said, still not looking back. "This was followed by three of your wheeled conveyances tumbling through from the thoroughfare above. One of them landed on me." This time, he looked back, shooting me the dirtiest glare I'd seen from him.

"Maybe next time you invade an enemy lair, you won't stand up on a railing like a pompous stump orator running for office."

"I do not know what that means, but if you insult me, I will not save your life again."

"I saved your life, too, buddy!"

We'd passed through the last hatchway, and Zav reached the airlock chamber ahead of us. The dark elf who'd driven the submarine had been removed from the tunnel. Zav twitched his sword, and the lever to open the door threw itself.

I realized he was about to escape, and I'd been too busy arguing with him to ask him for the blood I still needed. If I didn't get it, Zoltan might refuse to make the formula, and all of this would have been for naught.

"Wait, Dragon!" I called as he stepped into the airlock and strode for the second door. "Zavryd-thingy," I corrected myself the best I could. A cat hacking up a hairball would have a better chance at getting close to the pronunciation of the whole name. "I got your artifact for you. Will you give me a vial of your blood?"

Zav opened the second hatch, and I swore when I realized he hadn't thought to close the first. Water gushed into the tunnel, passing the parked submarine and flowing toward us.

"Hold your breath," I told the girl and rushed forward. We would have to swim to the surface.

Or not. The submarine lid lifted as I brushed against it. The water hadn't yet risen high enough to flood the interior.

"In." I lifted the girl inside, pushing her behind the single seat. "Unless you know how to drive this thing, Shoreline, you get to ride in the back."

Where will I ride? Sindari asked me dryly.

Uhm, on my lap? Like a house cat?

I believe I shall swim.

He bounded out, and I was positive he would have no trouble meeting us above. I also would have opted for swimming if I hadn't had the girl with me, but I didn't know how well she could swim.

Fortunately, the labels on the console were in English, not dark elven, and I spotted the big hatch button right away. I hit it, but it came down with ponderous slowness.

The water kept rushing in, rising even as it spread into the tunnel. A distant clang sounded, and I had a feeling one of those hatches had shut itself as part of some emergency system to prevent flooding. As if that mattered when half the complex had collapsed.

Finally, the lid was down all the way, sealing with a satisfying sucking sound. The water kept rising, and the sub bobbed, rising with it. The current pushed us farther back into the tunnel instead of out into the lake. I cussed like a drunken sailor, worried some of the dark elves would catch up with us, especially if we couldn't get *out*.

Zav was long gone. Not only that, but I could sense that he'd changed from man to dragon, flying up out of the lake with his recovered artifact.

He would probably open a portal any second and whisk it and himself back to his home world.

We were on our own.

I found the controls for the engine and fired up the submarine. It hummed to life, and I did my best to turn it against the current. Thankfully, whatever thrusters powered it were strong. We pushed our way out into the lake, and the first hint of light reached us, city lights filtering down from above.

My first instinct was to try to find the kayak, but it only seated one, and the submarine was faster now that we were out in the lake. Besides, the east side of Lake Union would probably be chaotic, if cars truly had fallen through what would seem to be a huge sinkhole to the rest of the city. I sped toward the north. I could have Dimitri pick us up at Gas Works Park.

We brushed against something on the bottom, a jolt going through the craft. One of the submerged wrecks.

I found the sub's headlights and turned them on, their beams illuminating thousands of fish and the humongous kraken. The girl shrieked. I almost did the same.

I pulled us to the left, hoping we wouldn't run into the giant bulbous squid, its long tentacles flexing and shifting behind it like seaweed in a current. It and the fish were still feeding on the bait. Whatever it was had been dropped into a hole in the hull of a hundred-year-old steamboat tipped sideways on the bottom of the lake. I imagined those big blocks of compressed corn one could set out in the woods for deer.

"It's busy eating, Shoreline," I said, hoping that was correct as we sailed past, far closer to those tentacles than I would have liked. "We'll be fine."

"Jennifer," she mumbled numbly.

"Your name?"

"Yeah."

"Nice to meet you."

The kraken didn't seem to notice us. Finally, something was going my way tonight.

I brought the submarine to the surface, saw the dark bank of the park, and took us in that direction.

You think you will escape after your heinous crimes, mongrel human? a voice thundered in my head.

At first, I thought it was Zav and that he was angrier with me than I thought, but this was someone new. One of the dark elves. It had to be.

You will not escape, Ruin Bringer. You will suffer for all the carnage you left in your wake.

I decided it would be wiser not to give a snarky retort. We were almost to the park, but who knew what the dark elves could do with their magic? Even from afar.

Half-expecting a tidal wave to come roaring after us, I twisted to look behind us. The surface of the water stirred, not with a wave but with a huge dark shape. The kraken. It was chasing us.

Sindari? I asked silently as I pushed the acceleration to maximum, envisioning those long tentacles grabbing the little submarine and dragging it down to the bottom. *Are you nearby? We may need a little help.*

The submarine was faster than I expected. We roared toward the dark bank like an out-of-control semi barreling down from a mountain pass. The headlamps flashed over something—a rock? We slammed into it, and the impact sent me into the domed lid. My head hit hard, and pain blasted through my skull. Jennifer cried out in fear.

I forced bleary eyes to focus. We were almost to the shore.

"Where's the— there." I was practically sitting on the console, so it was easy to slam my elbow against the button to raise the top.

It only went up halfway. That would have to do.

As I grabbed my passenger and squirmed out through the gap, a monstrous tentacle slapped down on the lid. Another one wrapped around the base of the submarine. The hull ground against rock as the kraken pulled it away from the shore.

The girl and I tumbled out. I reached for the ground with my boot, hoping we were close enough to touch. Yes. The water was at waist-level. Low enough to run, albeit tediously slowly.

The kraken drew the submarine out into the depths and lifted it into the air. I heard shouts from across the lake, from the houseboats, and wondered how many reports of a Loch Ness monster there would be tomorrow. The kraken hurled the submarine twenty feet before it smashed down into the water.

"Better it than us." I had my arm around Jennifer, helping her slog to shore, and kept Chopper in my other hand. I didn't think the kraken would be able to reach us once we were on land, but I wasn't positive.

And we weren't there yet.

My new friend is coming for you, the voice taunted in my mind.

I glanced back as we plowed the last few feet to the bank. Yes, there was the dark shape of the kraken, and two tentacles reared up into the sky, silhouetted against the Space Needle and the lit cityscape to the south.

The tendrils came down toward us like axes.

"Go, go." I pushed the girl toward the shoreline as I stood in the shallows, waiting with Chopper poised.

I scrambled to the side, the water slowing me down, as the first tentacle hammered toward me. I sliced upward, cutting into it with the magical blade. But the thing was massive. Even as I sliced through it, the force of the rest of it striking the water created a wave that hurled me to the side. I stumbled, struggling to get my feet under me and my blade up again as a second tentacle whipped toward me from the right.

I ducked, and it whizzed over my head, pouring a waterfall on me. The one that had crashed into the water, its tip now missing, rose up and slapped at me. I pierced it with the tip of my blade, but it still clubbed me in the stomach.

Out in the lake, more tentacles rose. If they all came at me at once, there was no way I could parry every one.

Orange light flared on the shoreline behind me, and I glanced back in horror, imagining a dark elf hurling a fireball at the girl I'd worked so hard to save.

But Zav stood there in his full dragon form, his jaws open wide as fire flared from his mouth like a blowtorch. A ball of spinning flame sped toward the kraken, quadrupling in size as it flew. It slammed into the giant squid, and all of the tentacles reared back, jerking away from the shoreline.

I sensed tremendous power as a wave of magic crashed into the kraken. The massive creature was lifted from the water and thrown even farther than it had thrown the submarine. It struck down on the other side of the lake with a splash that had people in their houseboats shouting and pointing.

The kraken soon slunk below the surface, disappearing from sight. As silly as it was, I hoped it wasn't dead. The dark elves had been using it all along. All it had wanted was some food.

By the time I slogged to land—land that I wanted to collapse on and kiss repeatedly, but wouldn't because of my dragon witness—Zav had changed back into human form. The artifact was nowhere to be seen. Maybe he'd already opened a portal and thrust it through.

"Where's Jennifer?" I looked around but didn't see the girl.

"What?" Zav looked at the bank—the shoreline—behind me.

"The girl," I said.

"Ah." He pointed to the massive tanks of the park's old gasification plant and the chain-link fence around them.

I could barely make her out, but she was there. I sagged with relief, then focused on Zav.

"Thanks for the help," I said. It didn't come out as grudgingly as I'd intended. I wouldn't admit it to him, but I was relieved he'd shown up. Both times. I was exhausted.

"You found the entrance to the dark-elf lair."

"I did. There are probably a lot more entrances now though." I pulled out my phone, relieved the baggie had kept it dry, and texted my location to Dimitri.

Hopefully, Jennifer would recover enough to tell us her address, so we could drop her off at home. That would be better than the police station, given my dubious criminal status these days.

"This is true," Zav said. "Whether you wish it or not, you draw the magical to you, including those who have committed crimes. I will continue to use you as bait."

I glared at him. Just when I'd been hating him a little less…

"You will save yourself pain and might live longer if you agree to come with me to serve this purpose." Zav gazed at me with his cool violet eyes.

"To be dangled as bait at your convenience? And do your bidding? I haven't forgotten that spell you cast on me." I prodded my temple with a finger. "It almost compelled me to get myself killed. I hate to break it to you, but I'd die before being some dragon's slave. Before being *anyone's* slave."

Without any hint of apology in his voice, he said, "You can atone for your many sins by assisting the Dragon Justice Court in apprehending criminals for rehabilitation. I was unable to find Yemeli-lor and Baklinor-ten before the collapsed tunnels forced me to leave."

"Atone for *my* sins? Killing bad guys is not a sin."

"Bad guys, as you call them, should be rehabilitated, not executed by some mongrel with a stolen sword." His gaze flicked toward my shoulder, where Chopper's hilt once again poked up.

"It's not stolen," I snapped.

Admittedly, I'd killed the brain-munching zombie lord who'd been carrying it and then claimed it for myself, but that had been more than ten years ago. I'd made sure the undead guy was truly dead, dismembered and beheaded with bits of him scattered in the woods all along the highway back to town. Someone had once told me that since zombies were already rotten, they decomposed quickly and made excellent fertilizer.

"It is an ancient dwarven blade of great power. I doubt you even know how to call forth its magic."

I scowled at him. "I know it does a good job of beheading monsters. That's all I need."

I wouldn't admit that his comments were stirring my curiosity. It wasn't as if the zombie lord had given me a user manual for the sword after I killed him. Could this arrogant dragon know more about my sword than I did? And was it true that it had been stolen?

Zav sneered. "It does not belong in this vermin-infested world."

"You're like a broken record. What do you even know of Earth? Is this your first time here? We have amazing stuff. You should go to the theater or to a symphony. Or a wine-tasting. Do dragons drink?"

"I will leave now, but if you refuse to work for me and continue to roam free, know that I will not save your life again."

"You didn't save my life this time. I had everything under control. And I'm the one who helped *you*. You didn't even know how to get down there, did you? You waited until I figured it out and then followed me, like the crazy purple-eyed stalker you are."

"I knew where the dark elves were located."

"But not how to get down there."

"It would have been a simple matter to break through the streets and jump down on them."

"But you didn't, because..." Because why? He thought humans were vermin, so why would he care if he wrecked our city? "It's against the rules, isn't it?" I asked, enlightenment brightening my mind. "The rules of your little court. They don't want you killing people or wreaking havoc on the civilizations of the natives."

"It is against *my* rules." Zav pressed his palm to his chest. "*I* am not a criminal. I enforce the law; I don't flaunt it. *I* do not wantonly destroy things or take lives unnecessarily."

He squinted at me and stepped closer, his chest only inches from mine, his powerful aura crackling in the air and making my skin tingle with electricity. I probably should have sprinted away as fast as possible, but my feet were rooted, and I wasn't even sure it was because he was holding me with a spell. I felt mesmerized by his eyes, his presence—trapped even without a cage.

"But if you keep killing the criminals I'm sent to arrest, I *will* make an exception. They should be punished and rehabilitated so they can be useful members of society, not slain by some vigilante executioner." He thrust an arm in the direction of the tunnels and the chamber—the chamber now filled with rubble and cars. "You're an anarchist, and your methods are unacceptable." His eyes blazed, boring into mine.

I had thought he'd given up on wanting to kill me, but now, I wasn't so sure. A shiver of fear went through me, but I made myself lift my chin and glare back at him. "My methods are legal here on Earth, and you have zero jurisdiction here, so butt out, Dragon."

Ah, Val? Sindari had found his way to shore and was sitting by the fence and watching over the girl. *Remember what I said about goading dragons?*

No.

Don't.

Oh, was that it? You'd think I could remember something so short and simple.

Yes, I would.

"The Dragon Justice Court has jurisdiction everywhere. Just because your ignorant people don't know it, does not mean it's not true. Be afraid of the day when they decide to make their rule known here." Zav looked at the cloudy night sky and his voice grew softer. "Or destroy the infestation on this world so that someone besides criminals and law enforcers will be comfortable visiting again."

I swallowed. He didn't mean humans, did he? Even these dragons couldn't truly have the power to wipe out all of humanity. I sure hoped that wasn't something being discussed among his arrogant kind.

Zav reached for me, and this time a spell *did* hold me. I tried to spring back, but I couldn't move. My boots turned into hundred-pound weights. His hand slipped into my duster, knuckles brushing my side through my wet shirt.

"What are you doing?" I blurted, horrified and shocked at the thought that I might get felt up by a dragon. Well, maybe not entirely horrified. He made a handsome human, and all that tingling and electricity could make sex interesting.

I scowled fiercely at him and at the thoughts. Was he *putting* that in my mind?

His hand went to my inside zip pocket, not anything more personal, and he drew out the sample case that Zoltan had given me, where I'd carefully tucked my painfully acquired vials of blood. If he took the case as some punishment, I'd clobber him. Some way or another, I'd clobber him.

Zav flipped it open, drew an empty vial and syringe, then closed the case and returned it to my pocket. He studied the syringe, his brow furrowing slightly. I doubted he'd ever seen one before. But he must have gotten the gist, for he pushed up his sleeve, then jabbed the needle into one of the veins snaking down the top of his forearm.

"That's not the vein people usually use."

Zav operated the syringe one-handed, filling it without trouble. A few seconds later, he pulled out the needle, ignoring the blood streaming down his arm, and gave me the syringe. "I assume you can handle pouring it from one container to the other."

"Yes. I can dress and feed myself on my own too."

He eyed me coolly.

Shit, I hadn't meant to be sarcastic. "Thank you," I made myself say. Why was it so hard to force those words out?

Leaving me with the syringe and vial, Zav stepped back and turned away.

"Think about my offer," he said over his shoulder as he walked toward the parking lot.

"Your offer of slavery?" I was thankful he'd given me the blood, but that didn't mean I was going to become his faithful minion.

"To work on the side of the law and atone for your sins."

"As a slave."

"As bait." He kept walking, the shadows swallowing his dark hair and dark robe.

"So much better. Thank you for this gracious offer. I'll definitely think about it, probably while I'm throwing axes at a picture of a black dragon stapled to the wall."

He looked back over his shoulder, those glowing violet eyes gleaming out of the darkness. *I will have a picture of myself delivered to your domicile so that you needn't use anything inferior for the purpose.*

"I can't wait," I muttered.

Even before he'd said that, I'd been positive I would see him again. It might be a good idea to find out what powers Chopper had that I didn't know about. If only for self-defense purposes.

As Zav shifted into his dragon shape, I realized that the gouge in my side from the dark-elf crossbow quarrel was gone. Completely healed. Had he done that when he touched me?

Before I could think of thanking Zav, he sprang into the air, flying over the empty parking lot and heading out toward Puget Sound. Or maybe flying to the local print shop to have a huge poster of himself made for me.

CHAPTER 24

D imitri was relieved to see me. He must have been *especially* relieved to see Sindari, because he patted the passenger seat and gave the tiger the prime position. I sat in the back with Jennifer as we headed up I-5. With the lake and her awful experience falling behind, she managed to give us her address. She also admitted my tiger was really gucci, which I gathered was not a suggestion that he be made into a handbag.

Someone's stomach rumbled—it might have been mine—and Dimitri handed out paper-wrapped meals of beef and rice with Nin's trademark sauce. By the time Jennifer had eaten, she almost seemed like a normal kid. Aside from the haunted look in her eyes.

I didn't ask what she'd gone through, but it was sure to leave lasting marks. Since I had my own issues to work through, I'd let someone more qualified help her with her emotional scars. My job—my legal, noble, and definitely not criminal job, thank you very much, Zav—was only to kill the bad guys and bring their kidnap victims home.

"I totally dug the submarine too," Jennifer added. "But I could have swum almost as fast. I'm on the swim team at school."

A pang went through me as I thought of Amber. I wondered if she had another meet coming up. Maybe, if I wasn't too busy dodging the law, I could go watch. Something about everything I'd been through made me want to watch *and* speak with her and tell her how well she was doing. But I doubted she wanted anything to do with the mom who'd walked away all those years ago. That hurt, but I stood by my reasons. If tough-as-nails Willard had nearly been taken down by my enemies, a teenage girl wouldn't have a chance. It was better if I stayed away.

"Are you in high school?" I asked.

If so, Jennifer was older than I'd thought, but I didn't think the middle schools here had swim teams.

"Yeah, a freshman. I know, I'm short."

"You ever compete against Edmonds-Woodway?"

"Of course."

"Did you swim against Amber Stavropoulos?"

Dimitri glanced back at me but didn't say anything. He drove us off the freeway and onto tree-lined streets full of ranchers from the 1950s.

"Yes," Jennifer said. "Oh my gosh, she's such an Amazon. She is *not* short."

"Does that mean she beat you?"

"Yeah, but she's already varsity. She's on a year-round team. I just do summer league. But I still could have out-swum that... What was that thing? A giant squid?"

"More or less. You might want to avoid Lake Union for a while."

"Or forever!" She shuddered dramatically.

We pulled over to the side of the street, the house dark. It was well past midnight. Jennifer hopped out and reached in the window to ruffle Sindari's head before running up to the front door.

Val, I do not approve of children, Sindari informed me.

Why not? She thinks you're gucci. Isn't that better than being called a pet?

They are presumptuous with their hands.

It's a sign of affection. You loomed protectively at her side while a dragon manhandled me.

Did he not give you his blood?

Yes, but he could have asked for the vial instead of freezing me to the grass and sticking his hand in my jacket. You want to talk about presumptuous—that's presumptuous.

We waited to make sure someone came to the door and let Jennifer in—judging by the hugs I saw, she'd been missing more than a few hours—and Dimitri took off before anyone could come out and question us.

"Where to next?" he asked.

"Woodinville."

"So dark elves can shoot crossbow quarrels at us again?"

"I think they're going to be busy repairing their home or finding a new one. I've got all except one of the vials of blood that Zoltan asked for. I'm hoping we can just add Willard's to the formula when we bring it to her instead of making two trips." Especially since she'd mentioned being under guard.

As we drove out east, I eyed my phone, tempted to call or text Willard and check on her, but I didn't want to get her hopes up. And a part of me worried that we might be too late. What if she was already past the point of no return? Or what if she wasn't yet, but it would take Zoltan weeks to make his formula?

To my surprise, Zoltan was standing out in the street when we arrived, the crime scene tape and security car—and body—from the previous night gone. He held a suitcase large enough to be a portable massage table.

I slid open the van door as we pulled up. "Were you expecting us or are you waiting for any stranger to chance by and pick you up?"

He stepped in, leaned his suitcase beside the seat, and sat next to me while casting my neck an admiring look. Up front, Dimitri located his cervical collar and snapped it on.

"Many videos are already up on the internet showing a massive—" Zoltan made air quotations, "—*sinkhole* that opened up in Eastlake. Nobody mentioned seeing any dark elves, but someone caught some shaky footage of a dragon flying over the area and also a kraken in the water—it was termed the Loch Ness monster by those recording. I presumed that this apocalyptic chaos was your doing and that, since the dragon is your ally, you would ultimately be successful and come back in need of my services."

"He's not my ally. He wants me to be his slave."

"His aura is even stronger about you than before."

I swore. You shower, you loofah, and you douse yourself in a lake, and you *still* can't get rid of dragon aura...

Zoltan leaned close and inhaled deeply. I tensed, my hand gripping the butt of my gun.

"You also have his blood. If he has made you a slave, you must be a very favored slave."

"I'm not his slave. I told him to go screw himself."

"Dragons, in their natural form, are not properly equipped for that."

"He was in human form."

"Hm, then I suppose it would depend on how excited he was by the night's activities." Zoltan leaned back. "You also have the kraken blood and the blood of the alchemist. Excellent. I will also need the blood of the victim."

I winced at hearing Willard called that.

"We can go there next." I gave Dimitri the hospital's address. "Is there any chance that suitcase means you can make the formula on the spot?"

"It's entirely possible if the lighting is sufficient. Or insufficient, I should say."

"We'll figure something out."

Figuring something out entailed going in through a locked fire escape door—I'd returned my lock-pick charm to my necklace, along with the night-vision one—and turning out the lights so Zoltan could follow me. Dimitri waited outside in the getaway vehicle, as he insisted on calling it.

He seemed to think this whole adventure in Seattle was fun. I was too busy worrying about Willard and my future to share his enthusiasm. Every time I heard a police siren in the distance, I flinched. If Willard survived, turning myself into a criminal wanted by the law would have been worth it. But if she didn't...

I shook my head as we climbed, not willing to contemplate that.

Sindari padded along at my side. I could have sent him back to his realm, and he was probably tired after infiltrating the dark-elf compound with me, but I was reluctant to do so. If Willard was worse off than I thought or Zoltan couldn't do anything, I wanted to be able to lean on him and maybe cry into his fur.

There was a window on the fire escape door, so I could make sure the hallway was empty before leaning out and looking for a light switch. This late at night, I wasn't worried about running into that many staff in this relatively quiet wing, but Willard had mentioned a guard outside her door. I could see to her door from the stairs, and there was nobody standing outside it. Did that mean the guard had taken a break? Or that she was so weak that they didn't see a point to keeping someone here?

"I cannot go in with such blazing brightness present." Several steps back, Zoltan had his hand up, guarding his face from the hallway light slashing in through the window.

"I know. I'm looking for a light switch. If nothing else, you can set up on the landing down there, and I'll go get a blood sample." I pointed through the doorway. "Those look like switches. Halfway down. Right in front of that security camera on the wall. Well, let's see if my charm works on technology as well as it does on magical beasties."

I will do it, Sindari told me. *Go see your boss.*

Thank you. I held open the door for him. With his natural magic, he camouflaged himself from my view and probably the view of the security cameras as well. *You're a good friend.*

Not just a service animal?

You are *of service.*

A service friend, then.

Yes.

I headed out after him, hurrying to Willard's door. As I opened it, the hallway lights went out, save for a few indicators glowing here and there, along with the illuminated exit sign over the door. Zoltan rushed in with his big suitcase and his hood pulled low over his face. I opened the door so he could hurry inside where it was dark, aside from the glow of the monitor above Willard's bed.

"I wouldn't do this for someone who hadn't just delivered five-hundred-thousand dollars in dragon blood into my hands," Zoltan muttered as he entered.

I almost fell over. "Five hundred *thousand* dollars?"

"Easily. Since there haven't been dragons on Earth for centuries, I'm not positive about the market rate. It may be much higher. Oh, the formulas I'll be able to mix up. The world will be mine."

"That's not at all alarming to hear from a vampire." I hustled in, realizing Willard was both awake and looking over at us.

"Since it's you, Val," she said, "I'm going to keep myself from being afraid of the vampire stalking in with a— Is that a massage table?"

"A chemistry set." I almost asked her what she had to be afraid of at this point but caught myself. Usually, Willard appreciated my snark, but

I doubted a dying woman wanted to be reminded of her fate. "He needs some of your blood to make an antidote."

Willard was silent, and it was too dark for me to read her eyes. Did she believe it was possible? *Was* it possible?

"You wouldn't believe what I had to go through to get the rest of what he needs. A dark elf used kraken blood and some other ingredients to make you sick. Sindari and I had to raid their lair, steal the alchemy components, stop a ritual sacrifice, and create a sinkhole that brought a lane of traffic in through the roof of their church. I'd say I deserve a combat bonus, but at this point, I'd be happy just to have you back on the job, my police record cleared, and Lieutenant Sudo shipped off to the worst duty station imaginable." Since Zoltan was coming over to get his blood sample from Willard, and she might find that alarming, I kept talking to distract her. "Also, if you could finagle a car for me, that would be amazing. I got a final letter from the insurance company. They closed my case and aren't going to give me money for the Jeep. My comprehensive coverage isn't as comprehensive as the television ads promised. They have an Act of God clause, but a dragon flinging your vehicle into a tree doesn't fall under it. What kind of world do we live in?"

Willard's eyebrows twitched at this uncharacteristic chattiness, and she didn't miss Zoltan slipping a needle into her vein. "Your hands are cold, vampire."

"Your veins are like shriveled husks." Zoltan gave the glowing light from the monitor a cross look. "Don't they give you any water for hydration in this place?"

"I guess that means I'm not in danger of having him drink my blood." Willard looked back at me. "Why did you *admit* that a dragon did it?"

"Because of a foolish bout of honesty. I later tried to amend my story, but that didn't help either. I wish I'd started out saying a tornado had landed on me, but there's a dearth of them in Oregon. Next time, I'll go wyvern hunting in Nebraska."

"No chance of losing your Jeep to a tree there."

Zoltan whistled as he took his sample and headed over to the table he'd set up. The suitcase *had* folded out into one, but instead of holding massage implements, there was a complete chemistry lab tucked away in niches and racks. He pulled out a tiny infrared light and set it on the corner.

"Don't vampires see in the dark?" Willard asked.

The red light showed how sunken her eyes were and how much weight she was losing. I hoped this worked.

"Certainly," Zoltan said, his back to us as he worked. "But not well enough to read labels or the hash marks on graduated cylinders. I *assume* you want me to be precise."

"I suppose." Willard leaned her head back against her pillow.

I could tell she wanted to ask if she should get her hopes up. I wished I knew. "I think those lights are good for your skin. Maybe you should cozy up to that one, Willard."

"What are you implying, Thorvald?"

"That the sands of time only go one way, my friend."

"Tell me about it."

Sindari slinked into the room, visible once again. He pushed the door shut behind him with his tail.

"If I live, I'll do my best to clear you of trouble." Willard closed her eyes. "You may recall that I've been labeled a suspect, too, but I heard a few things while Sudo was in here questioning me. More precisely, after he was done questioning me, thought I'd fallen asleep, and took a call while looking out the window over there." She slid her phone out from under the sheets. "I recorded it."

"Was it as incriminating as I hope?"

"More so for his superior, General Nash, someone I've butted heads with over this department before. Interestingly, he's retiring this year after buying a yacht and a beautiful house on the water in Medina. Polite of Sudo to use speakerphone for his conversation. He must be one of those people afraid that cell waves irradiate the brain."

"Medina? Isn't that where Bill Gates has his mansion?"

"Yes, I believe it's just down the street. Nash's general's retirement pay must be more substantial than anyone else's."

"I assume he's being bribed?"

Generals made good money by military standards, but I was positive one couldn't afford even the median home in Medina, much less waterfront property there. Even Seattle proper wasn't exactly an inexpensive place to live.

Oh, wait. The dark-elf alchemist had mentioned bribing someone to close Willard's office. That must have been Nash.

"Yes, and I can prove it." Willard smiled and pulled something else out from under the sheets. A MacBook Air. "I've been doing research in between sleeping and puking. I was determined to get to the bottom of this, if only to clear your name, before I bit it."

A lump formed in my throat at this admission, and it was a moment before I could find my voice. "Thank you. But I'm afraid there won't be any biting here. I forbade Zoltan to unleash his fangs."

"Given the shriveled huskiness of my veins, it didn't sound like he was tempted."

"I don't know. He keeps eyeing my throat."

"Half-elven blood is almost as good as elven blood," Zoltan murmured without looking back. He had numerous flasks and beakers and even a recipe book out now. "And I am tempted to find out if that dragon aura would convey any extra potency to your blood."

"Dragon aura?" Willard asked.

"It's a long story. Tell me more about this skeevy general."

"I sent a note to another general that oversees his division and ours. I'm hoping something will break soon. I called in favors and gathered a *lot* of data." She patted the small laptop.

I eyed the sheets. "What else do you have hidden under there? A printer? A scanner? A file cabinet?"

"Just charging cords. I've had to be discreet. Sudo and his investigators have visited often."

"Is he getting a house in Medina too?"

"Not that I could discover. I think he's just one of those young pups eager at the chance to take down a senior officer and make a name for himself."

Or Sudo had simply been following Nash's orders. A general could easily have assigned a lowly lieutenant to dig up—or make up—incriminating evidence on Willard. Enough to put suspicion on the whole office and order its closure? Maybe so.

I still didn't know what *plans* Synaru-van had been referring to, plans she'd wanted me out of the way for, and I made a mental note to do some more research later. We might have taken out the alchemist and that vile priestess, but there were still the two criminals Zav was looking for and however many hundreds more dark elves lived in those tunnels. I had a feeling I hadn't seen the last of those people.

"Also," Willard added, "Sudo loathes you."

"We only met once."

"At which point you stole his car."

"Because he wouldn't arrange for me to borrow one when my vehicle was clearly obliterated. I'm dismayed at the all-around lack of sympathy I'm getting from people in regard to this dragon I keep having to deal with."

Zoltan wandered around the room to poke into drawers. He found an IV bag and returned to his chemistry set to fill it with the concoction he'd made. My stomach did a nervous flip-flop at the idea of this strange person—strange *undead* person—siphoning some weird alchemical potion into Willard's veins.

Judging by the skeptical curl of her lip, she wasn't pleased by the idea either. I reminded myself that Zoltan's advice about manticore venom clearing lungs had been accurate. If that dragon blood was as valuable as he said, he had a reason to be thankful to me, so hopefully he didn't have any treachery planned.

"I can't drink your concoction instead?" Willard asked as Zoltan returned to her side, preparing the IV rack already in place from some earlier fluid delivery.

"This will be far faster. Besides, my formula would find the inhospitable acid of your stomach a challenge to deal with."

"This vampire thinks everything about me is unappealing," Willard told me.

"Next time I see the dragon, I can have him rub some of his aura on you if you want. Zoltan is into that."

"Next time?" Willard didn't watch as Zoltan set up the IV. *I* watched, making sure there were no vampire shenanigans. "Are you seeing him regularly? This sounds like the start of a relationship."

"It's a long story. He wants to use me for bait to help catch the criminals he's after here on Earth."

"Do you have a favorite song yet? A place to make out? Do I need to book a wedding on my calendar?"

"You're hilarious for a mortally ill person."

"I'm always hilarious."

"That's not what your neighbor said. He thought you were a humorless drill sergeant."

"You have to be appropriately firm with young people."

"That should do it." Zoltan left the IV draining into her vein and returned to put his equipment away and fold up his table.

"What exactly is it *doing?*" Willard asked.

"Removing the magical triggers embedded in your system that told the DNA in your replicating cells to unravel while refusing to obey their programming for apoptosis," Zoltan said. "You'll still need your conventional treatment to get rid of what's there, but it should be *much* more effective now. I also used a drop of the dragon blood to mix into a potent immune system enhancer. The dragon blood alone would fill you with youthful vigor. If I had more of it, I would be tempted to hook up an IV for myself."

"Can vampires feel youthful vigor?" I asked.

"The better the quality of the blood we consume, the better we feel."

Willard prodded my arm. "This is the same reason I always tell you to eat organic."

"You and my mom would get along great."

"I'll see myself out." Zoltan picked up his suitcase and started to open the door but lurched back, crying out in distress. He pinned Sindari with a disapproving look. "The lights are back on."

I didn't do it, Sindari told me.

If there's nobody out there, would you mind turning them off again?

It's a long hallway, and I'm past the time I should be returned to my realm.

A service animal would do it. And bring a couple of beers back on the way.

Funny. Sindari padded into the hallway, and it soon grew dark.

Zoltan, mumbling something about his burned retinas, walked out.

I texted Dimitri. *If the vampire comes back to your van, will you drive him home?*

Without you?

I want to stay and keep an eye on Willard.

It's a good thing Nin let me borrow one of her weapons. I was hesitant to take it, but now I'm glad I did. I'm not convinced the cervical collar is enough to save me.

I'm not either. Carry whatever weapon she gave you in your lap.

Actually, it's on my finger. It's a pistol ring.

Is that more manly than it sounds?

No, but she wasn't willing to lend me the submachine gun since I only had forty dollars for a deposit and she doesn't take credit cards. She promises it packs a big punch though.

You can trust her. But make sure to take pictures if you have to use it. I snorted, imagining a pistol ring on one of Dimitri's big sausage fingers.

It was only after Zoltan and Dimitri were gone that I remembered the notebook I'd taken from the dark-elf laboratory. I assumed it was written in that special alchemical language of theirs and that Zoltan was the only one around who could read it. I wished I'd thought to ask him to take a look. Oh, well. He hadn't needed it to concoct Willard's formula. If I saw him again, I would ask him about it. It was probably just a recipe book, but one never knew.

"Feeling any better?" I waved at the nearly empty IV bag.

"I'm not sure," Willard said, "but my veins are tingling."

"That must be the dragon blood. Zav is…" I groped for a way to explain the electricity of having his aura nearby. "Tingly."

"Tingly?" Willard raised her eyebrows. "When the wedding invitations come, make sure you spell my name right."

"Ha ha. I don't even know your first name."

"Good."

She lay back and closed her eyes. I dismissed Sindari for a night of rest, then pulled up a chair for myself.

EPILOGUE

"I must admit, I didn't think you'd be back," Mary said.

"It's been a rough week." I sat in her chair—this time, she had it turned so the back didn't face the door—and looked out on the sun beaming down on the lake.

From here, the sinkhole in Eastlake wasn't visible, but recent news reports promised that construction crews were working around the clock to fix it. The media hadn't mentioned dark elves, statues made from bones, or upturned vats of blood, but a few citizen reports had made it onto the various social networks. The Loch Ness monster—now the Lake Union monster—was being blamed even though the damage was several blocks inland. Tourists and locals were flocking to the sinkhole for closer looks, and the police were busy shooing them away. Nobody had tried to arrest me. I kept expecting it, but maybe Willard had pulled some strings.

To my surprise, only a couple of people had posted footage of a black dragon in the night sky, and all of it was blurry. There was an argument in the comments section of one video about whether it was a dragon or a UFO streaking chemtrails over Seattle to poison us all.

"Do you want to talk about it?" Mary asked.

"Not specifically, but maybe we could look at some ink blots or something."

She snorted. "We don't use those anymore."

"You're disappointing my preconceptions."

"So sorry. Do you want to talk about your family this time?"

I bit down on my instinct to say no. If I wanted to figure out how to master my stress and get healthier—and make sure my new weaknesses weren't a liability when fighting bad guys—I had to take this seriously. And probably all the other stuff my doctor had recommended too. Yoga. Deep breathing. Meditation. I wanted to gag, but I would try it all. I had to try. I couldn't afford to have weaknesses.

"Sure," I made myself say.

"Good."

I let myself talk about my daughter and admitted that I didn't *like* the distance I'd created, but after so many years, I didn't know how to fix it. Besides, nothing had changed as far as my job went. It was still dangerous to know me, or even stand next to me. I wondered if Mary would one day be used against me, and a half hour into the session, I felt more bleak instead of better.

A honk came from the street below the window. At first, I didn't think anything of it, but my phone buzzed. Mary frowned at the interruption when I checked it and lurched to my feet.

"I'll be right back. You can keep billing me."

I ran down the stairs instead of waiting for the elevator and burst out onto the sunny sidewalk. Corporal Clarke, one of the army couriers who occasionally delivered orders and physical materials to Willard's office, stood next to a black Jeep almost identical to the one I'd lost. It was *newer* than the one I'd lost.

"Ms. Thorvald? This is for you, from Colonel Willard." He waved at the Jeep and handed me an envelope.

Pleasure spread through me for more reasons than my fondness for Clarke's Jamaican accent.

"She said to show you the manual, PMCS forms, and mileage log, and to make sure you know it's a government loaner until you replace your personal vehicle. Or until a dragon hurls it into a tree." His dark eyes twinkled. Clarke had always been someone I could sense coming, so I was certain he had a magical ancestor.

"Are you supposed to know about the details of my missions?"

"I'm the courier. I know everything."

"You're a corporal. Corporals rarely know how to find their asses in the dark."

"I'm special, ma'am. And my ass practically glows." The eyes twinkled again. *Definitely* magical blood. Probably fae.

"Colonel Willard isn't back at work already, is she?"

"Still receiving treatment, but she's doing better. I witnessed her issuing orders briskly over the phone while blowing open a scandal that… will be classified, so I'm supposed to pretend not to know about it."

I imagined a pit-bull version of Willard taking a chomp out of General Nash's ass—I was sure his didn't glow—and approved, even if Willard should be resting.

"Much like with dragons hurling Jeeps into trees?"

"That's right. Colonel Willard also said to inform you that your name has been cleared with the police, and you're back on the job. You can expect new assignments soon."

I wanted to hug him. No, I wanted to hug *Willard*. But now that she was on the mend, she'd probably go back to barking orders and being terse with me, no touching between colleagues. And that was fine with me.

"Here you go." Clarke tossed me the keys, waved at the binder on the seat, and headed to a waiting car that looked a lot like the one I'd borrowed from Lieutenant Sudo.

"Corporal. Is that Sudo's vehicle?"

"Not anymore." He smirked over his shoulder. "He's been reassigned to South Korea, up near the DMZ."

"Has he? That's a shame."

"The shame is mostly that he didn't clean his vehicle before dropping it off at the motor pool. There was weird cat and dog hair all over the inside."

"That *is* weird."

I clasped my hand around the keys, tempted to take the new Jeep for a spin. But Mary was waiting for me to return for the second half of my therapy session. If Willard was contemplating new assignments for me, I needed to get as healthy as possible as soon as possible.

As I walked back toward the building, the twang of a familiar aura plucked at my senses. High above, almost indistinguishable from an airplane, a black dragon flew over the city.

I needed to get as healthy as possible for a *lot* of reasons.

THE END

The adventure continues in Book 2, *Battle Bond*.

CONNECT WITH THE AUTHOR

Have a comment? Question? Just want to say hi? Find me online at:
http://www.lindsayburoker.com
http://www.facebook.com/LindsayBuroker
http://twitter.com/GoblinWriter
Thanks for reading!

Printed in Great Britain
by Amazon